# KILL

# TWO

# BIRDS

BY

THOMAS BJØRN

2024 Slow Horse Books

Text copyright © 2024 by THOMAS BJØRN
Cover art copyright © 2024 by ALEXIA C ROY



Library and Archives Canada Catalouging in Publication
Title: Kill Two Birds / Thomas Bjørn ; cover by Alexia C Roy.
Names: Bjørn, Thomas, author. | Roy, Alexia C – illustrator.

Library of Congress Control Number: 2024908999

ISBN 978-1-7383500-0-1 (Paperback Edition)
ISBN 978-1-7383500-1-8 (Hardcover Edition)
ISBN 978-1-7383500-2-5 (eBook Edition)

Cover art by Alexia C Roy, ACR Marketing
Interior design by Integrative Ink
Printed in the USA by IngramSpark

Visit Thomas Bjørn at www.thomasbjornbooks.com

*For Geoff*

# Contents

*They lied*
*People died*
*Now she's going to make them pay*

*What can I remember? Not much and always the same. It's a gray day, heavy with clouds and cold. There's a tire swing, and my small hands in red wool mittens struggle to hold onto the swing chains. A woman screams. Or is it me? Then there's the feeling of being lifted off the swing and pinioned against a rough wool coat rank with the stink of cigarette smoke. I remember a gloved hand pressed too hard over my mouth, mashing lips against teeth until the salt-penny taste of blood touches my tongue. There's a struggle, a muffled sob — mine? — and one red mitten on a snow-dusted ground before everything becomes suddenly dark. Then I wake up.*

Tuesday, September 27th, 2022
Five days before Brasil's presidential election

# 1.

---

## THE JANGLES

*RIO DE JANEIRO, BRASIL*

I woke tangled in sheets, wet with panic sweat and a heart trying to pound its way out of my chest. My head, the only part of me free to move, whipped side to side, looking for something —anything — familiar. Then I saw it. Pinned to the wall was a photo of Corcovado Mountain with its 100-foot-high statue of Christ the Redeemer. Scrawled across the picture in fat red marker — October 2nd. My pulse began to slow. Rio. I was in Rio.

After wrestling out of my cotton prison, I made my way to the kitchen to find Dad. He wasn't there, but Marcos was, sitting at the island reading the paper.

"Bom Dia," Marcos said without looking up.

"Where's my dad?"

"In Portuguese, Leah," he said, eyes still down, reading the news.

"Marcos, I need to run." My words squeaked out small and tight, making me sound like a scared little kid and not at all how I'd come to think of myself — intrepid high school senior, world traveler, adventure-sport junkie.

Marcos dropped his newspaper and looked up.

"Need to?"

There was no hiding from Marcos. He knew me too well and for too long. My knee jiggled. Wild strands of still-damp hair were stuck to my face and neck.

"Ah, kid, you've got the *jangles* again, huh? I'm sorry."

I've had the same nightmare since I was a kid. When I was little, I didn't have the words to describe how the nightmare left me feeling. I'd called it the jangles then, and the name stuck.

"Look at me," he said. When I didn't move, Marcos lifted my chin with a gentle finger. "Come on, kiddo. Lift those eyes and look at me."

I did.

"Good girl. Now breathe with me." He began slow, deep pranayama breaths, willing me to do the same. In through the nose ... one, two, three, four. Hold it ... one, two, three, four, five, six, seven. Exhale through the mouth ... one, two, three, four, five, six, seven, eight.

"Better?" he asked.

"Yeah." I nodded. "A bit. Thanks. But I still want to run."

Marcos walked to the fridge and reached inside. He broke off a square of dark chocolate and handed it to me.

"You haven't had an episode in a long time. How bad was it?"

I held up four fingers before popping the square of chocolate into my mouth. Green tea would be next. Dark chocolate, green tea, and bananas. All three had been my constant companions for as long as I could remember. Three things that helped settle me until I could purge the glut of unwanted panic hormones from my body. For me, that came from running and rock climbing.

"Did it start at four, or is it four now?"

"It's four now. I'm feeling better, Marcos. I just need to run. Where's Dad?"

"Since you're well enough to notice he's not here," Marcos said, "again … in Portuguese, please."

It was a thing between Marcos and me. He'd speak to me in the language of whatever country we were stationed in and insist I answer him the same. I didn't squawk about it anymore. I'd learned long ago that routines helped.

"Onde está o minha pai?" I answered. "Is that right?"

"Close enough for eight weeks in-country," he said, graciously not wincing at my word choice or pronunciation. "Your father left already. He's training my replacement, remember?"

How could I forget? After fourteen years with our family, Marcos was leaving us. Leaving me. He'd been my nanny, driver, cook, personal trainer, climbing buddy, and when Dad worked crazy hours or left on business trips, Marcos was my *in loco parentis*. Now he was leaving, getting married to a woman he'd met when we were posted to The Netherlands. I thought of Marcos like a brother, a very much older brother, and I was going to miss him like crazy. But I was happy for him too. He was like family, and you want the people you love to be happy, right? So when Marcos broke the news about leaving to marry Basia, I'd told myself it was all good. She made him happy, and anyway, I was leaving too. This time next year, I'd be in college.

"Marcos, I'm going to run the beach. Do you want to come?" I asked, even though I could see that he was already dressed in his non-uniform uniform of khaki pants and a white dress shirt with two military-sharp creases ironed in.

"No beach run today, kid. Not for you or me. Sorry."

"Why?" I asked, my level four panic inching up a decimal point or two. I put my hand out for another square of chocolate and then popped it into my mouth.

"The election is in five days," he said, as if I needed any reminder. Brasil's presidential election had crowded out any other news. People talked about it in shops, restaurants, and on the beaches. If the hum in Rio was any indication, Sunday's election was going to upend things. But I didn't know what that had to do with my morning run.

Marcos tapped his finger on the stack of newspapers on the kitchen island. I didn't have to look to know there would be a copy of the Rio Times in English for my dad, and the Folha de S. Paulo in Portuguese for Marcos.

"So?"

"João Matheus Pereira. Do you know who that is?"

I rolled my eyes. We'd only been in Rio eight weeks, but you'd have to be a cave dweller to live here and not have heard of him. An orphan from one of Rio's most crime-ridden *favelas* — Brasil's word for a shantytown — Pereira had risen to become one of the wealthiest people in the country. He owned a huge agribusiness based in Mato Grosso — a large state bordering Bolivia. During the worst of the pandemic, when the Santos government was either unable or unwilling to help the favelas, Pereira started a feed-the-children campaign, sending truckloads of food to favela schools. Any child who stayed in school would get a hot lunch. He'd bankrolled the whole thing himself. Now, Pereira was challenging Santos for the presidency and everyone — oddsmakers and pundits — believed he could win.

"Pereira's making one last delivery today before Sunday's election, and the paper says he's agreed to stop at Praia Leblon and say a few words to his supporters en route to the favela. People have already started to arrive. The beach will be a zoo soon."

I walked to the window and looked out. Sure enough, there was a steady stream of people heading toward the beach. Denied a run, my leg started to jiggle again. Then it hit me.

"Which favela?"

"Rocinha."

"My field trip!"

"I know, but Leah ... there is a chance the school might cancel."

Our AP World Geography class was supposed to take a walking tour of Rocinha favela this morning. Janneke and I were counting on it for more video footage to finish our documentary. The submission deadline was just around the corner.

"They can't!" I said, anxious now for a completely different reason. "We still need shots."

"I thought you two finished your documentary last weekend," Marcos said.

"We had until I convinced Janneke we needed to change some things in the script. Now it's in pieces until we get new footage."

"I'll take you both to Rocinha this weekend," Marcos offered. "We can each take a mototaxi. You should get some great footage that way."

"I've got SATs on Saturday, remember? And Sunday, we're climbing Corcovado. After that, you'll be gone."

"Right," Marcos said, shaking his head. "I forgot about the SATs. But it will be okay, Leah."

"You don't understand, Marcos. The documentary isn't just for the film festival. Janneke is counting on submitting it with her college application. I don't want to be the reason she doesn't get into Yale."

"Breathe," Marcos said, hands on my shoulders, willing me to meet his gaze. "Just breathe. I know it doesn't feel like it right now, but there *is* time, and kiddo, your school trip might still be a go. We simply don't know right now. But we do know that you need to purge that adrenalin and cortisol. How about we go to school early? If we can leave in the next ten minutes, we'll have time to do some bouldering on the school wall. Would that help?"

I nodded.

"Good. Go grab a quick shower. I'll pack our climbing shoes, grab some cereal bars and bananas for your breakfast, and put your green tea in a Yeti. Deal?"

"Thanks, Marcos," I said and headed back to my room to get ready. My level four had already dropped to a three.

❧

After a short shower, I felt better. I was still worried about the documentary, but Marcos was right — I needed to climb. It was the nightmare and the flood of panic hormones it generated that made me feel that things were spinning out of control. Bouldering would help.

Banking that the field trip would still happen, I slipped on a loose pair of shorts and an ultra-light cotton tee. On a walking tour of Rocinha favela, I'd be dripping sweat by noon. So even though I was the new kid at school — again

— and normally would be taking great care with my clothes, hair, and make-up, I knew that if there was ever a day where comfort counted more than looks, this was it. Reluctantly, I scraped my shower-wet hair into a tight ponytail.

Ponytails were something I tried to avoid. They drew attention to my more unflattering features. I have long, floppy ear lobes that an old cow of a biology teacher (thank you very much, Mrs. Jeffries!) warned me would only get bigger and floppier with time. But that wasn't the worst of it. I also have one blue eye and one brown, and with my hair pulled back into a tight ponytail, my heterochromia is more noticeable. So is my chin. An American classmate once described it as Jay Leno-esque. Seriously, what teenage girl wants to hear that?

My chin may not be pretty or feminine, but my marine-square jaw looked just enough like my dad's that people often commented on the family resemblance. Sometimes I'd correct them, explaining that I was adopted. Most of the time, I'd simply smile and nod.

The truth was, I had no idea who I looked like. The face that looked back at me from the mirror was nothing more than a random composite of genetics inherited from two people whose identity I would never learn.

My ten minutes were up. I shoved my cell phone in my shorts' pocket and grabbed my camera — a tiny GoPro. Marcos was waiting at the door with my climbing gear. He handed me a Yeti filled with green tea and a breakfast-to-go bag, then we headed to *The Tank*.

I'd nicknamed it *The Tank* because it was more tank than car.

"This is Rio," Dad had said, defending his purchase. "Bad things can happen here." I accepted that Rio was a city where you needed an armored car. Even the average person would shell out an extra ten to fifteen grand to armor their personal cars. But *The Tank* was over-the-top, even for my safety-obsessed Dad. It was made by Land Rover's Special Vehicle Operations team. Who even knew there was such a thing?

*The Tank* rounded the corner to my school and headed uphill.

"Just drop me off at the gate, Marcos."

"Not today, kiddo," he said. "I'm bouldering with you."

I nodded. Truth was, I was grateful for his company.

My new school took security as seriously as my dad. From the outside, it looked more like a prison than a school. Bordered by a four-foot stone wall topped with six feet of chain-link and razor wire, it had an entry gate manned by an armed guard. Marcos greeted the guard like they were old friends. They had a brief, friendly conversation, all in Portuguese, then Marcos and I headed to the bouldering wall at the back of the school.

Forty minutes later, my hands were sore and my muscles tired, but the jangles were gone. I'd cleared the last vestiges of panic hormones from my system.

"Feeling better, kid?"

"Yeah, I do, Marcos. Thanks."

"Good."

He steered me toward the shade of a giant cannonball tree, its trunk wrapped with vines thick with rose-pink flowers and ping-pong-ball-sized fruits. It was hard to imagine that those small fruits would grow to be the size of cannonballs by graduation. By then — so I'm told — the fruit will be too heavy for the vines. I imagined them falling one after the other, striking the ground in a noisy rat-a-tat barrage, and splitting open on impact to reveal their smelly blue insides, each one teeming with seeds for the next generation. But for now, it was safe to sit here.

I sat down beside Marcos, leaned back against the trunk, and breathed in the flowers. Morning was the best time — their scent was always strongest in the morning. By the end of the day, all the flowers would be dead.

As I took off my climbing shoes and slipped them into their carry bag, Marcos asked, "So kiddo ... any idea what triggered your nightmare today?"

I shook my head. I didn't know, not really. Except maybe it was because Marcos was leaving next week, and I'd miss my nanny, slash driver, slash climbing buddy.

"I'm really going to miss you, Marcos," I said.

I knew he'd miss me too, but I also knew that he was chomping-at-the-bit excited to get back to Europe and to his fiancée, Basia. I could see it in his face every time he talked about her.

"You know we'll see each other in December," Marcos said. "You're in the wedding party, remember?"

"Of course, I remember. Who could forget a trip to Poland in December?"

I winked and gave him a shoulder bump. Marcos knew how much I hated the cold. We'd had two separate postings to Moscow. The first after Mumbai and the second after Myanmar. For a young kid, the contrast between sandals and sundresses to having to wear boots, hats, mitts, and snow clothes just to play outside turned out to be too much for me, and it had been Marcos more than my dad, who suffered through my continuous litany of complaints. I didn't want him to think I was complaining now.

"It was really nice of Basia to ask me to be a bridesmaid."

Marcos returned my shoulder check, like a confirmation that we were good. It was nice sitting there with him like that. Just the two of us, post-bouldering. I was really going to miss this.

"I've got something to tell you, kid."

He sounded serious. I turned to look at him.

"About the field trip?"

Marcos met my gaze. "No. Something else."

"Okay?"

"This is turning out to be a big work weekend for your dad. He's not going to be able to make the climb."

The climb.

Corcovado Mountain.

The picture on my wall with October 2nd slashed across in fat red marker. I'd been looking forward to this since we arrived in Rio eight weeks and two days ago. We'd hired a climbing guide to take the three of us up the mountain. It was a going-away present to Marcos from Dad and me. The prize at the end of the climb — Christ the Redeemer. That thirty-meter-high hunk of concrete covered in soapstone tiles which was always the first shot featured in movies set in Rio. It was going to be epic. It was also going to be our last climb for a long, long time.

"Dad *has* to be there. It's our last climb. You're leaving Monday."

"We'll have others. Your father is a busy man with a big job, Leah."

I snorted and rolled my eyes. "Come on, Marcos. Dad's a cultural attaché. That's like being a booking agent for countries." Before Marcos could object, I added, "And Brasil has virtually the same time zones as North America, so it's not like he has to accommodate weird hours or the international date line." I raised my eyebrows as high as they would go to make sure Marcos knew what I thought of his defense of my dad's absence.

"There is some good news too."

"Yeah, right," I said, too annoyed with my dad to behave like the diplomats' daughter he'd raised me to be.

"Your father pulled some strings, Leah. He's getting you a Yale alumni interview with Christina Ramos."

Christina Ramos. Pulitzer Prize-winning investigative journalist.

"Really? When?"

"TBD kid, but the US Consulate opens at 0800 hours, and he's pushing to get you in and out before school tomorrow morning. And Leah, this is all on the q.t. okay? No bragging to your friends that you scored an interview."

"I would *never* brag." I was insulted he would think that. "But Marcos, there are only three of us applying to Yale. Couldn't Dad ask Ramos to squeeze in two more? Janneke's my closest friend here, and Teebo is ..."

"Oh, I think I know what Teebo is," Marcos said, his mouth ticking up at the corner. I blushed.

"But Ramos is in Rio to cover the election, not interview high school kids. Your father moved mountains to get *you* an interview, kiddo. The old man is still under the delusion that Ramos is your number one role model and that your dream in life, your one big goal, is to become a journalist like her."

I felt a familiar knife-twist of guilt as I looked up at Marcos. The way he stared at me, with eyebrows raised ... Marcos knew exactly what I was thinking. And feeling. We both knew the only reason Dad even tried to *move that mountain* was because of my *Big Lie*, and both Marcos and I knew how Dad felt about liars.

**2.**

---

## CALLUSES, CHALK DUST & LIES

My dad hated lies. And liars. If Dad had been Pope in the sixth century instead of Gregory I, there would have been *eight* cardinal sins instead of seven, and lying would have landed somewhere near the top.

I'm not naive. I'm sure my dad has told a lie or two in his life; he's a diplomat after all, and occasionally has to find creative, truth-adjacent ways to make things happen or deliver bad news. But he's never lied to me. With me, he's the ultimate straight shooter. A truth-teller. An ardently honest, pull-no-punches kind of guy that tells the truth even when it hurts.

Exhibit A: My adoption. Dad told me from the get-go that I was adopted. He never pretended otherwise, and he could have. I was three, almost four, when he adopted me, and I have zero memories of TBD. Time Before Dad. Once I was old enough to ask questions about my birth parents, Dad even brought out my adoption papers. He wanted me to understand that a sealed adoption meant that even he didn't know who gave me my screwed-up genetic cocktail.

15

Exhibit B: Dad never hid his sexuality. He's gay and open about it. He has a life partner who's been around longer than me. His name is Dr. Walid Masri, but I call him Uncle Wally. Born in England to Palestinian parents, Uncle Wally is capital-P *Passionate* about his work. Officially, he's a professor at the Centre for Palestine Studies, which is part of London's Middle East Institute, which is part of SOAS — School of Oriental and African Studies — which is part of the University of London. Impressive, right? When he's not teaching, Uncle Wally travels to the Middle East for research or to someplace glamorous or important as a guest lecturer. He's even got a TED Talk about Palestine that went viral.

Dad loves Uncle Wally's passion. I figure that's part of why Dad pushes me so hard and also why I'd told him my *Big Lie* despite knowing how he feels about the truth. In my defense, I only lied because he'd been ragging on me for months, and I desperately needed him to stop.

That was three years ago, almost to the day. We were living in Wassenaar in the Netherlands and having dinner at my favorite pannekoek restaurant, Boerderij Meyendel, when Dad announced that we'd been posted to Turkey. Two days later, I was sitting in a classroom in Istanbul. That's how fast things can change in my world.

In Istanbul, I went to an international school stuffed with consular kids, and all anyone could talk about was Jamal Khashoggi — the Washington Post journalist who'd entered the Saudi consulate on October 2nd and never came back out. When you have a parent who works for a diplomatic mission, you notice things happening at other consulates. Especially the scary stuff. And when your dad's office is only a few minutes' walk from where a guy *was disappeared*, you really pay attention!

The whole city felt tense. Just doing ordinary things like walking to the coffee shop had me checking over my shoulder half a dozen times. Worse, I began having my nightmare again. The same nightmare that sent adrenalin flooding my system and left me shaking and panicky. Finally, Dad suggested a weekend break from the city — a climbing holiday to Finale Ligure in Italy.

We'd just finished a climb of Bric Pianarella, the biggest climb I'd ever done. My muscles ached in a good way, a way that told me I'd achieved something.

"Leah," Dad said as we packed our gear, "I want to talk to you about something."

"Sure. What's up? Wait, we're not moving again, are we?"

"No. You'll get to finish your freshman year here. I promise."

"But?" There'd been a hitch in his voice and a pinch between his eyebrows that told me something big was bugging him.

"You'll be a sophomore next year. I need you to consider what you want to do with your life."

"What? Like a job?" I snorted. I figured he was joking.

"I want you to think about college and careers, yes."

"I'm a freshman, for crying out loud. We don't even get college counseling at school until junior year."

Dad pressed his lips together and stared at me. He was serious. He was giving me *The Look*. Like oxygen fuels a fire it stoked a growing inferno inside, and fourteen-year-old me exploded all over him.

"This is crazy! Are any other ninth graders being asked to make a *career choice*?" I hammered my point home with exaggerated air-quote-fingers. "Not a chance!"

Dad hesitated. "I know, Leah. But you're ..."

"I'm what?" I was indignant. But I was also embarrassed by my outburst, and I couldn't look him in the eye. Instead, I focused on his Adam's apple rising and falling as he swallowed the words he'd left unsaid. I watched his chin swing slowly from side to side as he shook his head. When I finally looked up, the look on his face was too much. Disappointment. I'd disappointed him, and *that* hurt more than any lecture or punishment. I looked away.

"This life," he said, opening both arms to the scenery in front of us, "is artificial in so many ways."

"It doesn't feel artificial," I said, holding out my hands. The calluses and chalk dust were very real. So was the lovely lactic acid build-up in my muscles left over from the climb.

Diplomat Dad found the words he wanted and continued. "Leah, most kids your age live in the same place their entire life. They don't go on holidays like ours. And they certainly don't have a Marcos. You understand that, right?"

"Yeah," I conceded. "I know."

Lots of expat kids had nannies when they were young. Most were dailies — women who came in the morning and left at night. A few even had live-in help if they were posted to a place where that kind of thing was common and if their villa or apartment included a maid's room. But Marcos lived *with* us as part of the family, and he'd been with us since Dad adopted me. No other fourteen-year-old at my school had a driver who took them rock climbing, zip-lining, dirt biking, kayaking, karting, skiing, parasailing, hot-air ballooning and more. Marcos also cooked meals and took care of me when Dad traveled or worked strange hours. No one I knew had a Marcos. Dad was telling me I was spoiled, and that hurt.

"Okay, I get it," I said. "You're worried that if I don't find a good job, I won't be able to do stuff like this, and then I'll be unhappy with my life. Right?"

"No, Leah. That's *not* what I'm saying. I'm saying that work gives a person self-respect. And it's always better if that job is something you believe in."

"Like Uncle Wally."

"Yes. Like Walid. But what matters, the thing that is *truly* important, is being able to live by your own efforts. Leah, I don't want you to faff around from one thing to the next without purpose like some bored socialite."

"Socialite?" I said with another snort. "Dad, please. You're showing your age. Anyway, I'm not an influencer or some New York blue blood. I'm a diplomat's kid. A regular run-of-the-mill foreign service brat."

He gave me a funny look, leaned back against the rock face, and stared out over the pine trees that gave Pianarella its name. His face slowly softened, and when I felt the danger had passed, I relaxed against the rock face with him. We sat there together, enjoying the scenery and letting the lactic acid leech out of our muscles. But it turns out Dad wasn't finished with me.

"Things will ... change when you come of age, Leah. That's only four years away. And as silly as it might seem to you now, you really do need to start thinking about the future. About college and careers." He turned to look at me. "It's important, Leah. More than you realize."

Dad was being weirdly intense, and if that wasn't peculiar enough, he said, "Don't you have a dream? A goal in life?"

*A goal in life?* Please! We'd barely unpacked the boxes in our Istanbul apartment. I was still making friends and figuring out my new school. If I had any goal, it was to fit in, cement fast friendships, and get good grades. But Dad was giving me his *Dad look.*

"Okay," I conceded. "Okay, you're right. I do love my life. I love everything I get to do with you and Marcos. Uncle Wally too. But Dad, it's not easy, always moving like we do. Especially in the middle of a school year. And I never complain, right?"

Dad nodded. His eyes softened, and the corners of his mouth ticked up into an almost-smile.

"I *don't* complain because even though it's hard moving so much, I love it. I love my life. I love living in all the different countries and making friends from around the world."

Dad took my hand and gave it a small squeeze.

Encouraged, I added, "Of course, I'd love it a whole lot more if you'd let me have some social media."

"Leaaaah," Dad said, drawing out the last syllable of my name until it sounded like a question.

I winked at him so he'd know I was joking. Sort of joking. I *would* like a few socials, but I'd accepted long ago that they were off-limits. It was never going to happen. At least not while I was living at home.

"Seriously though, Dad," I said. "I like lots of different things."

"Climbing, running, and hanging out with friends doesn't count, Leah. You can't pay rent and buy food doing those things. You need a job that will allow you to be independent. Self-sufficient. Ideally, it should be something you take pride in. And that only happens when you're passionate about something. Like your Uncle Wally is about his work for Palestine."

This was worse than English class. It was never enough to actually enjoy the book they made you read; they killed it first, then made you take it apart piece by piece. I'd wanted to fall inside Harper Lee's Alabama and live there for a while, but no. We had to analyze the life out of it, picking the book apart until the magic was gone and that mockingbird was not just dead but dissected bone by bone and ligament by ligament. I definitely did *not* want to do that with my life. I fought back.

"You're a cultural attaché. Are *you* passionate about your job?" I figured I had him there. Everything about Dad's job sounded deadly dull.

"Yes."

If it was anyone but my dad, I wouldn't have believed them, but Dad doesn't lie. Not to me. I was losing this argument. I wanted it to end, and with Dad, honesty was always best.

"Okay. It's true," I confessed. "I don't love anything. Not yet, anyway."

When he looked like he might launch into another lecture, I added, "Hey, I'm being honest. That's what you always insist on, right? The truth?"

"Always."

"See? I know that, and I told you the honest truth. I'm just not there yet. But I will think about what you said. I promise."

I'd hoped the combination of honesty and a promise would be enough, but I was wrong. When we returned to Istanbul, those discussions continued, augmented by a campaign of Post-it Notes. I'd find them everywhere.

Slid inside in my shoes:

*Find something you're passionate about and keep tremendously interested in it.* Julia Child

Stuck to my laptop screen when I opened it at school:

*No matter how carefully you plan your goals, they will never be more than pipe dreams unless you pursue them with gusto.* W. Clement Stone

Even hidden in my cereal bowl:

*The will to win, the desire to succeed, the urge to reach your full potential ... these are the keys that will unlock the door to personal excellence.* Confucius

I never knew when or where they'd show up, but I always knew what they'd say. More or less. They were all versions of my dad's *favorite* saying:

*Life doesn't hand out participation medals, Leah. You need to play to win.*

What I wanted, what I needed was for Dad to back off. So, ignoring my commitment to honesty, I picked my moment, stood tall, and announced that I wanted to be a doctor. With all the sincerity I could muster, I told him, "I've dreamed about medicine my whole life." What parent's chest doesn't swell with pride at the thought of their kid becoming a doctor, right?

Mine.

He saw through it right away. In hindsight, it was a pretty dumb thing to declare since I had no interest in chemistry or biology and couldn't give him one plausible reason why I'd chosen medicine.

Next, I professed a love of the law. He doubled down on *why* I wanted to be a lawyer. Unsatisfied with what he called my *superficial answer*, he shook his head and sent me away to think about it some more.

He flat-out laughed at me when I said I wanted to be a teacher.

"Actress then," I spat back, more than a little angry.

"At least you have a talent for that," he said.

I think I hated him a little then. I stormed off. Minutes later, I was marching into Marcos's room carrying a stack of Post-it Notes. Marcos put down the newspaper he'd been reading and watched without comment as I slammed his door shut. Then, with a theatrical flourish meant to show just how angry I was, I stuck each of Dad's Post-it Notes one at a time onto the back of Marcos's door.

*"Wheresoever you go, go with all your heart."* Confucius

*"If you aim at nothing, you'll hit it every time."* Zig Ziglar

And on they went until they formed lines across and down the face of the door ending with the queen of all Post-it Notes, plucked from Madeleine Albright's Doability Doctrine.

*"Where our interests are clear, and our values are at stake, and we can make a difference, we must act, and we must lead."*

"Look! Look at these!" I said. Each note was a nagging finger poked into my fourteen-year-old ribs. "No one else my age has parents insisting they pick a career!"

"I understand, kiddo," Marcos said with an infuriatingly calm voice. "But why fight it?"

"Because it's not fair," I'd whined. "I don't want to decide my whole future now. I'm fourteen. I just want to be a teenager. Why won't he let me be like everyone else?"

"Maybe because you're *not* like everyone else," Marcos answered. That only fanned the flames of my frustration and anger.

"Look, kid, you've tried doctor, lawyer, teacher. As far as I can tell, you've tried the full cast of the Village People."

He was not wrong.

"So why not try reporter?"

Marcos turned to his desk, picked up an article he'd cut out of the newspaper, and handed it to me. It was from the New York Times, written by Christina Ramos — the journalist who broke the story that Jamal Khashoggi had been murdered inside the Saudi Embassy.

"Why not? Because I don't want to be a reporter, Marcos. And it would be a lie. Dad hates lies, remember?"

Marcos rolled his eyes. "Kiddo, come on! You weren't exactly telling him the truth when you offered up all those other careers, now were you?"

I had just enough good grace to look abashed.

"Okay, fair enough. But Marcos, Dad didn't believe any of my other choices. Why would he believe this?"

"He'll believe it because being a reporter suits you."

"How does it suit me?"

"Leah, how many years have we been together?"

Marcos rarely used my name. He almost always called me kid or kiddo.

"Fourteen."

"Fourteen years. That's right. And for fourteen years, I've watched you. You're brave, adventurous, and, most importantly, you're naturally curious. Not to mention, you've got a pretty fine bullshit detector, kiddo. Fourteen years, nine different schools, and not once have you been conned into choosing a bad friend. You have a real knack for reading people. Your dad agrees; being an investigative journalist suits you to a tee."

"You talked about this with Dad?"

Marcos stood up, walked to the door, and began peeling off the Post-it Notes, collecting them in a stack.

"Tell him I suggested it, and you liked the idea."

"Okay, but what happens if Dad believes me and *then* finds out I was lying?"

The memory of our talk at Bric Pianarella and the disappointment on his face haunted me.

It was probably stupid, and any shrink would say my fear was the same fear that all adopted kids lost sleep over. Despite knowing in my heart of hearts that Dad loved me, deep down, I still worried about being abandoned and alone. After all, I'd already had one parent — the woman I'd been physically corded to for nine months — give me away.

But if he *did* believe me, it would get him off my back.

And if I was ever going to discover something to be passionate about, telling Dad that I wanted to be a journalist could buy me the time to *actually* figure that out. At least, that's what I told myself.

Even with that logic dance, I hesitated. I looked up at Marcos.

He was smiling down at me. His great big, benevolent, big-brother-type smile. Then he plucked the Ramos article from my hand and placed it on top of the Post-it Notes.

"He won't find out from me, kid."

"Leah!" Dad called from the living room. "Leah, we're not finished talking. Can you come out here, please?"

I squeezed my eyes shut and made a choice. I turned to Marcos.

"You promise you won't squeal? You won't tell him that I've got no intention of becoming a journalist?"

"I promise."

"Okay then."

Armed with the Ramos article atop my pile of Post-it Notes, I steeled myself for The Big Lie.

Marcos had been right. Dad approved. Marcos was right about something else too — keeping his promise. He backed me up in Istanbul, and he continued to back me up through moves to Hong Kong, Belarus, and all the way to Rio. In fact, Marcos did more than just back me up. He aided and abetted by cutting out Christina Ramos articles for me so I could pin them to my bulletin board like a stage set. Three moves and three years later, I had a wall of select Ramos articles and a dad who proudly believed I was an aspiring investigative journalist.

Just like Christina Ramos.

**3.**

---

## THE REPORTER

The reporter stood on her hotel balcony and stared across Praia do Leblon — a perfect stretch of beach bordering the ocean, spanning every shade of blue, from the palest forget-me-not to evening's darkest cobalt. It was a postcard view, but the reporter was no tourist. She was Christina Ramos, Pulitzer Prize-winning investigative journalist, in Rio to cover the presidential election. For the journalist, the rapidly gathering crowds were far more interesting than any beach.

Coffee in hand, Ramos watched as the crowds swelled, doubled, then doubled again and again until bodies packed Avenida Delfim Moreira and overflowed inland onto streets running perpendicular to the ocean. They came on foot from the closest Metro station, Antero de Quental, and from Rocinha Favela in a seemingly unending stream of mototaxis. They all came to see their hero, João Matheus Pereira. If the odds-makers were correct, on Sunday — five days from now — Pereira would become Brasil's president-elect.

A large delivery truck appeared, driving slowly along the beach road. The police waved it over. Anticipating the arrival of their hero, the crowd swam toward the vehicle like schooling fish. The truck door opened, and there he was, João Matheus Pereira. Wearing his trademark look, blue jeans and a white shirt with rolled-up sleeves, Pereira looked every inch the working man's friend. It was the look Ramos had made famous in her New York Times article one year ago.

She watched as Pereira climbed onto the truck's hood and then turned to face his people. Like a wave rolling toward shore, a collective, breath-holding silence moved across the masses. It was eerie. Ramos felt a shiver run up her spine. Then Pereira stretched both arms out toward the crowd as if inviting them into an embrace, and the streets erupted with a cheer that could be heard from Copacabana to Barra da Tijuca.

Ramos watched the scene below with interest and a healthy dose of reporter's skepticism. Putting down her coffee, she pulled out her phone and snapped some pictures. Just then, her cell phone rang. Her call display showed a laughing young woman in a cap and gown sporting a fake mustache. It was Valerie Soto — her old college roommate from Yale and the current US Consul General in Rio de Janeiro.

"Valerie?"

"Christina Ramos, you old Bulldog. When were you going to tell me you were in town?"

Ramos chuckled. "Who are you calling an old Bulldog, puta? And how in hell did you know I was here? I just got in last night. Wait. Don't tell me that you're tracking American citizens in-country now?"

"I wouldn't tell you if I was. But no. I heard it from the new guy over at the Canadian Consulate. James Teague. Heard of him?"

"No. Should I have?"

"I'm not sure. Maybe. Teague only parachuted into Rio eight weeks ago, but he's clearly wired up. He seems to know everyone already. He called me specifically to ask about you."

"Me? Why?"

"His daughter. Leah. Says she's a senior at a local international school. According to Teague, she has journalistic aspirations, and for some unfathomable reason, you're her hero. Personally, I have no idea what she sees in a hack like you."

Ramos snorted. "Glad to hear success hasn't gone to your head."

"Seriously, Christina. About Teague ..."

"What about him?"

"His kid is applying to Yale. He asked that you do an alumni interview with her while you're here."

"I don't have time, Valerie. I'm on call for an interview with —"

"João Matheus Pereira. I know. James Teague told me."

Ramos hesitated. How the hell did James Teague know that? Pereira's people had only contacted her Sunday, and the only other person Ramos had told between then and now was Tyrell, her editor.

"Christina, are you still there?"

"Yeah."

"Good. Because I need to ask *you* for a favor this time," Soto said, her tone reminding Ramos that between the two old college friends, the favors had historically been a one-way stream flowing toward the reporter.

"I've already told Teague you'd do the interview. Tomorrow morning at 08:00 hours."

"What the hell, Val?"

"Do this for me, Christina."

"Why?"

"I need to know how it is that a Canadian Cultural Attaché is more informed about the comings and goings of US citizens than we are. I'm hoping that your interview with the girl, Leah, can give me some answers."

"You have people for that," Ramos countered.

"I'd like to think you would do it as a friend without me having to remind you that you owe me. What do you say, *puta*? Will you use those wily reporter skills that earned you a Pulitzer to help me — and possibly your country?"

It only took Ramos a split second to agree, but not because Valerie Soto was an old friend. And not because this old friend held a high consular rank that could prove useful someday. Ramos was curious how this Teague guy, a newcomer at the Canadian Consulate, knew she was in Rio. And even more mysteriously, how in hell did *he* know she'd scored an interview with João Matheus Pereira? Still, getting some high school senior to talk, especially one angling for an alum recommendation, would be like shooting fish in a barrel.

"Sure, Val. I'll do it."

"Good. See what you can get out of the kid tomorrow, okay?"

"What's her name again?"

"Leah. Leah Teague."

*It's the ugly truth: She was their puppet.*

*And it's impossible for a puppet to cut the puppet masters' strings if they don't even know they're a puppet.*

**4.**

---

# DON'T WORRY — IT'S A MUSTACHE

My school wasn't at all worried about a group of high school seniors going on a field trip to Rocinha. Fifteen minutes after leaving the school gates, Mr. Mudaris, our AP World Geography teacher, was herding us off the bus and onto the sidewalk to wait for our guide. No one had mentioned João Matheus Pereira, his rally, or that he'd be making a delivery to Rocinha's schools today. Instead, we talked about weekend plans, complained about homework, SATs and the pressure of college applications.

I'd just switched my cell phone from my back pocket to the front when Janneke said, "I hope we can get everything today. Did you bring the list of shots we need?"

"It's all in here," I said, tapping my finger on the side of my head.

A crease lined Janneke's forehead. I grinned.

"Het zit wel snor."

She laughed then. Literally, what I said was, *It's a mustache*, but in Dutch it's how you tell someone not to worry.

"For someone who lived only eighteen months in de Nederlands, you have a remarkable command of our idioms."

It was my turn to chuckle. Sometimes when Janneke spoke English, it was that formal classroom English. Still, I didn't want her to worry; I knew how much she was counting on me. Like Janneke, I was applying to Yale, but unlike her, I didn't need to get in. I had no big plans. I could happily go somewhere else. Uncle Wally hoped I'd go to one of the England's Oxbridge schools, while my dad thought the sun rose and set over his alma maters, Queen's and U of T in Canada. But Janneke dreamed of studying film in America. After much persuading, her parents reluctantly agreed to Yale and its chokingly high foreign student tuition, but *only* Yale and *only* if she got accepted. It was her one chance. It was also the only way she could spend the next four years with Nick — the boy she loved, who was doing his senior year in Maine at some snooty boarding school.

I wasn't about to let her down. I had our list of desired shots committed to memory. I'd not only helped write the script, I was also its narrator. I'd rehearsed so much that I knew it inside and out, frontward and backward. I knew exactly what shots we still needed. I also knew that if another potentially better shot presented itself today, I'd be ready for that too. I'd find a way to make it happen. Whatever it took. Because if there was one thing I'd learned from changing schools as much as I had, it was to protect your friendships. It didn't matter that I'd only met Janneke two months ago. We met. We clicked. We had each other's back. That was Survival 101 for kids like us.

Janneke, Teebo (short for Tyberius), and I met the first week of school during college counseling classes. They'd put us together because we were the only three applying to Yale. Janneke liked that I could speak a little Dutch, thanks to Marcos. And she liked being able to talk about her home with someone who knew it well. I liked Janneke's tell-it-like-you-see-it honesty and that she knew precisely what she was passionate about. Dad would have loved her.

Janneke and I became instant friends, and Teebo ... well, we weren't anything yet, but maybe someday. I'd promised Marcos I wouldn't say anything about my Yale alumni interview. Still, it pinched to keep that secret from these two. It didn't seem right that I was getting an interview, and they weren't, just because they didn't have parents who could pull strings like mine. Janneke's mom was a geologist at Shell, and Teebo's dad worked for PSA Group. Neither were high enough up in their companies to have any political clout. But a promise is a promise, so I swallowed my secret with a drink of water from the bottle clipped to my belt loop and turned my attention to identifying potential shots.

The roads were paved but narrow with no painted lines. Old model cars and trucks parked along the road were covered in a thin film of dust. Pedestrians owned the center of the streets. Shopping bags in hand, they shuffled up and down the steep road. A mototaxi station operated out of a small storefront nearby. A few drivers straddled bikes under a corrugated tin awning while others flew in and out like bees searching for their next flower. But what caught my eye were the electrical wires. They crisscrossed streets and alleys, strung between buildings in crazy random patterns, meeting at power poles in a fat snarl of cables and connectors that made me think of dendrites from biology class. Not for the first time, I shook my head at how crazy unsafe this was. It was no wonder people died trying to steal power from the grid.

That twigged something in my brain — something I'd read about João Matheus Pereira. It was a Ramos article from early in the pandemic when Pereira first began delivering food to favelas. That same article was pinned on my bulletin board next to the picture of Corcovado Mountain — the one with our climbing date scrawled across in red. Curious, I looked the article up on my phone.

Underneath Ramos's byline was a picture of Pereira in a white dress shirt with the sleeves rolled up. Pereira was a compact man, small but powerfully built. His face was tanned and weathered, with ink-black hair slicked back from his forehead. I scrolled through the interview until I found the part about Pereira's father.

**Ramos:** As a child you lived in Vila Cruzeiro. I believe at the time it was one of the poorest and most brutal favelas in Rio.

**Pereira:** Sim (Yes).

**Ramos:** And you were a member of the Red Command.

**Pereira:** Sim (Yes). Since I was twelve years old. I wanted to stay in school. I had dreams of going to university, but after my father died trying to bring us electricity, there was no money. My mother could not find work, and because we must have money for food, I joined the Comando Vermelho. Estevãoran was its leader then. He took in boys like me and gave us jobs. Small jobs at first, but it was never charity. To earn we had to be useful. We had to prove ourselves.

**Ramos:** What could a twelve-year-old boy possibly do for Comando Vermelho?

**Pereira:** Some boys took naturally to the selling of drugs. Some were more suited to the violence — they seemed to like that. Me, I was smart, good at sums, and observant. I saw things.

**Ramos:** Things?

**Pereira:** Things happening in his organization that interested Estevãoran. Even then, I was good at — how you say — planning a few moves ahead?

**Ramos:** Strategy.

**Pereira:** Estratégia. It is close, yes? Estevãoran took an interest in me, and I found more and more ways to make myself useful to him. Too useful. Other boys resented how quickly and how high I climbed in Comando Vermelho.

**Ramos:** How did you go from being a teenager working for a favela drug lord to living in Mato Grosso and owning the continent's largest private agribusiness?

**Pereira:** Ah, well ... I had to leave Vila Cruzeiro. You see, I might have killed two of Estevãoran's men. Not men. Boys like me. Boys who resented me for having Estevãoran's ear. They had decided to teach me a lesson. One day, I returned home to find them taking turns beating my mother and doing things to her no son should ever have to witness. You can see that I am not a big man, Miss Ramos. As a boy, I was also small. But I was powered by rage. I beat those boys very badly and left them for dead.

**Ramos:** They died?

**Pereira:** Maybe they lived. Maybe not. I did not stay to check.

**Ramos:** And your mother?

**Pereira:** She was already dead.

**Ramos:** And so you ran away?

**Pereira:** Sim (Yes). There was nothing left for me in Vila Cruzeiro.

**Ramos:** I am so very sorry you had to face all that, Senhor Pereira. But I am also very surprised you would tell me this. Aren't you afraid I will include it in my article, and the police will arrest you?

**Pereira:** My story is well known. This happened a long, long time ago, Miss Ramos, and as I have said to you, maybe those boys lived, maybe they did not. There is no way to know now, and I no longer remember their names.

**Ramos:** This explains why you left, but how did you go from being a runaway and a fugitive to the sole owner of a mega farm?

**Pereira:** How can you explain luck? I was in the right place at the right time."

I put my phone back in my front pocket. As interesting and dramatic as Pereira's life was, Janneke and I had decided *not* to put this year's election politics into our documentary. It would distract from the story we were trying to tell. Still, pictures of Rocinha's pirate electrical connections might be useful spliced in somewhere. I shot some video, switched off my GoPro to save batteries, then turned my attention to a group of motorcycles waiting at a mototaxi station. The drivers sat straddling their bikes, waiting for fares. They wore vests to identify themselves — plain fluorescent yellow and green, or red with the Claro telecom logo emblazoned across the back. I saw them daily zipping along Av. Delfim Moreira. The bikes were small, around 200 to 250cc. I'd ridden motocross bikes that size at a club in Gouda, The Netherlands.

"You're smiling," Janneke said. She moved to stand beside me again.

"Me? Yeah. I was thinking how much better it would be to ride than walk."

"You can take tours, you know."

"I know. Marcos suggested it would be a good way for us to get some footage." I frowned and fanned myself with my hand. It was still early, but the temperature was already over 80 degrees. Heat rolled down the cement walls of the surrounding buildings and radiated off the pavement.

"I wish today's tour was on a motorbike. It would be a lot cooler."

"I sometimes forget that you moved here from Belarus," Janneke said. "Your driver is right, though. A moving shot from the back of a mototaxi would be excellent, but since we need to get all our video today, and since neither of us can come back here this weekend ..." She shrugged. "We can't put off the editing any longer."

"Helaas pindakaas," I said. It means *that's too bad*, but the literal translation is, *Too bad, peanut butter.*

"We should speak more Dutch together, Leah, so you don't forget."

"Probably. But Marcos is making me learn Portuguese. I don't think I can manage both."

Just then, our guide arrived. Tall with dreadlocks, baggy shorts, hemp sandals, and a loud Hawaiian shirt, the guide shook hands with our teacher. They exchanged a few words that were impossible to hear over the traffic and people-noise, then the guide motioned everyone to follow. He led us uphill in a loose line. To wrangle strays, Mr. Mudaris circled near the back like a mother duck. There weren't any strays. Even at this hour, it was far too hot and humid to wander. A mototaxi whizzed past, leaving a welcome but short-lived breeze in its wake.

When we were far enough away from the traffic and noise, the guide began his spiel about how wonderful it was to live in Rocinha, how much the favela had changed from the bad old days before *pacification*, and how now that the army had cleared out all the gangs and organized crime, Rocinha was a great place to live. He said that people who squatted here years ago could now legally claim ownership of the homes they built. I made a mental note to fact-check that later. It was too late to add that to our script, but it could be useful for an essay later.

"Rocinha has AirBnBs. Tourists *love* to stay inside Rocinha for the full *favela experience*." The guide didn't actually do air quotes with his fingers, but he certainly did it with his voice.

Next, we toured a building that housed an after-school program.

"See all the children doing their homework, arts and crafts, and computer? It is all funded by a wealthy expat who saw a need here in Rocinha. An expatriate like most of your parents, yes?"

Not my dad. He was not a big money earner. He worked for the feds.

After leaving the after-school program, we walked on, the tropical sun blasting us. Sweat dripped down my neck, trickled into my cleavage and down my back. My deodorant wasn't working the way it was advertised. I wasn't the only one.

As our class lined up to buy water from a shop so small only two of us could enter at a time, my senses were assaulted by a wet soup of body odor and something else. Something foul. I looked for the source of the stink. Nearby, an old white pickup truck had pulled to a stop. The truck bed was stacked with sun-faded, pastel-colored crates, each one crammed tight with once-white chickens and covered in poop and molting feathers.

"Anyone for frango tonight?" Josh called out, then feigned gagging.

Like me, Josh was new to the school this year. But unlike me, this was his first international posting. He still held his old life in Houston as the benchmark for how things should work everywhere. He'd wise up by the end of the school year —most everyone does —but right then, the look on the guide's face as Josh stood beside the truck making fake retching noises made me cringe with embarrassment. I wasn't keen on eating chicken either, not after seeing and smelling that, but there were people walking past. People who lived here in Rocinha. I looked around to see if any passers-by had overheard or understood. One woman shot our group a dirty look.

"Me desculpe sobre isso," I said haltingly, hoping I'd just apologized for my classmate and not unwittingly added to the injury. She walked on.

Our next stop was outside the freshly white-washed offices of the UPP, the Unidade de Polícia Pacificadora. In English, the Police Pacifying Units. Popular opinion may be that Rocinha is a safe place, but the concentration of heavily armed, flack-jacketed officers filing in and out of the building, and their patrol cars carrying automatic weapons, was hard to ignore. Safe places shouldn't need that much firepower.

Reading the crowd, our guide pasted on a smile and said, "We are so lucky to have the UPP. It keeps Rocinha safe so tourists can come, stay in our AirBnBs, and visit our many wonderful cantinas. We have talented artisans here also," he said, looking pointedly at each of us. I fully expected that we'd be led to some street vendors before the tour was over. He motioned for us to begin walking when a UPP officer waved to the guide and approached. The two exchanged some friendly words in Portuguese. I tried to listen, but after only eight weeks here, their conversation was too fast for me.

"Did you get any of that, Janneke?" I whispered.

"Some. He told the guide we couldn't visit the school today. Something about João Matheus Pereira and his food delivery."

"Does that mean the tour is over?" I asked, worried.

"I don't know."

"I still need some shots. You?"

"Yes. Me too."

Janneke motioned me to follow. Together, we edged forward, closer to where the guide was talking to Mr. Mudaris.

**5.**

---

# A MILLION DOLLAR VIEW &
# ONE CRAZY IDEA

João Matheus Pereira's visit to Rocinha meant we couldn't tour a favela school as planned, but our guide assured Mr. Mudaris there was another, better stop. And that meant another chance to get the footage Janneke and I needed for our documentary. With a pasted-on smile, the guide waved us to follow him up more hills along increasingly narrow and winding roads.

This high, the houses were fewer and farther apart. Even the sidewalks had disappeared. A profusion of jungle-green plants and trees clung stubbornly to every square foot of undeveloped slope and verge. By now, the sun was almost directly overhead, and everyone gravitated to the road's edge, seeking patches of shade. A bead of sweat dripped down my forehead, slid sideways off the bridge of my nose, and landed in the corner of my eye. The mix of salt-sweat and sunscreen stung. I wiped it clean with a knuckle.

Our trek ended in front of an unlikely spot — a one-bay garage where a man in overalls stood bent over an old car. The guide signaled us to follow him inside. We did, walking single-file and hugging the garage wall. As we passed a door-less washroom with a rust-stained toilet and dirty sink, I silently willed Josh to keep his trap shut. This was not a place to mouth off about the locals.

Everything about this stop had my safety antennae tingling, their sensors honed by years of security lectures from Dad and Marcos. This was an unplanned, unknown stop at an out-of-the-way location, and the guide was leading us toward a door at the rear of the building that led who-knows-where. But Josh stayed mercifully silent, his attention split between the mechanic and a large dog that lay sprawled and panting across our path. The dog barely looked up as fourteen pairs of feet stepped over him. One by one, we filed through that rear door onto a flat cement roof.

Clearly my antennae were faulty. We weren't in danger. We were being gifted something few people get to see — a spectacular view. Rocinha's massive horseshoe valley spilled out below us, bordered by a mammoth wall of sheer rock to the north, which made the rock climber in me itch for my carabiners, quickdraws, chalk bags, and rope. To the east, a fat, lush stripe of vegetation marked the end of Rocinha favela. Beyond that, I could see Leblon's luxury high-rises and the blue waters of the Atlantic Ocean.

I lived in a pretty swank apartment in Leblon. I'd wager every expat kid in this class also lived in equally great digs, either in an apartment or nearby villa. Still, I didn't have ocean views like this rooftop house *cum* auto repair shop.

From all the work Janneke and I had done on our documentary, I knew that a hundred years ago, this valley would have been a lush green, tropical rainforest brimming with the thorny *favela* plants that gave these cities-inside-a-city their name. Not anymore. There was almost no vegetation left. Every available inch was packed tight with two, three, and four-story cement buildings. From where I stood, those boxy buildings with their flat roofs looked like wobbly-stacked building blocks. The only color besides cement-gray came from the occasional building painted canary yellow, hot pink, Dutch orange, pale purple, or toothpaste green. Or from the white satellite dishes and stubby blue water tanks that dotted the thousands of flat roofs.

"What do you think, Janneke?"

"I think we are *very* lucky to come here instead of the favela school. This was not on our list, but we can use this."

I thought so too.

"I'm going to film," she said and left to claim a place at the edge of the rooftop where our classmates were already busy taking pictures of the view, each other, selfies. I had no doubt Janneke would get great footage for our documentary. She had a Fujifilm X-T4, perfect for aspiring filmmakers. I just had my GoPro, but I had an idea. Something that could add an interesting perspective.

I slipped away to the rear of the rooftop where a short, steep slope ran up to the road above. The slope was green and peppered with trees. If I climbed high enough in one of those trees, I could show more than the view. I could film *where* this amazing view originated - the rooftop of a favela home and business.

My GoPro was securely mounted to a small, lightweight monopod that hung from my wrist on a loop, kind of like a pocket umbrella. With a backward glance to ensure everyone was still looking the other way, I slid the monopod handle up my arm until the camera and pole hung from my shoulder, then I scrambled up the slope toward the road. Once there, I studied the available trees the same way I'd study a rock face to pick the best route up a cliff. Confident of my choice, I began to climb.

The tree bark was rough, but that was not a problem for me; my hands were calloused from years of climbing. Ten feet up, however, the trunk began to narrow, and I stopped. Lifting the camera, I looked through the viewfinder. I needed to be higher.

I hitched up until the trunk began to bow. I didn't dare go further. Lifting the GoPro, I began filming. First, the view of the ocean, then zooming out, I got footage of the flat cement roof and the garage beside it. I might not have Janneke's practiced eye or her high-end camera, but I was pretty sure my shot's story was what we needed. At least it would be if there weren't a dozen high school seniors milling on the roof, talking and taking selfies.

Behind me, I heard the high-pitched whine of a small two-stroke motorbike. I swiveled to look. As the mototaxi whizzed past on the road below, an idea hit me. The road was right there, below and behind me. If I waited until the class filed back inside the garage, I could repeat the shot without anyone littering the view *and* there would still be plenty of time to climb down to the road and meet everyone as they exited the garage. But when I turned back toward the cement rooftop, I saw the guide, angry-faced and marching toward me.

Scrambling like a seasoned arborist, I hurried down the tree.

"Nem fodendo," the guide cursed.

I'd been here eight weeks; I knew what that meant. It meant he was pissed. As he turned and walked toward Mr. Mudaris, I held my breath, but all the guide said to my teacher was, "We go now. I will walk you to where your bus waits. There is a cantina where you can buy cold drinks and food."

The guide shot a last warning glare my way, but he hadn't ratted me out and Mr. Mudaris was too busy taking his own pictures to notice where I'd been. We filed back through the garage and over the dog, who had yet to move a muscle.

The guide never let me out of his sight until we reached our destination — a multi-story sprawl of cement buildings painted Colgate green. Our bus was parked on the road, door open with our driver sitting on the bottom step. When the bus driver saw us, he stood and headed our way.

"The cantina of my friend," the guide said, pointing to a kiosk tucked into a shady overhang. "He will take care of you." Then he shook the teacher's hand, hailed a passing moto-taxi, and left just as our school bus driver arrived.

"The UPP was just here," our bus driver told Mr. Mudaris. "They have closed all roads out of Rocinha. We cannot leave yet."

"Did they say why?" Mr. Mudaris asked.

"João Matheus Pereira is delivering food to a local school."

There was a collective groan from the entire class. Everyone was ready to return to the air-conditioned comfort of our classroom.

"How long do they expect us to wait here?" someone called out.

"They said maybe an hour." The driver shrugged. "That was twenty minutes ago."

"The guide just left," Josh said. "If he got out, why can't we?"

"He's from Rocinha, remember?" Teebo said. "It's the roads *out* that are closed."

Mudaris nodded. "Class, it appears we're stuck here. We'll have to make the best of things. The canteen is open. I suggest you find something there to eat or drink. And for those of you who are new to Rio and Rocinha — Josh, Leah — these places only take cash. So if you need some *reals*, let me know."

I always carry cash — cash in my wallet and a secret stash of emergency cash. It's one of the many safety practices and protocols drilled into me since I could tie my own shoes. Dad and Marcos claimed their protocols were common sense because of the places we've lived and visited, but seventeen-year-old me was beginning to think they were over the top. But a habit's a habit, and today, Brazilian *reals* were tightly folded and tucked in my pocket, shoe, and bra.

"I'm fine," I said. Everyone turned to look at Josh.

"What?" he said. "I've got cash money."

"Good," said Mudaris. "Because we may be here a while. See if you can make a lunch out of what's on offer. I'll let the school know what's happening."

With that, twelve seniors made for the cantina and the promise of cold drinks and food while our teacher hung back and made a call. The first few kids brazenly ordered caipirinhas — the Brazilian cocktail made with fresh limes, extra-fine sugar, and cachaca rum. I unclipped the water bottle from my waistband before remembering I'd drained it *and* the bottled water I'd bought an hour ago. I joined Janneke at the back of the line.

"How's your list, Janneke?"

"See for yourself." She lifted her camera to show me the film she'd taken from the roof. It was good. Really good. I showed her mine.

"How did you ...? Never mind," she shook her head and grinned. "Did Mr. Mudaris see you climb?"

"No. But the guide did, and he was pretty pissed. He dropped the F-bomb in Portuguese. He didn't think I'd understand," I added.

She laughed, then got serious. "Getting this footage was a nice surprise. It's perhaps the best view of Rocinha we could have hoped for."

"Yes, but I'm still missing some shots. We wanted footage of a typical residential street in the favela, remember? Something with no businesses or stores."

She shrugged. "Perhaps we can get something from the bus window as we leave. If not, we will have to make do with what we have."

I nodded even though I wasn't ready to settle. Then I heard the sound of an approaching motorcycle. The Doppler effect told me it was heading toward us, fast. Moments later, I saw the neon vest.

"I have an idea," I said and stuck my arm out to wave down the mototaxi. "Cover for me?"

"Are you crazy? The roads are closed."

"Just the roads out, remember? But I don't want to leave Rocinha. I'll get the driver to take me through a few nearby streets. Who knows, maybe I'll get lucky."

Her brow furrowed, but she finally nodded. "Okay, Leah, but keep your phone close. I'll call you when it's time to get on the bus."

"Thanks."

"And Leah?"

"Yeah."

"Je bent gek."

"Crazy like a fox," I said, laughing. Feeling electrified at the idea of doing something more exciting than sneaking a rum drink during school hours, I sidled off toward the road and the approaching mototaxi.

## 6.

---

# TRINTA MINUTOS, POR FAVOR

As the mototaxi slowed, I felt that same thrill I got before a big climb. The neon-vested driver wasn't much older than me. Cute too, but I didn't have time for cute. He, on the other hand, was giving me the up-down. Considering how sweat-baked I was after three hours under a tropical sun, it's a fair bet he wasn't checking me out. Just trying to decide whether I had the money to pay.

I pointed to the bus with my school's name emblazoned across the side, then tapped that same finger against my chest. Even though I wore plain shorts, a T-shirt with no logos or labels, and a beat-up pair of Chuck Taylors, the boy shrugged as if he already knew where I was from. I suppose I reeked of *other*; my GoPro alone would tell him that.

"English?" I asked.

He shook his head.

In my best Portuguese, I made a halting request. "Um tour, por favor. Vinta minutos."

A tour. Twenty minutes, please.

He nodded his understanding, so I tried my luck with a few more instructions, Google Translate at the ready on my phone just in case.

I pointed my finger first at me, then my GoPro, and then I pointed at him.

"Mostre-me, sua Rochina." Show me your Rochina. At least, I hoped that's what I said. "Turistas — não," I added. Tourists. No. "Sua casa?"

I didn't know how to say "nothing touristic." Instead, I asked to see his home. I really hoped he didn't take it the wrong way.

He nodded and tipped his head for me to climb on the back. With a last glance toward my classmates and teacher to make sure I wasn't seen, I climbed on quickly and signaled the boy to drive. He kicked the bike into gear, and we were off.

He drove fast. After hours of walking and standing under the hot tropical sun, the breeze from the ride was glorious. With my knees vice-gripping the driver, I started filming. I held the camera high in my right hand while my left hand held tight to the metal grab bar at the back of the seat.

He followed a labyrinthine path of left and right turns, the uphills and downhills canceling each other out and keeping us at the same altitude. Sometimes there were buildings on both sides of the road. Sometimes it seemed like we were on the edge of a forest jungle with nothing but green rising on one side or dropping off the other.

Everything looked different from the back of a bike. Maybe it was because there were no shops and businesses up here, but this Rocinha didn't just look different. It felt different too. Like a living thing. It was in the music leaking through open doorways. It was in the faces of little kids playing in the streets. It was in the buildings themselves, where almost every structure was painted a hopeful color. It was even in the posture of the boy driving this mototaxi.

We turned onto a quiet street with no music and no people. The boy slowed to a stop and every muscle in my body tensed. For the first time since I'd climbed on board, I was nervous. I reached for my cell phone and then hitched as far backward as possible just in case I needed to jump off in a hurry.

"Minha casa," the boy said and pointed to a building.

My house.

The tension leached out of me. He *had* understood.

I had so many questions then. I wanted to know whether he lived here alone or with his family? How much of the house was his? How many people did he share it with? Did they have to pay rent to someone, or had they built it them-selves? But I didn't know enough Portuguese yet. All I could manage was a sincere smile, a nod, and "Obrigado." Thank you.

"Foto." I pointed to a three-way intersection at the top of the street. "Lá."

The boy understood my one-syllable request. He squeezed the clutch, kicked the bike back into gear, and drove to the top of the street, stopping just before the three-way intersection. I climbed off the back of the bike, aimed my camera downhill, and shot what I was sure would be the last footage I'd need. But before going back to the bus, I needed to make sure. I was head-down, checking my video when a blue and white UPP police cruiser drove past, then turned uphill at the next street.

"Espere aqui." Wait here, I called, already moving to see where the police car had gone. The boy shook his head and revved the throttle to underscore his objection.

"Por favor," I begged.

He shook his head again. It was clear he wanted to keep his distance from the police.

Turning back, I reached into a front pocket, I pulled out a cream, brown, and yellow banknote — two hundred *reals*; about forty US dollars — and showed it to him. He stuck his hand out for the money.

I shook my head. Holding up two fingers, I said, "Dois minutos. Then bus."

The boy shook his head. I pulled out another two hundred *real* banknote.

I was offering him eighty US dollars. As much as he'd make in an entire morning. Maybe even an entire day!

Actually, that was a guess. I had no idea if it was true, but I *did* know that he could have it all for a measly two minutes more.

It seemed like forever before he nodded. Stuffing the banknotes back into my pocket, I ran to see if I could catch a glimpse of the cruiser. It was still there, parked on a narrow road, barely wide enough for two vehicles to pass side by side. Parked above it was a tired-looking truck. It was like the chicken truck I'd seen earlier, except this cargo bed held a boxy load covered by a sun-faded tarp. I was about to move closer when loud and angry voices tumbled downhill, raising hairs on my arms and the back of my neck.

I hesitated. I could still turn away, get back on that mototaxi and return to my classmates and school bus. Instead, I started my GoPro, and stepped fully around the corner.

Check me out, Dad. I'm *pursuing my goals with gusto.*

**7.**

---

# IN CASE OF EMERGENCY

By the time I stepped around the corner and looked uphill, some of my *gusto* had leaked out. The two UPP officers had exited their cruiser and were fast approaching the rear of the old truck, where two rough-looking men stood by the truck's cargo bed. Maybe it was the way the men slouched. Maybe it was their lazy gestures or how they spat on the road between drags of their cigarettes. Or maybe it was because those men did not look at all concerned about two heavily armed, Kevlar-wearing UPP officers walking toward them with a swagger. Everything about those men from the truck screamed shady.

One of the *disreputubles* (that's how I'd labeled them) clamped his cigarette between his lips and, using both hands, lifted the sun-faded tarp.

Boxes. Just boxes.

I don't know what I expected. Maybe deep down I thought I'd stumbled on a UPP bust. Instead, the only thing beneath that tarp was pulpy cardboard boxes, limp from humidity. Those cardboard cartons could hold anything from black beans to beauty cream.

I was about to switch off my camera and return to my waiting mototaxi, when one of the disreputables unsheathed a knife, sliced open a box and pulled out a tightly wrapped cellophane package. He stabbed it with the tip of his knife, then offered it to one of the UPP officers, who tasted the tip with his tongue.

Holy eight balls, cocaine! It had to be. If I believed the kids at school, Rio was filthy with the stuff.

Then, one of the disreputables took out his phone and moments later, a small two-stroke motorcycle with a passenger on the back appeared at the top of the hill and headed down toward the two parked vehicles.

My neurons were firing over time. Adrenalin coursed through my body, but this was nothing like the jangles. The jangles was the monster hiding in the closet, the bogeyman under the bed. It was the unknown danger that lurked in dark corners waiting to grab you. Unlike my dream, this adrenalin dump made sense and understanding *why* something scared me always made it easier to manage that rush of fight-or-flight hormones.

In hindsight, leaving right then would have been the sensible thing to do. But sensible people don't climb mountains, I've been told, so I kept filming as the passenger climbed off the back of the motorbike and took off his helmet.

I only saw him in profile. From the glimpses I got through my GoPro I'd say the man was about the same age as my dad, but where my dad's hair had turned an elegant silver, this man had a head of thick dark hair slicked back from his forehead. He wore a white dress shirt with the shirtsleeves rolled up. He held a fat envelope which he handed to the UPP officer, who opened it and looked inside. Were those banknotes? What else could they be? The envelope was too thick to be coveted tickets to the city's favorite soccer team, FC Flamengo. After all the crap we'd just been spoon-fed about favela reforms, here were two UPP officers accepting a bribe, presumably to let cocaine into Rocinha.

This changed everything. I needed to leave. Keeping my arms and camera locked in place, I began to shuffle slowly backward an inch at a time — moving quickly was a sure way to be spotted. Meanwhile, uphill, the UPP officer erupted in a string of angry Portuguese profanities. I froze. I held my breath as the officer waved the envelope in the face of the white-shirted man. What happened next changed my life.

In a rapid, practiced move, the man with the white shirt reached behind his back, pulled out a gun, pressed it against the belly of the UPP officer just beneath the bottom of his Kevlar vest, then fired. Even before the officer hit the ground, the *disreputables* had guns out and aimed at the remaining policeman.

I've read that gunshots sound like a car backfiring. Maybe to some, but I heard firecrackers — those small red cherry bombs that looked like teeny tiny sticks of dynamite and to me were synonymous with New Year's Eve in the Netherlands. The second firecracker sound came so fast after the first that if I hadn't seen it with my own eyes, I wouldn't have believed it. I watched in horror as the second officer's neck snapped backward, and he fell.

I must have screamed because, through my GoPro, I saw the white-shirted man turn and look right at me.

Behind me a motorcycle engine fired –– my ride!

I ran. I didn't know if my driver would wait for me, but when I rounded the corner, he was there. His mototaxi vest was off, and he was busy shoving it down the front of his T-shirt with one hand and madly waving at me to hurry with the other. I jumped on board. Even before my butt hit the seat, we were moving.

"Bus," I yelled in his ear. Like I needed to tell him that.

He didn't answer, but he drove like a fiend, dodging and weaving through up-down streets, taking a crazy convoluted route. I had no idea where we were until we rounded a corner smack into the backside of my school's bus. I jumped off the bike, took every banknote I had tucked in my pockets and inside my bra, and stuffed them down the neck of the boy's shirt. Then I ran toward the bus, the *hin-hin-hin-hin* from his bike's two-stroke engine fading into the hills of Rocinha as he sped away.

My classmates were already on board. Janneke was staring at me through the window, pointing to her phone. Crap. I'd put my phone on silent at the start of the walking tour. Janneke had called to warn me, and I'd missed it.

A red-faced Mr. Mudaris stood on the bottom bus step, his expression cycling from disbelief to shock, making a hard landing on seriously pissed. He launched into a lecture that was gathering a head of steam when I heard another motorbike, followed by that firecracker sound. Something whizzed past my ear, exploding into the ground in front of me. I flew up the bus stairs, past Mr. Mudaris, just as a second bullet shattered the side mirror.

"Go!" I shouted at the driver. He didn't need to be told. He was a local. He recognized the sound of gunfire and had the bus moving before the doors were even closed.

I dropped to my knees and pulled out my cell phone. It had three pre-loaded I.C.E. — In Case of Emergency — numbers. Dad was ICE 1, Marcos was ICE 2, and ICE 3 was just a name to me, Max Klein. I called him "Birthday Max" because I only ever spoke to him once a year on my birthday.

Technically, he was an emergency contact, but he was thousands of miles away in Toronto. He couldn't help me now.

I selected ICE 1 and sent a text.

*911*

## 8.

---

## LEAVING ROCINHA

The bus was filled with the screams of my classmates. I couldn't hear myself think. To make matters worse, the bus driver was racing down hills and swerving around corners like a Formula One driver at Interlagos.

I pushed up to all fours. I didn't dare stand. At these speeds, around these turns, I'd be tossed from one side of the bus to the other. Instead, with my cell phone still clutched in my hand, I flipped over to sit on my butt. That's when I noticed the GoPro recording light was blinking. Steadying myself, I started to reach for the off button when my phone rang.

Dad. Thank God!

Heart thumping, I answered.

"Dad!"

He said something, but I could barely hear him over all the panicked yells and screams.

"You have to talk louder, Dad. I can't hear you."

"Leah, can you hear me now," he said, his voice louder but preternaturally calm.

"Yes, I hear you."

"Good. Your 911 is confirmed. I have you. I can see you're moving. Are you on the school bus?"

"Yes, but —"

"Are you in danger, Leah?"

I cupped my hand over the phone to make sure he could hear me.

"There was a man on a motorcycle shooting at our bus."

Technically, he was shooting at me, but that was best kept secret. At least for now.

"Are you currently in danger?" he asked, his voice annoyingly like a 911 operator.

"I ... I don't know." That was the truth. Since my initial dive onto the bus floor, I hadn't looked out a window. Not even once.

"Are there any motorcycles near your bus now?" Dad asked, still with that 911 voice.

"I don't know."

"Please check your surroundings, Leah. Do it carefully," he added. A wiry edge had crept into his voice. I would have missed it if I didn't know him so well. But it was there; he was worried, and that added to my own fear. Cautiously, very cautiously, I assessed the situation. The screaming had stopped, replaced by nervous murmurs — frantic questions being whispered back and forth. Most of my classmates were still hunkered down in their seats. Only three heads were visible — Janneke, Teebo, and Josh — peering around their seatbacks and looking at me. I knew I'd have to explain everything later, but first I had a job to do.

Pulling myself up just enough to look out the nearest window, I could see that we'd left Rocinha. I swiveled to look in all directions — through the side, back, and front windows — then I reported to Dad.

"We're okay. We're out of Rocinha, heading for school," I said.

The bus driver nodded, but his eyes stayed locked forward, his fingers vice-gripped on the steering wheel.

"And the motorcycles, Leah? Do you see any?"

I looked again. "A few."

"How many? Describe them."

"Two. Both mototaxis with passengers on the back. Carrying shopping bags, I think. They're heading the other way."

"Are you sure they're mototaxis, Leah?"

"Both passengers are old women, and the drivers are wearing red Claro vests."

"Are there any motorbikes following your bus?"

"No, sir. There's nothing behind the bus."

"Any casualties?" Dad asked. "Does anyone need an ambulance?"

"No, sir, but —" I looked at Mr. Mudaris, who was talking on his cell phone and simultaneously sending me dirty looks. I was in so much crap right now, I couldn't see how I'd ever dig my way out.

"Leah?" Dad was talking again. "I need you to listen carefully. Can you do that?"

I nodded.

"Leah, are you still there?"

Stupid, stupid, stupid. Of course, he couldn't see me nodding.

"Yes, sir," I said.

"I have your location. I can see that you're eleven minutes out from school. Marcos is already on his way."

"You're not coming?"

"Marcos is closer."

My heart was still racing from everything I'd just experienced — the drug deal, the shooting of the policemen, the harrowing motorcycle escape, and the gunshots aimed at the bus. I wasn't clearheaded enough then to piece together the right questions.

"Do what I tell you, Leah. You'll be fine. Everything will be fine."

When I didn't answer, he said, "Listen to me, Leah. This is very important. The Rio police are *en* route to your school. You are *not* to talk to them without me there. Do you understand?"

"Why not?"

"Just do as I say, Leah." Dad's voice was as stern as I'd ever heard it. "No police. Promise me."

"I promise."

"One more thing. Remember, do not hang up your phone."

He didn't need to remind me of that. Living in volatile places, his emergency protocols had been drilled into me. I answered him anyway.

"I remember, Dad."

"Good girl. Keep your wits about you and your eyes open. Marcos should be there when you arrive or very soon after." There was a pause, and then he added, "You can do this, Leah."

I hoped he was right.

**9.**

## ONLY AT AN INTERNATIONAL SCHOOL

The bus made a sharp turn at high speed into the school grounds, sending everyone tumbling across their seats, some into the aisle, some into the windows, depending on which side of the bus they were on. Once inside, the gate closed firmly behind us. All those fortifications I'd once thought were overkill — stone perimeter walls with chain-link and razor wire, the heavy iron gate, the guards — none of it seemed excessive now. It felt like safety. My classmates clearly agreed. Their whoops, hollers, and fist pumps echoed inside the small bus. Not me. Not yet.

I scanned the small parking lot looking for any sign of Marcos. Nothing. I did, however, see a police car and two policemen. They were standing next to the headmaster — a woman who, so far, I'd only ever seen at assemblies. Mr. Mudaris spotted them too. Even before the bus stopped, he was on his feet.

"Wait here," he ordered, his voice much louder than the size of our small sixteen-seat school bus required. Despite his instructions, some students stood up.

"Sit down!" he barked, then shot a last, daggered look my way before heading down the steps and off the bus.

With Mr. Mudaris gone, our driver shut off the engine and escaped down the steps. I watched him through my window. He leaned against the bus with a thud, then suddenly hunched forward as if punched in the gut, his back rapidly rising and falling over and over.

I recognized panicked breathing when I saw it. This was no nightmare reaction for him. If I had to guess, I'd say he'd been shot at before. Lifting his head, the driver looked toward the police, but their attention was on Mr. Mudaris, who was hustling across the parking lot toward the police, chest out and with the side-to-side wiggle of an Olympic race walker. Seizing the moment, the driver scuttled quickly around the nose of the bus and out of sight. He clearly didn't want to talk to the police.

And I wasn't supposed to.

Mr. Mudaris continued across the pavement toward the headmaster and the squad car. Once there, he turned and pointed at the bus. At me! I shrank back and down in my seat, one hand slipping protectively over my GoPro, but not before I saw two Rio police heading toward the bus. Mr. Mudaris tried to follow, but the headmaster grabbed his arm.

*Do not talk to the police.*

Those were Dad's exact words. But he'd also promised Marcos would be here, and Marcos was nowhere in sight. Think, Leah, think!

I turned to my classmates, most of them friends by now. They were all staring at me. I owed them something, but I needed them too.

"I'm really, *really* sorry," I said, meaning every word. "This is my fault. I should never have taken off. I know that, but come on ... Mr. Mudaris can't expect us to stay inside this tin can, right?"

I looked around at my classmates, my friends. Janneke was staring at me. I could see that she had questions — *lots* of questions. I pressed my palms together under my chin. Prayer hands. Namaste. Anjali mudra. However, she saw it, Janneke understood.

She nodded, then stood up and addressed the class. "Leah is right. With the engine off, there's no air conditioning. It is too hot to stay here. We need to leave. Now."

"Yeah, this blows," Josh said.

"I'm thirsty."

"I have to pee."

"And Mudaris is a dick." That was Teebo. Good old Teebo. "C'mon, let's go," he said.

Where Teebo led, people tended to follow, and this time was no different. Everyone stood up and headed for the door.

"Thank you, Teebo," I mouthed. He winked, then joined the rest of the class, already heading down the bus stairs and pouring onto the pavement outside.

Quickly, I removed the data card from my GoPro and replaced it with a fresh one. I slipped the used card into its small plastic case and tucked the case inside my bra. I can't say what made me do that. Instinct, maybe? Or maybe it was Dad's warning not to talk to the police, but with the data card secured, I hustled down the aisle to the bus steps because one thing I knew for sure ... I needed to be off the bus *before* the police got here. Trapped inside with them, I didn't think I'd be able to avoid talking. Not without Marcos beside me.

Outside, my classmates had surrounded the two police officers and were busy peppering them with complaints.

"How could you let this happen?"

"Wait till my dad finds out."

"Yeah! Shit's gonna fly, man."

I hadn't asked my classmates to do this. And I don't think they were doing it for me. This was a gut reaction to being shot at. The idea that this sort of thing shouldn't happen to *us* was unacceptable. We were expats. Protected. Entitled. Which in our world meant someone was to blame. Someone needed to be held accountable, and my friends had decided that someone wasn't me; it was the police.

I almost smiled then. This could only happen at an international school. Where else could a group of high school seniors feel so entitled they would dare to scold the authorities?

Ignoring the very vocal indignation of my classmates, the police pushed their way through and headed toward me. I willed Marcos to materialize. Instead, it was Mr. Mudaris who appeared. He'd extricated himself from the headmaster and was scurrying rat-like toward the police. Behind Mudaris, and moving as fast as her high heels would allow, was the headmaster.

These two policemen were very different from the ones I'd seen in Rocinha. They didn't wear flack jackets or carry automatic weapons. One wore a uniform. He was taller, wiry, and pock-faced, the more dangerous looking of the two. The other one was a plain-clothes policeman. He was old, maybe fifty, squat and chunked like those over-the-hill Hollywood actors who insist on doing shirt-off scenes long after they should. He had a thick chest and cheeks so full I swore his eyes would disappear into porcine slits if he tried to smile. His hair was curly and dark brown, but only at the roots. Either it had been kissed by the sun, or he'd paid someone to frost his tips. My money was on vanity.

The pork-faced policeman spoke first. "You are Leah Teague?"

"Yes, yes. That's her," Mr. Mudaris said.

Creep.

"We must talk to you, Miss Teague."

*Do not talk to the police.* Dad's instructions had been clear but following them wasn't easy. Little me. Big them. And they were intimidating.

That's when I saw him. Marcos. He strode toward me, looking so much like a coiled spring that I wouldn't have been surprised to see his picture in a physics textbook as an illustration for potential energy right next to the pictures of a stretched rubber band, water behind a dam, and an archer's bow with the string pulled back. Letting go of a breath I didn't realize I'd been holding, I turned to the detective and shook my head.

"Two policemen, two brothers in arms, were killed today," he pressed. "You will tell us what you saw."

Just then, the headmaster arrived. She pushed through and squared off between me and the police.

"This girl is a minor and in my care. You will not speak with her until she has a parent present."

I couldn't even remember the headmaster's name right then, but I wanted to hug her until the juice ran out.

"Por favor, Madame Principal." It was the uniformed policeman who spoke this time. He aimed a snake-smile at her. "It will take only minutes, and it will help us catch a killer. You must want that too." He turned his viper smile on me next. "You want to help us catch a killer, don't you, Miss Teague?"

The next thing I knew, Marcos was there. He placed a protective hand on my shoulder, giving it a warning squeeze.

I looked up at him. He caught my eye, then leveled the smallest of nods. Dad had briefed him too.

The policeman turned to Marcos, stared, and started speaking in Portuguese. Marcos had that kind of face. With dark hair, dark eyes, and olive skin, he could be Brazilian, Italian, Greek, Spanish, even Middle Eastern.

Marcos pretended he didn't understand (and I pretended not to look surprised at that). The policeman switched back to English.

"Are you her father?"

"No," Marcos said. "Her father sent me. I will be taking Miss Teague home now."

"I am afraid she cannot go until she has given us a statement. We believe she is witness to a police shooting."

My eyes bugged wide. How did *they* know what I'd witnessed? Alarm bells rang in my brain. Turning to Marcos, I tried to look pitiful and scared. I was a fair actor when called upon, but it didn't take much acting at that moment.

"I want my dad," I said in a whining voice. Marcos rewarded my theatrics by wrapping his beefy arm around my shoulder and pulling me close. Then he turned to the police.

"Miss Teague is the daughter of James Teague, cultural attaché at the Canadian Consulate. They're here in Brasil on diplomatic passports."

Marcos pulled a card from his shirt pocket and handed it to the policeman.

"You can contact Mr. Teague at the number on the card," Marcos said. "He's instructed me to tell you that he intends to cooperate fully with the police once his daughter is over the trauma of today's events."

"And when will that be?" the uniformed policeman asked. Something about his voice convinced me that he was *definitely* the more lethal of the two.

"You will have to ask him. Now, if you'll excuse us," Marcos said and steered me away. The uniformed cop, undeterred by Marco's burly presence, stepped in front of us and pointed at the GoPro I'd been clutching protectively against my chest.

"That camera. The light is on. It is recording, yes?"

Unsure, I looked down. It was. Huh? I must have turned it back on after I loaded the new video card. I don't remember doing that.

I didn't answer. Instead, I did my best to look traumatized, which wasn't hard considering.

"Has it been on the whole time? Tell me!"

I didn't look up at the policeman, but I did nod.

"I am taking that," he announced, and reached for the camera.

But I was holding the GoPro against my chest between my breasts, and when he tried to grab it, his knuckles couldn't help but touch places they shouldn't. I recoiled at his touch, and whip-quick, Marcos's hand shot out, vice-gripping the policeman's wrist.

"Take. Your. Hands. Off. Ms. Teague."

Now there were *two* large, man-hands fighting for control between my breasts. The plastic case inside my bra — the one that held the data card — pressed so hard against my skin that I worried it might draw blood.

The policeman only snarled and pulled harder at my GoPro. Marcos doubled down also. This close to Marcos, I could feel him vibrate with anger. I worried he might do something stupid to protect me, like punch a policeman. I had to stop this.

Yelling loud enough for everyone in the parking lot to hear, I said, "Take your hand off my breast!"

The uniformed officer curled his upper lip and snarled at me like a feral dog.

"I am not touching you," he spat between clenched teeth.

"Yes, you are!" I said, my eyes locking his. With a head-tip and a downward glance to remind him that the recording light on my camera was still on, I mustered as much umbrage in my voice as I could and yelled, "You did too! You grabbed my breast!"

Furious and red-faced, the uniform yanked his arm back as if he'd accidentally touched fire, which he kinda did. By this time, Marcos was a pyre of blazing anger.

I was furious also but made sure my next words sounded wounded and afraid.

"I'm scared. I want to go home, Marcos."

Marcos's eyes never left the policeman, but he nodded.

"We're going, kiddo," he said. Once again, he draped his beefy arm protectively across my shoulders. I was happy to let him lead me toward the front gate. I stole a look back at the uniformed officer. He was bent over his mobile phone, making a call. I was pretty sure that whoever he was calling would mean trouble for me. The kind of trouble that Dad would have to clean up.

# 10.

## MOTOTAXIS & MACHETES

At the school gate, Marcos stopped briefly to say goodbye and thank the guards. It hadn't escaped my attention that, other than the police, Marcos was the only person the guards had let inside. I relaxed the death grip on my GoPro and let the whole camera-monopod assembly dangle from my wrist. Between the walking tour, the insane bus ride, and my face-off with the camera-grabbing cop, I'd sweated so much that my T-shirt clung to my skin like Saran Wrap. Grabbing the hem with my free hand, I peeled the tee from my body and flapped it in and out. The guard waved us through the gates, then we headed for *The Tank*.

"That was quick thinking back there, Leah. With the police and the camera."

"Thanks."

"Thank *you*," Marcos said. Then with a wink he added, "Your quick thinking *and* your acting skills probably saved me from doing something incredibly stupid."

I gave him a sisterly shoulder check. "Yeah, well, I spent all my cash in Rocinha. I had nothing left to pay your bail, so ..."

"Brat," Marcos chuckled. As we approached the car, he said, "Back seat today, kid."

I shook my head. "I'm sitting up front."

He hesitated.

"It's *The Tank*, Marcos. It doesn't matter where I am. Every seat is safe."

"It's not because of safety, Leah. We have an audience."

Marcos tipped his head toward the school gate. I swiveled to look. Sure enough, the two policemen had followed us to the gate and were watching from just inside. Despite the tropical heat, I felt a sudden chill. I began to tremble.

"Breathe, Leah," Marcos said. "Everything's going to be fine. Just hang on. I'll get you some dark chocolate." He pulled open the door and leaned across the front seat.

I shouldn't need chocolate, green tea, or bananas. Those were for the jangles, and I was wide awake now. Sure, I'd witnessed two murders and been shot at today, and that was scary and shocking and horrible, but honestly, it didn't feel real somehow. Almost like I'd been watching a movie or tv show. Maybe that was because I saw the murders through my GoPro lens. I dunno. The bottom line was that I knew I was safe because Marcos was here. And even if I *had* been afraid right then, I was no stranger to fear.

In my waking life, I was a risk-taker and proud of it. Not just rock climbing, either. In the Netherlands, I'd skydived and rode motocross. I did a cage swim with great white sharks in Gansbaai, South Africa. I'd lied about my age in Turkey to join a white-water trip on the Dalaman River. Being able to deal with the rush of adrenalin from extreme sports made me feel strong and capable. I needed to know that, when awake, I was in control of my body and its reactions. I told myself that I was only shaky now because I was hungry. I put my hand out for some of that chocolate.

While Marcos was reaching across the seat, I heard the familiar *hin-hin-hin-hin* of a two-stroke engine. I turned in time to see a motorcycle rocket around the bend. It flew downhill straight at me. For one panicked moment, I thought the driver had lost control. I called out for Marcos.

My cry for help came too late. In the next heartbeat, the motorcycle was beside me. A passenger on the back of the bike grabbed my GoPro and ripped it from my wrist, nearly pulling me with it. Then the bike accelerated downhill and away. It all happened so fast. Before Marcos could reach my side.

"Leah! Leah, are you okay?" His face was worry-creased.

"I'm fine, Marcos. But those creeps got my camera!"

I stared down the empty stretch of pavement, rubbing my wrist against the friction burn from the monopod handle. Marcos's eyes narrowed, his jaw set in a hard line. I was furious at the motorcycle thieves, but I was angrier with myself for having dropped my guard. I knew better. It was why, when we'd arrived in Rocinha, I'd switched my phone from my back pocket to my front. It was why I never hung my purse on the back of a chair at restaurants, especially outdoor restaurants. Security precautions had been ingrained in me, along with my ABCs and 123s.

I turned to Marcos, but he was staring at the school gates, furious. Then it dawned on me.

"The police?"

They'd wanted my camera. The uniformed cop even tried taking it from me.

Instead of answering, Marcos barked an order. "Get in the car. Now."

Just then, a second bike flew down the hill toward us. It came fast, even faster than the first. This one also carried a passenger with a bare, outstretched arm that held something long and silver. Sunlight flashed off its metal surface, temporarily blinding me.

Everything that happened next happened faster than my brain could process. One moment I was standing beside *The Tank* staring at an outstretched, blade-wielding arm on an approaching motorbike. Then Marcos picked me up, pivoted me around, and shielded me with his body. The next thing I knew, I was on the ground with Marcos on top of me like a dead weight and my face pressed against the pavement. I never lost consciousness, but the force of the impact and the weight of Marcos's body winded me. There wasn't enough air in my lungs to do more than squeak his name.

"Marcos."

He didn't answer. He didn't move. I wriggled out from under his dead weight. That's when I saw it.

Blood.

The back of Marcos's shirt — always a white shirt and always starched with two military-sharp creases from the laundry — had been sliced open. A giant flower of red blood blossomed across the white cotton, growing bigger and bigger. I screamed.

"Marcos!"

He still didn't move. What I did next was reflex, a rote response from years of training.

I spotted a woman stepping out of her car clutching a cell phone.

"You," I yelled at her. "Yes, you! Dial 192 and demand an ambulance."

Only when I saw her start to dial did I turn back to Marcos. Sending a silent prayer of thanks for all those first aid classes and refresher courses I'd been forced to take, I pressed down on the gash on his back.

There was so much blood. I knew I needed to quell the bleeding, but my bare hands weren't cutting it. Blood oozed through my fingers. Desperate, I looked up for help. Like an angel, the headmaster arrived.

"Use this," she said. She pulled off her suit jacket, rolled it into a tight ball, and placed it over the gash.

I nodded my thanks, tears rolling down my cheeks.

"Ambulance?" I managed to ask.

"Soon," she promised. "I called too."

I looked through the school gates and saw the police heading toward us. The headmaster noticed also. She placed her hand atop mine and said, "Don't worry, Leah. I'm here. I've had my secretary call your father. I'll stay with you until he arrives."

The rest was a blur. The ambulance came first, loaded Marcos onto a stretcher, and whisked him away. True to her word, the headmaster stayed with me, her arm wrapped around my waist, keeping the police at bay.

Then Dad arrived with Raphael, my new, soon-to-be replacement driver.

Dad swooped in, wrapped me in a blanket, and bundled me into the backseat of his car.

"Get us out of here," Dad said to Raphael as the police speed-walked toward us.

"Sir?" Raphael said, pointing to the uniformed cop who had almost reached the front of our car.

"Go!" Dad barked. He slapped the back of the driver's seat hard.

Raphael hit the accelerator, just missing the officer.

Once we were clear, Dad turned to me. "Phone," he demanded.

I handed it over.

He looked at the screen.

"Good," he said. He disconnected the call, then reached across the backseat. He took my hand and squeezed it briefly, then let go and turned around, looking outside the car windows and behind. Was my dad checking to see if we were being followed?

Finally, he turned back to me. "Leah," he said. His eyes were shiny with held-back tears. I'd never seen him like this before. He reached across the seat and took my hand in his once more.

"Listen to me, Leah. I'm proud of you. So very proud. You kept your head and remembered everything Marcos and I taught you: the 911 text and maintaining the phone connection. I could hear everything, including when that policeman tried to take your camera."

I nodded.

"You didn't give it to him, Leah. Why?"

"I dunno. You didn't want me to speak to them. I guess I figured that included not letting them see what was on my camera." I shrugged. "But Dad, when I wouldn't give the policeman my GoPro, he called someone. I think maybe it was the policeman who sent those guys on the motorbikes."

I felt my face flush. Was it tinfoil-hat crazy to suggest a Rio policeman arranged the *theft-by-motorbike*?

Dad didn't say anything at first. His face was stony. Finally he said, "I think you're right."

"Then ... that means the second bike, the one that hurt Marcos ... that was *my* fault." Tears poured down my cheeks.

"It's done, Leah. It's over. We'll talk about it later," Dad said. "I'm sorry you had to go through this, but let's get you home and cleaned up. Okay?"

It wasn't okay. Nothing was okay. Marcos was hurt. His blood was on my hands. Literally and figuratively. I had to make it right.

I reached inside my bra, pulled out the plastic case with the memory card, and handed it to my dad.

"What's that?" he asked.

"I'm pretty sure this is what the police were after."

"Why do you think that?"

"Somehow, they knew what I'd seen in Rocinha, but ... they couldn't have. It doesn't make sense."

"What exactly *did* you see in Rocinha?"

I collected my thoughts, organizing the story as best I could.

"Drugs. There was a truckload of drugs. The UPP came. I thought they would arrest the guys with the drugs, so I started filming. Then this man showed up, an old guy with an envelope of money. I think he was trying to pay off the two UPP officers, but there was an argument, and the old guy shot the UPP officers. Both of them."

"Did he see you? The gunman?"

I nodded. There it was — a crack in the stone that was my dad's poker face. Blink, and you'd miss it. A moment later, he was himself again.

"Whatever possessed you to hide the card from the police, Leah?"

"You said don't talk to them, so ..."

The driver, Raphael, let out a small hoot.

Dad ignored him, pulled out a laptop, and loaded the video card. I couldn't get a good look at the screen from where I sat belted on the opposite side of the car, but for the briefest moment, I could have sworn Dad's face paled. Then his *diplomat face* returned.

"Should I have given it to the police?" I asked. "Was I wrong to hide it from them?"

"You were *not* wrong," he said. "Change of plans, Raphael. Take us to the consulate."

"Not the apartment, sir?"

"The consulate."

"Yes, sir," Raphael said.

"But Dad ..."

I wanted to go home. My hands and clothes were covered in Marcos's blood. I desperately wanted to wash the blood away. Then I fully intended to go to whatever hospital Marcos had been taken to and wait for news. But Dad wasn't listening to me. He was on the phone.

"Damn. Voice mail," he muttered. "Phil, it's James Teague. There's something you have to see. I'm en route to my consulate now. Call me ASAP. Better yet, meet me there."

# 11.

## GO BAGS & DAD-CLOTHES

Dad was a million miles away. Whatever was eating him was bad. I knew it when he reached across to take my hand. I knew when he leaned over to touch my cheek more than once. And I knew it by the set of his jaw and how rigidly he sat. Like a jaguar on the Pantanal, every muscle tensed and ready to pounce. It hurt my heart.

My dad was my protector. He always made me feel safe. Sure, part of it was his physical presence. Even though he was old, he was still kind of a beast. Super fit, a medal-winning triathlete, Dad was a smidge over six feet tall and solid muscle. He made ladies swoon at each new posting and left us giggling together because we knew that sooner or later, those same ladies would learn that he was gay and become pink-cheeked with embarrassment at how brazenly they'd flirted.

I always trusted him to be straight with me. Even as a kid, Dad never flinched when I'd questioned Santa Claus, who left the Easter chocolate, or who really replaced my baby teeth with money? He would always tell me the unvarnished truth when I asked a question. Every. Single. Time. I could always count on him to give me facts, not fantasies. And I loved him for that.

When we arrived at the consulate, Raphael signaled and drove down into the parking garage below. Underground, inside a car with tinted windows, my pupils couldn't dilate fast enough. I was Jonah inside the belly of the whale, which I found morosely fitting. Good old Jonah had wanted things his way and damn the consequences. Kind of like me and my impromptu mototaxi adventure in Rocinha. In the story, it took God three days before he forgave Jonah. I wondered how long it would take for Dad to forgive me.

Right now, it was clear that he was worried about something else entirely, and I wanted to be there for him the same way he was always there for me. I reached over and squeezed his hand. Two things happened then, one right after the other. Raphael turned off the engine, then Dad's phone rang.

"Hang on, Phil," Dad said into the receiver. "Raphael, I need you to take Leah upstairs. She needs to get cleaned up. Her go bag is in my credenza — it's the navy backpack."

To me, he said, "Leah, you'll find a change of clothes in there. Raphael will show you where the showers are. I'll meet you both in my office as soon as I'm done." Then he put the phone to his ear. "Okay, Phil, I'm back."

In an instant, Dad was all business again, and Raphael was out of the car, opening the rear door for me. The last thing I heard before Raphael closed the door behind me was my dad asking, "How soon can you get here, Phil? Leah shot a video of our man. It's going to change everything."

*Our man.* That blew me away. I had so many questions. I wanted to stay and get answers, but answers would have to wait. Raphael's hand was on my back, firmly shepherding me toward the elevator.

Raphael Thibault. My new driver. I'd met him only once before and then only briefly. That was *my* choice. Dad asked me if I wanted to be part of selecting Marcos's replacement and I'd declined. I told him it didn't matter; whoever he hired would only be with me until the end of this school year. After that, I'd be at university. But truth was, I didn't want to get attached to anyone again. It was too hard when they left. So Dad did all the interviews, and Dad chose Raphael.

I didn't want to be told anything about Raphael either. I figured everything I needed to know I'd see for myself. Like the fact that he was young, and young meant less experienced than Marcos. Or that he was kinda gorgeous and close enough to me in age that more than a few of my classmates would be tripping over each other to get his attention. *And* I'd figured out that he was French Canadian. Not at first. When he spoke English, it was completely unaccented, scrubbed clean as a crime scene. But once Dad switched to French, Raphael's roots were unmistakable.

In France, especially Paris, words are filtered through continuously pursed lips as if the speaker has newly sucked on a lemon. It's always been my contention that anyone can sound Parisian French if they pucker up while speaking. Raphael's French wasn't at all lemon-lipped. It was earthy and a little dangerous in the same way that Acadian and Louisiana French always sounded just that little bit better, more mysterious, sexier.

The elevator doors closed, and I looked up at Raphael. "What's going on? Who's my dad talking to?"

"I don't know."

He answered without looking at me. Marcos would always look at me.

"But you have an idea, right? I know you do. I can see it in your face."

"You can, can you?" His mouth pursed. "I'll have to work on that."

Did I amuse him? This wasn't some joke to me.

"Who do you *think* my dad is talking to?"

He seemed to sense my mood and answered me this time.

"I don't know for certain. I haven't been here long, remember? But I overheard him say Phil. There's a Phil Millburn at the US Consulate. He's your father's American counterpart."

"A cultural attaché?"

Raphael nodded.

That didn't track. I shook my head.

"Come on, Raphael. Dad arranges cultural exchanges for poets and painters, musicians, and maritime fiddlers for *chrissakes*." I almost never swear, but I wanted his attention. I wanted him to take me seriously. "What does a video of a police shooting in Rocinha have to do with my dad's job? And why would it *change everything*? You heard him."

Raphael shrugged.

"Tell me!"

"I haven't seen the video, remember? I was driving."

The elevator stopped moving, and the doors opened.

"We're here," Raphael said. "Let's get you a visitor's pass, then I'll get your go bag and show you where you can clean up."

The mention of a go bag didn't alarm me. Go bags, or bug out bags as they were also known, were not the sole province of spy novels and Hollywood movies. Go bags were *not* routinely packed with untraceable guns, fake passports, and fat stacks of foreign currency. They were practical. Embassy people often kept go bags for themselves and their families. They were routinely filled with money (always US dollars), a change of clothes, toothbrush, toothpaste, and personal stuff like tampons or must-have medications: insulin, ace inhibitors, inhalers, angina meds ... whatever someone might need when bugging out. Dad and I didn't need meds, but we both carried dark chocolate and a box of green tea bags. Embassy people kept their go bags in their homes or offices, even in the trunks of cars. You didn't need one if you were posted to someplace like London, Paris, Stockholm, or The Hague. But if your posting was to a place where insurrections, military coups, or natural disasters might make it necessary to leave at a moment's notice, then people — prepared people — kept a go bag. And my dad didn't just attend *The Church of Be Prepared.* He was their Pope.

So when Dad told Raphael that he had a go bag for me in his office, I didn't question *why.* I was more concerned about what clothes my almost sixty-year-old father had selected for me and packed inside.

I clipped the visitor's pass to my T-shirt, then Raphael and I headed to my dad's office. Raphael opened the door and held it open for me.

"How gallant," I said, rolling my eyes. Being brassy was my way of letting him know I wouldn't be easily managed. I stepped into my dad's office like I owned it.

The truth was, this was only my second time in the consulate since arriving in Rio. Dad had hit the ground running, working crazy long hours, and I'd been equally busy with schoolwork, college applications, making friends, and working to fit into another new school in yet another new country.

As offices go, it wasn't impressive. My dad didn't rate anything fancy. The furniture, the view — or lack of, in this case — suited his midlevel consular rank.

There was a time I'd found him and his job borderline embarrassing. Consular kids have a pecking order for each other based on how important our parents' jobs were, and I never landed much above the middle. Put another way, being the daughter of a cultural attaché earned me no great status with my peers. But it also meant I was never under too much scrutiny either.

Keen to change out of my blood-stained clothes, I walked toward the credenza and reached for the door.

"Let me," Raphael said. "You're ..."

He didn't have to finish the sentence. One glance at my hands reminded me they were rust-stained from trying to staunch the bleeding on Marcos's back. Not just my hands, either. I wore Marcos' blood on the front of my T-shirt and shorts. Even my legs and face felt sticky with it.

Raphael removed the backpack from the credenza, slung it over his beefy shoulder, and nodded toward the office door.

"Come on."

Alone in the shower room, I peeled off my shorts, T-shirt and Chuck Taylors, crusty with dried blood. I didn't know what to do with them, so I shoved everything into the garbage can. I turned on the water and stepped under the spray, waiting until the water stopped running pink before soaping off. There was no shampoo in the staff shower, just an all-purpose liquid soap dispenser like you'd find in some of the cheaper European hotels. I declined to use it. Instead, I ran fingers through my wet hair over and over like a comb. Then I turned off the shower and stepped out.

Wrapped in a towel, I opened the go bag. Inside was a pair of jeans, my size, and a decent top. There was underwear, socks, a bra — also, surprisingly, the right size — and a new pair of Vivobarefoots. My running shoe of choice after Chucks. Kudos, Dad. There was a sweater too, but I left that in the bag.

Dressed, I slung the backpack over one shoulder, picked up the garbage can stuffed full with my blood-stained clothes, and headed out of the locker room. Raphael was waiting. He'd been on the phone but hung up hastily when he saw me. There was a crease between his eyebrows. Not worry. Guilt?

"Let's go," he said.

"Who were you talking to?"

Raphael shook his head and began to walk. I followed. Certain the call had been about me, I intended to press him for more information, but when we arrived back at my dad's office, Dad wasn't alone.

## 12.

---

## SOMETIMES THE TRUTH SUCKS

"Does she know about Berlin?"

"Does who know about Berlin?" I said, stepping around Raphael and into Dad's office.

"Leah?"

For one small second, Dad looked every inch like the kid with his hand caught in the proverbial cookie jar. But his face morphed back to its normal self so quickly that I almost questioned what I'd seen. Almost.

"There you are, Leah. You must feel so much better after that shower," Dad said in a candy voice, usually reserved for dinner parties and other hand-shaking events.

I did feel better, but I was starting to feel handled. Was Dad's cocktail party tone for me or the man he was talking to? And was this the mysterious Phil who'd called when we arrived at the consulate? As curious as I was about both things, I had a more pressing question.

"Is there any news about Marcos?"

"He's in surgery."

"How bad is it?"

Dad paused and took a deep breath. Right then, I knew I wouldn't like what I heard. That hesitation was my dad steeling himself to deliver bad news. I hugged the garbage can with my bloodstained clothes tight to my chest.

"It's not good, Leah. The blade nicked an artery and perforated a kidney."

And just like that, I was reliving that blinding flash of sunlight on steel raised to strike me until Marcos spun me around and shielded me with his own body.

"Leah? Leah, are you all right?"

I took a few deep calming breaths and nodded. "Marcos is going to be okay, though? Right?"

In two steps, my dad was there. Plucking the garbage can from my arms, he passed it to Raphael. Then Dad curled a finger under my chin, lifting my head. He looked me in the eye. I clamped my lower lip between my teeth to stop it from trembling. What he said next would be the straight truth — no unicorns or fairies, no storks or angels.

Sometimes the truth sucks. I wasn't sure I was ready to hear it.

"Rio has wonderful hospitals, Leah. Marcos is in excellent hands."

"Okay," I nodded, then took a deep, shaky breath. "When can I see him?"

"He's in surgery now. We just have to wait and be patient."

Patience was not one of my strengths.

"Dad, we have to tell Basia."

Marcos was supposed to be leaving next week to start a new life with his fiancée.

"Let's wait until we have something positive to tell her, okay?"

It was *not* okay. I knew Basia would want to be here for Marcos, and Marcos would want her here. But before I could argue, Dad kissed the top of my head, pushed me to arm's length, and pivoted me to face his visitor.

"Leah. This is Phil Millburn. Phil works at the American Consulate here in Rio."

"Hello, Leah."

"Hello, Mr. Millburn."

"Call me Phil, please," he said. Then he did something odd. He smiled. It was a genuine, for real kind of smile, but all the while he was smiling, he was slowly shaking his head side to side as if he was ... I dunno ... surprised?

"Goodness, look at you, all grown up. It's good to see you, Leah."

It didn't escape me that he said, "Good to see you" instead of "Good to meet you." Between that and the head-shaking smile, it felt like I was being handed a puzzle piece.

"I'm sorry, Mr. Millburn -"

"Phil. Please."

"I'm sorry, Phil. Have we met?"

Dad cleared his throat. "Phil's an old friend, Leah. I asked him here to look at the video you shot in Rocinha."

Mr. Millburn, Phil, pulled out the desk chair for me. "Why don't you have a seat, Leah."

"Sure. Thank you."

I sat at Dad's desk, facing his laptop with my favela video on screen. It was frozen at an image of Rocinha's crazy electrical wires and connections. This was the beginning.

"Do you want me to queue it up to where I saw the shooting?" I asked.

"Please."

I slid the progress bar across, stopping when I spotted my tree-climbing video. The mototaxi ride would be next. When I came to the footage of the residential street, I slowed, dragging the bar in tiny increments. I couldn't help but notice how freaking perfect it was. *Exactly* what we needed for our documentary. Janneke would be thrilled.

"How much further, Leah?"

"Sorry, Dad. It's coming up next."

I stopped the video at the first uphill shot of the police cruiser parked behind the old truck.

"Ready?" I asked.

Dad nodded, and I hit play. All three men leaned in closer to the screen. When the first gunshot came, there was a collective intake of breath, like an industrial vacuum sucking air out of a room. Then the second shot sounded, and the second policeman fell.

It was weird watching it. When I was there, standing at the corner filming, time misbehaved, stretched. In reality, the space between the two shots wasn't more than a second, maybe two.

"Stop it there," Dad said.

On the video, my screams had alerted the shooter, and he'd turned to look. He faced the camera full-on. I paused the video and leaned my nose closer to the screen. There was something disturbingly familiar about his face.

No, it couldn't be. Could it?

Fingers flying over the keys, I opened a browser window and called up the article I'd read on my phone. The Ramos interview with João Matheus Pereira. I didn't bother reading. I was looking for the picture I'd seen earlier. When I found it, I split the screen to compare the man in the video with the man in the New Yorker article. They were either the same person or a freaky likeness.

"Dad, what's going on? That looks like João Matheus Pereira."

I swiveled around just in time to see a look pass between him and Phil Millburn. A look I didn't understand. I thought I knew all Dad's looks, but I'd need a Rosetta Stone to decode what had just passed between those two.

"It *is* Pereira," Dad said finally. "And it's clear from what happened at your school — the theft of your camera and the attack on Marcos — that he wants this video very badly. Badly enough to risk a public attack."

"But he didn't get it. I switched the data cards."

"Yes," said Mr. Millburn. "And very well done, by the way. It was a remarkably clearheaded thing to do. Unfortunately, by now Pereira will have seen what was on your camera, and he'll know you still have the card with the video he wants. Needs."

"Or," I suggested, "he could think that I'm just some dumb kid who bungled the recording, and what he got is all there is."

No one spoke. Raphael and Phil Millburn just stared at me. Dad looked ... sad?

"It happens," I argued.

"Pereira won't take that risk," Mr. Millburn said. "He can't. He will have to act as if the recording exists. Which means he'll be actively looking for it. And it's pretty clear from what happened at your school that the Rio police, at least some of them, are helping Pereira."

Before I could argue or even ask a question, there was a knock on the door.

"Mr. Teague." A trim, middle-aged woman stood in the doorway. "There is a policeman downstairs asking for you."

"Thank you, Ágata," Dad said. *I* recognized the dismissal in his voice, but the woman showed no signs of leaving.

"He's very insistent, Mr. Teague. What should I tell him?"

"Have him leave his number. Tell him I'll call later."

She shook her head.

"I see." Dad tapped his mouth with the tip of his index finger. Something he often did when he was thinking.

"Tell him ... tell him I can't come downstairs at the moment. Tell him I'm waiting for the doctor to arrive and check on my daughter, but I'd be happy to speak with him on the phone. Then give him my cell number, Ágata."

When she left, Dad turned to me and announced, "The bottom line, Leah, is you're not safe here."

"Here where? At school? At home? I don't understand."

"Rio. Brasil."

"Dad?"

"We need to get you out of the country. You're booked on a British Airways flight to London."

"What? When?"

"Tonight."

I glared at Raphael. "That's what you were doing when I was in the shower, wasn't it?"

Raphael didn't answer. He didn't have to. The look he exchanged with my dad was enough of a confirmation.

But Dad wasn't finished. "You'll stay with Uncle Wally until this gets sorted." Dad added, "I haven't been able to reach him yet, but there's plenty of time still. It's a twelve-hour flight."

"But Dad ..."

"It's not up for discussion, Leah. Keeping you safe is my top priority. But I promise you, everything will be okay. I will make sure Uncle Wally is at the airport to meet you both."

# 13.

## A SUDDEN IMPULSE

I couldn't believe Dad was sending me away. Sure, Rio was dangerous. In the space of one morning, I'd witnessed a double murder *and* been attacked. Twice. But we'd lived in Hong Kong during the anti-extradition protests, and in Belarus during the Slipper Revolution, and he never sent me away from either of those places. I get that he was scared for me. I was seriously shaken up too, but I wasn't ready to leave Rio. Not when Marcos was still in the hospital, and definitely not eight weeks into my senior year. I was about to launch into a full-scale debate when the last thing Dad said finally registered.

*I will make sure Uncle Wally is at the airport to meet* you both.

"You both," I repeated. "What does that mean? Aren't *you* coming with me?"

He shook his head. "I need to stay here and sort this out. Raphael will bring you to London and deliver you safely into Uncle Wally's care."

"No! No way, Dad. I don't want to go with Raphael. I don't know him!"

I said it as emphatically as I could, but before Dad could reply, his phone rang.

The policeman from downstairs. It had to be.

Dad lifted a warning finger to his lips. When I nodded, he answered the call, putting it on speaker.

"Senhor Teague?" a voice said.

"Yes, this is James Teague."

"My name is Bruno Silva. I am Investigador Policial with the Polícia Civil."

I sucked in an involuntary breath. I recognized that voice. It was the detective from school. Plainclothes, frosted hair tips. Dad looked at me, and I mouthed the warning, "He was there."

Dad nodded.

"Senhor Silva?" Dad's voice rose at the end of the policeman's name, turning it into a question.

"I regret deeply what happened to your daughter today," the policeman said.

"As do we, Senhor Silva. As do we. To have something like this happen at an international school. And with the police only steps away? You can imagine how distressing this is for the students *and* their parents."

"Of course, of course. And I deeply wish I did not have to do this now, but I must insist on interviewing your daughter immediately. I was not permitted to do so earlier at her school."

"I completely understand," Dad said in the practiced voice of a diplomat. "We, at the consulate, want the criminals who violently attacked our driver to be apprehended. Of course, you may speak with my daughter."

My eyes bugged wide.

Dad winked, and I understood right away. This was a game. A ruse. This was Diplomat Dad working the room. I nodded my understanding.

"Unfortunately," Dad continued, "my daughter is in no state to speak with anyone currently. I understand eleven other students from her class were there as well. Not to mention the teacher, headmaster, and those parents parked on the street when the attack happened. Perhaps you could begin with them?"

"Your daughter is the only one who witnessed the murder of two UPP officers in Rocinha."

He'd said the same thing at school. It set off alarm bells then too, but it took me until now, until *after* I'd seen the video, to figure out why.

Even if the police had worn body cams — which they didn't — they would have had to face me to get me on camera, but they never once looked downhill. The video just proved that. And even if their cruiser had a camera pointed in my direction, I'd been standing at the bottom of the hill wearing a ball cap and sunglasses with a camera in front of my face the whole time.

So how did the Rio police even know to come to my school? There was only one way I could think of — and this is where things got sketchy and *really scary*. It had to be from the guy on the motorcycle who'd shot at me as I got on the bus. A bus with the school's name and crest painted across the sides. Since it was Periera who'd sent the shooter, it tracked that it was also Pereira who called the Rio police and sent them to find me. And if the Rio police were involved, Dad was right. I wasn't safe in Rio.

Phil Millburn's eyebrows were arched almost to his hairline, and he was shaking his head at my dad. Something had just passed between them. One more piece of information I couldn't decode.

"I'm sorry, Senhor Silva," Dad said. "Did you say my daughter witnessed a murder? I know nothing about that. I thought you were calling about the senseless attack on our driver. I thought this was about a violent crime on the doorstep of an international school."

"We have information, Senhor Teague, that puts your daughter at the scene of a double homicide in Rocinha."

"Information?"

And just like that, Dad's voice changed from silky diplomat to smoothly dangerous.

"What information?" he demanded.

"Senhor Teague, I must insist we interview her now. Speed is of the essence if we're to catch the perpetradores."

"My daughter is too distressed to speak to anyone."

"If I may, Senhor, your daughter did not look distressed at her school. She was remarkably composed. She gave first aid to her driver. And despite being new to this city, she remembered the correct telephone number for the Rio ambulance. I heard her call it out myself."

"She was wonderful, wasn't she?"

There it was. The diplomat had returned.

"I am so very proud of her," Dad said, smooth as butter. "Unfortunately, when I got her into the car, and she saw that she was covered in our driver's blood, she became hysterical. She is only a seventeen-year-old girl, after all."

Only a seventeen-year-old girl? It was my turn to raise an eyebrow. My dad never patronized me. This was for the detective's benefit.

"In any case," Dad continued, "a doctor will be arriving soon. I will be asking him to give her a strong sedative, after which I will take her home and put her to bed. Tomorrow will be soon enough to speak with you."

Dad was about to hang up when the detective said, "Senhor Teague, I recognize you have diplomatic status, but I must insist."

There was an extended pause. No one spoke. Not the policeman, nor my dad. If this was a game of chicken, the policeman swerved first.

"As I have said, I insist we speak with her. Even if it means intercepting her at the airport tonight, on her way to London."

I was stunned. Dad too, but he recovered far quicker than me.

"Fine. Give me a few hours. Once she sees the doctor and is checked over, we'll come to the station."

Without waiting for an answer, Dad ended the call.

He closed his eyes. He rubbed his forehead. When he opened his eyes, he looked at Raphael.

Raphael shook his head. "He didn't find that out from me, sir."

"They expected you to run," Millburn said. "This guy is wired in somehow. Someone at the airport?"

Dad nodded. "Okay. Here's what we know. It's clear we can no longer wait for the London flight. She's got to get out now. Raphael?"

"Sir?"

"Take Leah to the airport. The two of you need to get on the first flight to North America, preferably to Canada; we have more resources there."

"How do I get her past the police downstairs?"

My head yo-yoed from one speaker to the next. They were talking about me in the third person, as though I wasn't in the room.

"I can get her out," Millburn said. "From here, my consulate is on the way to Galeão Airport. Even if they follow me, it will look like I'm returning to work. If I do pick up a tail," he added casually, as if spotting a tail was second nature, "I'll stop at the consulate and wait them out. They can't watch me for long. They won't have the manpower. Not all Rio police will be in Pereira's pocket."

"Good," Dad nodded. "Thank you, Phil."

"You have diplomatic immunity, sir," Raphael said. "Why not simply tell the police they can't interview her. It's your right."

"Bad idea," Millburn said, shaking his head. "This is Rio. The lines here are ... blurry. Yes, you have diplomatic immunity, which extends to Leah. But refuse, dig in your heels, and you'll feel the blowback. We can't afford that now, James." Another cryptic looked passed between Phil Millburn and my dad before Millburn continued. "It would be best if you appeared to play along. You need to trust me on this. I know how things work in Rio. I've been here a few years."

Dad hesitated, then said, "Okay. Agreed. Top priority is to make the police believe we're cooperating. It will keep their focus away from the airport. At least until Raphael and Leah are airborne. What about a stand-in?"

"It's risky for your stand-in," Phil Millburn said, "but with the right person deployed at the right time, it could work."

"Then it's settled. Once Leah's flight departs, I leave here with a surrogate."

"What about Juliana in the visa department?" Raphael suggested. "She's young, with long brown hair. A close enough match."

"No. She's local."

"She might want to help, sir."

"I'm sure she would. But once Pereira's police realize she's not Leah, they won't hesitate to take it out on her." Dad shook his head. "No. It has to be one of us. A consulate worker *and* a Canadian. Someone who, if push comes to shove, can claim diplomatic status."

"James," Millburn said, dragging Dad's attention back to the matter at hand. "We've got to move."

"Right. Of course. Raphael, you and Leah leave now with Phil. Traffic should be light. You'll be at the airport in half an hour."

"What about you, sir?"

"Don't worry," he said. "I'll find a stand-in. Age and hair color won't matter much since my car windows are tinted. But the hair will. Silhouettes are still visible, and Leah had a ponytail when the police last saw her."

"And when you get to the police station?" Raphael said.

"Don't worry about that either, Raphael. Just let me know when you're safely on a plane on the runway and about to take off. I won't leave here until I hear from you."

"That could take a few hours," Raphael cautioned.

"I'll stall."

The three men exchanged a final look as if some shared history or agreement had passed between them. I had no idea what that could be. None of this made sense.

Phil Millburn headed for the door. "I'll be in the parking garage," he said, "getting the car ready and checking on available flights."

"No flights on LATAM, Avianca, Gol, or Azul," Dad said.

"Obviously," Phil answered, then left.

Raphael was a step behind. "I need to get my own go bag. I'll be right back."

That left Dad and me. At that moment, he looked all of his almost-sixty years. I expected some comforting words. An explanation. Instead, he said, "Wait here, Leah. I have to get something from the consulate safe."

When he saw the look on my face, he stopped and wrapped his arms around me.

"My sweet, wonderful girl. I was going to wait until your eighteenth birthday, but once this is over, we're going to have a long talk. I promise."

"A long talk about what?" I asked, pulling out of his hug so I could look him in the face.

The way he looked back at me was weird. I swear his eyes were wet. He just shook his head. "Not now, Leah. There's no time. You have to trust me, okay? Can you do that?"

I would have told him yes, *of course* I trusted him, but he didn't wait for my answer. He simply kissed the top of my head, turned, and hurried out the door, leaving me alone.

This was nuts. For one thing, it was all happening too fast. I was used to moving from country to country on short notice. Dad would come home from work and announce a new posting. Then a day or two later, we could be gone. But this ... this was different. Dad wasn't coming with me. He was sending me away. And with someone I'd met only once before. Maybe I deserved what was happening to me, but Marcos didn't. He shouldn't have to pay because I'd snuck off on a mototaxi to shoot a video. For that matter, neither should Janneke. She shouldn't have to give up on her college dreams because of me!

I looked down at Dad's laptop. After a quick glance over my shoulder to make sure I was still alone, I checked the file manager. Dad had uploaded a copy of the video. Perfect. *If Dad has a copy*, I reasoned, *it won't matter if I take the original.*

I wouldn't send the whole file to Janneke — I didn't want to upset her with a murder video. But I *could* edit out the footage she needed and send that to her. It might take me a few days, but at least Janneke would have it in time to complete our documentary for the contest and her college application.

Before my better self weighed in, I ejected the memory card. The case was nowhere to be seen, and there was zero time to look for it — I heard footsteps approaching in the hall. I grabbed a tissue from the box on Dad's desk. Then, turning my back to the doorway to buy a few more seconds, I wrapped the memory card in the tissue and stuffed it back inside my bra.

---

# DIPLOMATIC POUCHES & DAD QUOTES

Raphael arrived first, then Dad. He was carrying a small brown envelope the size of a 5x7 photo but easily an inch thick. He handed it to Raphael.

"You'll need this for exfil. And Raphael?"

"Sir?"

"Look after them. Understood?" Dad said.

"Yes, sir. But wouldn't this be safer in a pouch?"

"What is it?" I asked. "What's in the envelope?"

Dad answered Raphael like I wasn't there. "Normally, I would use the pouch, but it's clear that Silva has an information pipeline at the airport. One whiff that a diplomatic bag is coming through could focus their attention on more than the manifests of departing flights, and we can't risk that. I want Leah safely out of the country and out of Brazilian airspace before Pereira's people notice she's gone."

Only after Raphael nodded his understanding did my dad look at me.

"Time to go, Leah."

"But Dad ..."

"There's no time. We'll talk later, once you're safe in London with Walid."

When we reached the parking garage, Phil Millburn was standing beside his car with the rear door open.

"There's an Air Canada flight to Toronto in seventy minutes," he said. "The timing's tight, but if Raphael buys the tickets on the way, they might make it."

Dad nodded. "Good. You have the envelope, Raphael. Choose one. It doesn't matter which."

I should have had more questions then. Questions like, *choose one what*? Maybe if I'd known everything then, I would have made different, better decisions. But I didn't ask, and things were moving confusingly fast.

"Get her a phone, ASAP," Dad told Raphael. "Make sure her three ICE numbers are programmed in."

"Yes, sir."

"Text me when you're wheels up, then again when you clear customs in Toronto and have the details of your flight to London."

Finally, Dad turned to me and took both my hands in his.

"I know you're upset, Leah. But it's going to be okay. Raphael's with you, and he will stay with you the entire time. From when you leave here until Uncle Wally picks you up at Heathrow. Okay?"

I shook my head. Nothing about this was okay. Dad placed his hands on both sides of my face, fixed his eyes on mine, and said, "It *will* be okay, Leah. Your Uncle Wally will take great care of you. You know he will. And I know how much you love being there."

That part was true. If I had to leave, and it looked like I did, being with Uncle Wally in London was the best possible place I could think of.

I loved London. I knew that city inside and out. Uncle Wally's Mayfair house was the closest thing to a home I'd ever known. Dad and I had lived in so many different houses and apartments around the world, but Uncle Wally had lived in that same house my entire life. I knew it from top to bottom, from my attic bedroom to the massive ultramodern kitchen and tiny walled garden in the back where an ancient tree slanted over the garden wall. Since I was little, I'd scramble up that trunk, then step off and balance-beam-walk the length of that brick wall, adding jumps, spins, and cartwheels the older I got. It drove Dad and Uncle Wally bonkers, but it didn't stop me. I loved it. Uncle Wally's London house was my touchstone.

"James," Phil Millburn interrupted. "If they're going to make that flight, we have to go. Now."

My dad nodded but kept his hands on both sides of my face a moment longer.

"This is just a hiccup, Leah. Be strong. Be smart. Remember, *through perseverance, many people win success out of what seemed destined to be certain failure.*"

Any other day, his motivational one-liner would have made me groan, but right then it was oddly comforting. If I closed my eyes, I could almost pretend I was in the kitchen finding one of his Post-it Notes underneath my water glass.

"One of yours?" I asked, forcing a smile.

"Benjamin Disraeli. Do you have everything, Leah?"

"I don't have *anything*, Dad," I blurted. "Just the clothes on my back and this." I held up my navy backpack. My go bag.

"When you get to London, Raphael will help you sort out the basics — computer, tablet, and phone — and Uncle Wally will take you clothes shopping. Okay?"

It wasn't okay, but I nodded. He was trying to hide it, but this was clearly hard on Dad too.

"Leah, I know this is tough, but I wouldn't insist if it wasn't absolutely necessary. You understand that, right?"

I nodded. "Yes. But I have questions, Dad. A *lot* of questions."

"You wouldn't be you if there weren't questions," he said with a miserable smile.

Then Mr. Millburn opened the rear seat of his car and motioned for me to get in. "You need to lie down on the floor," he said.

"What?"

"It's either the floor or inside the trunk. And it will look strange if you're seen climbing out of the trunk at the airport."

Raphael's hand was on my back, pushing me inside. "Hurry," he said. "We're losing our window. And make room. I have to get down there too."

I crawled in headfirst and lay down. Raphael followed from the other side, his feet in my face, his body pressed against mine. I tried shifting, but there was no way to avoid touching him. There just wasn't enough room. Raphael was young, fit, and handsome, but everything about this was weird and incredibly uncomfortable.

Then Phil Millburn covered us with a blanket shutting out what little light there was. Shrouded in darkness, I heard the car doors close, and the engine turn over. Seconds later, we were moving.

# 15.

## LEAVING RIO

"Here we go!"

Phil Millburn drove out of the consulate parking lot and onto the street. What came next was a series of quick turns. If I hadn't been wedged so tightly in the rear footwell, I would have been thrown forward, backward, and side to side, flotsam on the floor of the car. To distract myself from the large male body sharing my small space, I kept track of each turn — left, right, left, left, right, left — until the turns stopped.

"Hang on," Mr. Millburn called. "We're almost there."

"Almost where?" I called back. "Are we being followed? Are we stopping at the American consulate? "

"Not the consulate. We're clear. We're almost at the tunnel."

"Oh. Okay, good."

Túnel André Rebouças-Maracanã. We had to drive through it to get to the airport. Once inside, it would be pitch dark again, but at least the road would be straight. No more being tossed backward against Raphael and him rolling forward into me.

"Once we clear the tunnel, you two should be able to sit up. Not all the way," Mr. Millburn cautioned. "You'll still need to stay on the floor, but you can at least rest your backs against the car doors. No more being sardines in a tin." He chuckled at his own metaphor, then called, "Here it comes."

Entering the tunnel was like turning off a light switch. The car went instantly dark except for a small patch under the blanket, where the light from Raphael's phone cast an eerie glow.

"How long until we reach the other side?" I asked.

"It should only take five minutes, but traffic is heavier than I expected. I can see a lot of brake lights ahead."

Brake lights could mean that there were police at the other end of the tunnel, stopping cars and looking for *me*. I closed my eyes and channeled Marcos. I pictured him standing in our kitchen, making me look right at him while he took deep breaths, willing me to do the same.

"Don't worry, Leah. It's probably just a little traffic congestion or a fender bender."

"Merde," Raphael muttered.

"What? Is something wrong?" I was wired, jumpy.

From beneath the blanket that covered both of us, Raphael replied. "I'm trying to buy the plane tickets, but I've lost the signal."

"You'll pick it up again on the other side of the tunnel," Mr. Millburn said. "It won't be that long. How about we talk about something else? So, Leah, you're a senior. You must be working on your college applications. What are your plans for next year?"

My college plans? Really? I knew Mr. Millburn was trying to distract me, but attempting small talk with the man smuggling me to the airport while I lay hidden in the footwell of his car? That was just too strange. Just then, the car braked hard, and Raphael was thrown against me.

"Ooof."

Okay. Strange or not, maybe a distraction was *exactly* what I needed.

"I'm applying all over. Canada, England, Yale."

"Yale? Is that your first-choice school?"

"Maybe. I have friends applying there. It could be nice to go to school with people I know for a change."

"My son is applying to Yale."

"You have a son in twelfth grade? I don't remember any Millburns at school."

"He used to go to your school, ninth through eleventh grade, but he's doing his senior year at a boarding school back home. Wentworth Academy, Maine. Do you know it?"

I'd never heard of Wentworth Academy, but that wasn't surprising. There were so many private schools in the US. If you weren't plugged in and paying attention, you tended to only hear about the big names. Places like Phillips Exeter, Choate Rosemary, and Groton.

"Does he like it? Wentworth Academy?" I asked, half to be polite and half to keep the conversation going. Raphael was busy repositioning himself, his hips, knees, and shoulders nudging uncomfortably against me.

"I'm embarrassed to say I'm not sure. Between his new school and my work, I've hardly had a chance to talk with him. But I'm sure he misses the sun, the beach, and his girlfriend."

*His girlfriend?* It was a long shot, but I asked, "Any chance she's a senior at my school?"

"Yes. Janneke van der Spek. Do you know her?"

"I do! She talks about Nick all the time. She just never said his last name. Mr. Millburn, may I ask you a question?"

"Of course you can."

"How come Nick went stateside for senior year? It sounds like he would have liked to stay here with Janneke. And you and Mrs. Millburn too, of course," I added.

"Ah, well, leaving was his mother's idea. She convinced him that if he was truly serious about getting into an Ivy League school, he'd need the boost that graduating from a place like Wentworth Academy would give his application."

"I guess that makes sense," I said. "But?"

"How did you know there was more?" Phil asked.

I didn't have a good answer for him. How do you explain to a stranger that reading people — their faces, body language, the inflections in their voice — came as naturally to me as surfers reading waves or Marcos learning another language. It was the math of all those small things added together. That sum was how I knew Phil Millburn's reaction to meeting me was hinky. I planned to ask Marcos about Phil Millburn once he got better. Marcos always said that reading people was my superpower, and I always countered that if my superpower made it easy for me to find friends and fit into every new school and posting, I was happy for it. But Phil Millburn was waiting for an answer. I had to tell him something.

"I dunno," I said. "I thought I heard it in your voice?"

"Well, you're right, Leah. There *is* more." Mr. Millburn took a deep breath. "Don't get me wrong, Janneke's a great girl. I admire her; she knows exactly what she wants to do with her life and career. Rather like you and your dream to become an investigative journalist."

I was glad to be hidden under a blanket right then so Mr. Millburn couldn't see my face.

"My dad told you that?"

"Yes, and he's very proud. But Nick ... Nick has no idea what he wants. He only chose Yale because that's Janneke's dream. Nick is barely eighteen. The *one* thing his mother and I agree on is that eighteen is too young to be planning a life with someone. He needs to keep his head down and get an education so he can figure out what he's going to do. After that, after he's sorted himself out, then he can choose who to spend his life with."

"And maybe absence *won't* actually make the heart grow fonder?"

As soon as the words came out of my mouth, I knew I'd gone too far. An extended, uncomfortable silence followed.

"So, Leah," Mr. Millburn finally said, "how are your SATs?"

Phil Millburn was proving to be a persistent conversationalist. This time I was keen to answer and steer the conversation away from my brainless comment.

"They're pretty good, sir. I've always liked taking tests."

"You do, do you?" Phil said. "Interesting. Then, may I offer a challenge?"

"What sort of challenge?"

"How about I give you an SAT-type word problem right now? To kill some time?"

"Challenge accepted. But don't use the word kill, okay?"

He chuckled. "You have a deal. Okay, here goes. You are traveling in a car on your way to Galeão Airport. Or, as it's now known, Antonio Carlos Jobim International. The car enters Túnel André Rebouças-Maracanã at — hold on, what time is it?"

I didn't think Raphael was paying attention, but he called out, "13:27."

"Thank you, Raphael," Phil said and continued. "Your car enters Túnel André Rebouças-Maracanã at 13:27. It maintains an average speed of 50 kilometers per hour through the 2800-meter-long tunnel."

"My turn," I piped in, grinning despite everything.

"If the brave, brilliant, and beautiful high school senior must stay hidden until after the car exits the tunnel, what time will it be when she is finally allowed to sit up?"

Phil laughed out loud. Raphael let out a snort.

"Keep going," Phil said. "If this is an SAT question, there should be multiple choice. So what are the choices?"

"All right. Let's see …"

I much preferred this game to overthinking the crap-pile of problems I'd created for myself since waking up this morning.

"Here are your four choices, gentlemen. A) 13:47; B) 5.6 minutes; C) 13:34; or D) Never."

"Never?" Raphael asked.

"Never," I said. "There's a bomb in the undercarriage that missed detection, and the car carrying our heroine, while bulletproof, is not bombproof because those cars belong to drug lords, the occasional president, and our heroine's overly neurotic father."

Raphael burst out laughing. He'd seen *The Tank*.

"It had better not be D," Phil called from the front seat, "or your consulate's security is terrible."

Obviously, I couldn't see his face, but I heard a smile in his voice.

"So what's the answer, gentlemen?"

"The answer is C. It's always C, isn't it?" Raphael said.

"Says the Canadian millennial who's probably never taken an SAT," I quipped.

"Millennial? How old do you think I am?"

In the front seat, Phil Millburn was actually laughing, and right then, I thought that was a pretty great sound.

Just then, sunlight flooded the car and seeped through the blanket. We had exited the tunnel.

"Hang on while I do a 360 check," Phil said.

I held my breath until he gave us the all-clear.

"You can sit up now. But keep your heads below the windows, please."

Raphael pulled the blanket off, leaving it in a puddle on the floor between us. We each sat up, retreating to our own sides of the car. Raphael returned immediately to his phone and, what I assumed, was booking our tickets.

With my back against the door, I had an angled view up and out the driver's side window to Corcovado Mountain and the massive statue of Christ the Redeemer. It was a sharp reminder that there would be no climb this Sunday; Marcos was in surgery, and I was leaving Brasil. Christ the Redeemer's outstretched arms no longer felt welcoming; they seemed like arms thrown wide in surrender.

"Damn. There's traffic ahead," Mr. Millburn said. "I don't think you're going to make the Toronto flight. What are your other options?"

"New York, Atlanta, Houston."

"Take New York," Phil said. "You'll find more connections to London. Plus, getting around the city and avoiding paper trails will be easier from JFK. It shouldn't be an issue, but better to plan for trouble than be caught by surprise."

"Okay. Thanks, Phil." Raphael returned to his phone.

I watched, curious, as Raphael removed a passport from the manilla envelope my dad had handed him back in the consulate. When he saw me watching, Raphael held a warning finger across his lips, then handed the passport to me.

It was American. I opened the cover. Below the *We the People* quote, and the colorful image of the eagle, flag, and three amber stalks of grain, was my picture. My picture, but not my name.

What the heck?

This passport said my name was Christine Louise Tyler. It wasn't just the name that was different. Christine Louise Tyler was fourteen months older than me.

I looked up at Raphael, but he shook his head and mouthed, "Shhh." Then he stuck out his hand for the passport. I handed it back, but as soon as we were alone I would definitely be extracting an explanation. If not in Rio, then once we landed in New York.

Like this was a regular, everyday occurrence, Raphael returned to what he'd been doing, presumably buying an airline ticket for one eighteen-year-old Christine Louise Tyler, born in Worcester, Massachusetts.

"Okay, you two. You can get up now," Phil said. "We're almost there. Antonio Carlos Jobim International Airport. A.K.A. Galeão."

Phil Millburn pulled to a stop in front of the International Departures. The place was crowded with suntanned holidaymakers, fortified by caipirinhas and sandy beaches.

"You go first, Leah," Raphael said. "Head to the Delta ticket counter."

"Alone? Why? Where will you be?" I asked.

"Following at a discreet distance, looking for anyone who may be looking for you."

I hesitated.

"Don't worry. They're expecting you at the police station, remember? And to further confuse them, I've purchased decoy tickets on a late-night flight to Amsterdam. They won't start looking until much later."

"Do you want me to wait here," Phil Millburn asked. "Just in case?"

"Thanks, Phil, but no. We'll be okay. Leah, it's time to go."

I nodded but leaned over the front seat and extended my hand.

"Thank you for all your help, sir."

"It's what friends do for each other, and your father and I are very old friends."

Yep. There was *definitely* something hinky about Phil Millburn. His voice, even his smile sounded in my brain like a distant echo.

"Mr. Millburn?"

"Phil."

"Phil. Have we met?"

"A long, long time ago. You'd be too young to remember."

"Was it in Mumbai?" Mumbai was the first place I'd lived with Dad after he'd adopted me. I remembered a lot about living there. But I didn't remember Phil Millburn.

"It was before that," Phil said.

Before Mumbai? That got my attention. I had almost no memories before Mumbai.

"Where did we meet?"

"Berlin."

I'd never been to Berlin. Not even as a tourist

*It's another ugly truth — parents lie. Oh sure, they say they're all about honesty, but honesty is a one-way road for them. They don't want you to know their story — their real story. Instead, they present you with a tale of family, a perfectly crafted ball of clay, and tell you this is what you're made from. They tell you everything you are and came from exists inside this lovely story-sphere they've offered up. They say, "Take this life-clay we've given you. Let it be your foundation to mold and shape into whatever you want." They don't tell you about all the stones and sticks, all the dirt and dross buried deep inside, the secrets and lies that taint the clay making it a poor foundation to build upon. And no one ever warned Leah Teague how, or when, those buried bits would surface and transform her life into something ... unrecognizable.*

# 16.

## JAMES TEAGUE — THE UGLY TRUTH

James Teague's phone pinged with the text message he'd been waiting for. *Wheels up.* He closed his eyes and breathed in a silent thank you. Leah's plane was in the air.

Of all the meticulous plans he'd made through the years, of all the scenarios he'd painstakingly anticipated or intercepted to protect his daughter, this was one not even the oddsmakers would have taken bets on. Leah had stumbled onto a double homicide committed by the very person Teague had been brought to Brasil to monitor. João Matheus Pereira. The fallout from this promised to be as big as that day seventeen years ago when the birth of a tiny child had upended his life in ways he could have never predicted.

James Teague never planned to be a parent, never pined for it. But when it happened, when a baby girl was born three weeks premature, jaundiced, with the barest tufts of black hair on her scalp, and a face so puckered that she looked more like a tiny Yoda than the chubby babies on diaper commercials, James Teague had fallen instantly and hopelessly in love. He knew that he would kill to protect this child. And he knew that he would willingly give his own life for hers.

Teague flashed back to his and Leah's goodbyes in the consulate parking lot. He could see how scared she was and how hard she'd fought to stay brave. It cut him to the bone to send her away like that. It would have been different if Marcos could have gone with her. Instead, Teague had been forced to put his faith in Marcos's replacement.

Raphael was a promising surveillance officer, intuitive and smart, but he was also young and green as a new shoot. He had no bond with Leah and knew nothing about her background. Teague had chosen not to read him in. Raphael's interaction with Leah was supposed to be limited to being her driver and minder until she left for college. In exchange, Teague would mentor the young CSIS officer.

To his credit, Raphael had accepted Leah's passports without question, though he was clearly puzzled why a teenage girl would have four farmed identities. Teague would handle Raphael later. He was more worried about his daughter's reaction. By now, she would have seen at least one of those passports. Her questions would be legion.

Teague always intended to explain things to Leah once she turned eighteen. He knew it wouldn't be an easy discussion; he'd told so many lies. And though he'd done it all to protect her, Teague feared his strong-willed daughter wouldn't see it that way.

Standing there in his office, he made a silent promise. The moment he'd cleaned up events in Rio, he would fly to London, and with Walid's help, he would sit Leah down and explain everything. Almost everything. There was one truth Leah could never be allowed to know.

Teague turned to look at the woman seated in his office. In her sunset thirties, Cecile Plante was nowhere near Leah's age, but she was trim like Leah, with long hair that could be pulled into a ponytail and threaded through a ball cap. Inside the car, behind darkly tinted windows, she could pass for Leah, buying his daughter enough time to get safely out of Brazilian airspace. He knew he could be putting this woman in harm's way, but he wouldn't let himself think about that. The only thing that mattered was Leah.

"It's time, Cecile."

The elevator pinged their arrival at the parking level. Once inside the car, Teague handed Cecile a ball cap and a pair of sunglasses, and she slipped them on.

"Ready?" he asked.

She answered with a tight nod.

"Ça va aller, Cecile. It's going to be all right. In a few hours, this will be over."

"I want to help, James. But won't the police be furious when they realize I'm not Leah?"

"At me, yes. Not you. I wish there were another way, but the police discovered Leah's ticket to London. They know I'm trying to get her out of the country. This will buy time to get her out of Brasil. But Cecile, if you're uncomfortable with this ..."

"I am — a little. But I want to help."

"Thank you. I promise to make this as easy as I can for you."

Cecile nodded as Teague pulled out onto the street and around a surprised policeman leaning against his cruiser, smoking a cigarette. Before the officer could recover, Teague made it to the Av. Atlântica, turned right and slotted himself into traffic, creating the buffer he'd need for his next move.

He was checking his mirrors when Cecile said, "You probably don't remember, James, but we served together before."

His brow knit together. He did not remember, and Teague was someone who, by professional necessity, kept a running inventory of contacts.

"Where?"

"London," she answered.

Teague took his eyes off the traffic for the briefest moment to steal a look across the front seat. How much did she know? Had someone talked? He thought all those loose ends had been tied up years ago.

"I wouldn't expect you to remember me," Cecile hurried to explain. "I had quite literally just arrived when you ..."

"When I what?" he demanded. Any other time he would have moderated his tone and found a more skillful and subtle way to determine what Cecile knew, but this involved Leah, and after a day like today, Teague was rattled.

"When you were sent to Berlin," Cecile said. "Then your cancer happened, and you had to take a leave of absence."

Teague kept his face blank, and his eyes fixed on the road ahead. Good. She'd heard only what he'd wanted people to hear, which meant he was free to concentrate on the troubles at hand. Still, these confluences left him with the unsettled feeling that the knot of lies he'd so carefully manufactured during Leah's lifetime was beginning to unravel.

"I'm sorry, James," Cecile said. "I should not have brought it up. Cancer is a personal issue. It's just that you look so well now, so incredibly healthy. It's good to see."

Teague managed a smile. "It's fine, Cecile. Thank you for your concern."

They continued their drive in silence, south along the Av. Atlântica toward Leblon. Teague's phone rang. The caller ID appeared on the car's display screen. It was Detective Bruna Silva.

"Senhor Teague," the detective said, ignoring niceties. "You are going the wrong way."

"Detective Silva, hello. Are you having me followed?" Teague asked, feigning surprise.

The detective ignored the question and asked one of his own.

"Where are you going?"

"Ah yes, well," Teague said. "I decided to go to the 14th DP. The Police Station on Humberto de Campos. It's closer to our home."

"But I am in the central station, and you, Senhor are already very much later than you promised."

The edge in Silva's voice was unmistakable.

"Do you have children, officer?" Teague asked.

There was a pause. "Sim."

"Then I know you will understand. We parents must protect our children. Today has been a horrible and difficult day for my daughter. But not to worry. I am still twenty minutes out from the 14th. You should be able to get there about the same time."

Teague hung up and quickly began another call; the police could not call him back if his phone was engaged.

"Call Walid."

The car's speakers beeped the long string of numbers — country code, area code, and phone number, followed by the distinctive British ringtone. After several rings, it went straight to voicemail.

"It's late. Where the hell are you, Walid?" James muttered.

"Problem?" Cecile asked.

"I hope not. I sent an email to my partner explaining Leah's arrival, but I need to speak with him before she boards her next flight."

"Dr. Walid Masri," Cecile said. "Remarkable man."

Teague glanced across at her. "You know Walid?"

"Of course. I'm Foreign Affairs, James. Dr. Masri is a pre-eminent scholar and one of the leading voices for Palestine. And I was posted in London once upon a time, remember? I've personally consulted Dr. Masri several times."

James said nothing.

"He's very good," Cecile added quickly. "His expertise in the area has proved quite useful. It's helped us develop a foreign policy on the region."

It all made sense, Teague knew, but he still didn't like it. Today held far too many overlaps and coincidences.

"I see. Of course."

"And you've been unable to reach him," Cecile said. It was a statement, not a question.

"It's odd that he's not answering his phone."

"It's only been, what, a few hours?"

She was right. It had only been a few hours since Leah had left for the airport. On the other hand, Walid was a lecturer, a professor in political science at SOAS. At this time of day, with classes having just begun and London four hours ahead of Rio, Walid should have been at home with a takeaway and up to his elbows with schoolwork.

"You still have plenty of time to contact him," Cecile suggested. "They won't even arrive in the UK until late tomorrow."

She was right, of course. Teague nodded, then made a quick right turn onto Rua Bolívar.

"Not here, James! You need to stay on the beach road. We're supposed to avoid Av. Epitácia Pessoa today. Didn't you see the memo? It's going to be a nightmare with all the roadworks!"

"I saw the memo," Teague said. It was the reason he'd made the turn. Getting stuck in traffic would buy more time for Leah.

"Oh," Cecile said, awareness dawning. She relaxed back into her seat. "Of course."

They drove in silence the rest of the stop-start way.

When they finally pulled into Leblon's 14th DP police station, two officers were waiting outside. One was in uniform, one in plain clothes — Detective Silva.

"Stay in the car," Teague instructed.

Despite nodding her understanding and despite her choice to help, Cecile's whole body tensed.

"Are you sure you're okay, Cecile?"

"Just go, James! He's coming!"

James gave her hand a quick reassuring squeeze before exiting. He heard the locks click before he'd even rounded the front of the car.

Detective Silva beat him to the passenger door. He jiggled the handle, trying to open it. Unsuccessful, the detective bent down to look inside but was hampered by the bright sun and the tinting on the glass. Cupping his hands around his eyes like a diving mask, Silva pressed them against the window. Then, realizing he'd been duped, he exploded a string of Portuguese epithets.

"Where is she?" the detective demanded.

"Detective Silva?"

"Where is she? Where is your daughter?"

"Gone."

"Gone where?"

"Leah is on a plane to Atlanta," Teague said.

"On a plane? Impossible!"

"Impossible, Detective Silva?" This man was an oaf. The only way he could have made detective was by graft and corruption. Wearing his practiced diplomacy like a mask, Teague offered, "I have a good friend at our consulate in Atlanta. My daughter will be staying with his family until you catch the ... what was that word you used? Perpetradores?"

Behind the detective, the uniformed officer had observed the exchange. Hearing that Leah was not in the car, he turned and made a call on his cell phone while a furious Detective Silva stabbed a finger against Teague's chest.

"That is not what we agreed!"

"No, it's not, Detective Silva. But it is logical, and it is fair. My daughter has nothing to offer you that could not be discovered over a video call."

"A video call will not give us the memory card!"

There it was. If he'd needed any more evidence of police complicity, Silva had just handed it to him neatly wrapped and tied with a bow. Teague needed every ounce of skill he'd learned from his NOC as a diplomat to stop him from punching this worm of a man in the face. Marcos was lying in a hospital, fighting for his life because of this corrupt piece of shit. Teague turned and walked away.

"You will wait here, Senhor Teague!" Detective Silva called after him, red-faced and furious.

"I think we both know that is not going to happen," Teague said with a veneer of calm. "Our diplomatic statuses aside, Detective Silva, neither myself nor my Canadian colleague," he was careful to include Cecile's diplomatic status with his own, "were present at either crime. We have nothing to add that could help your investigation."

The detective waved over a uniformed policeman who was tall, wiry, and pock-faced. The two men immediately launched into an animated, rapid-fire discussion in Portuguese. While the two policemen were busy arguing, Teague slipped back into the driver's seat. He started the engine and pulled quickly out of the police station parking lot, leaving a red-faced Detective Silva and a dangerously angry uniformed cop.

Once they were safely out of the parking lot, Teague turned to Cecile.

"Bar de Lado should be open by now. I could really use a drink. You?"

"Oh God, yes!" she answered in a gush.

"Good. You've certainly earned one."

"One?" Cecile said. "I think I've earned more than one."

Teague chuckled. The woman had spunk. He pointed the car toward the beach.

They hadn't gone far when a group of small cc motorcycles appeared behind them, each one carrying a passenger. One bike raced past and took up point directly in front of Teague's car. Teague checked his mirrors. A second motorbike had stayed behind, tailing them tightly. The third and fourth were flanking the left and right sides of the car, hovering menacingly close.

Teague saw an opportunity just ahead. When he was almost through the intersection with Av. Get San Martin, he made an abrupt, last-minute left turn, losing the motorbike in front and narrowly missing the one on his left flank. He was busy checking the position of the remaining bikes when Cecile screamed.

A white panel van had shot out from a side street, stopping directly in front of them.

Teague stood on the brakes, and the car screeched to a stop. Ahead, the van's side door opened, and men spewed out carrying automatic weapons.

"Bulletproof?" Cecile squeaked.

"Yes," Teague said, ice water in his veins.

"What do we do?"

"We stay inside the car."

Cecile slid down low in the seat. There is being told that something is bulletproof, and there is believing it. Teague believed it.

He assessed their situation. His sudden turn had landed them on an apartment-lined street. There would be people inside those buildings, he knew. People who would alert the police. Not that the police would respond; this attack was their doing. Teague knew his best move was to contact his consulate. Specifically, Consul General Jerome Hutchins. Hutchins could pull levers that Teague could not.

"Call Jerome Hutchins."

The call connected just as the shooting began.

Bullets hit the windshield. Dozens of large impact-snowflakes bloomed across the ballistic glass. The gunmen shot out the tires next. Teague peered through the few remaining spots of clear glass to check their perimeter.

"Look, James!" Cecile cried.

A gunman headed toward them. He had one arm tight around the neck of a teenage girl. The other arm held a gun that he used to prod a second teen, a boy, forward.

"Their shirts," Cecile said. "Look at their shirts!"

He was looking, but the logos on the shirts meant nothing to him.

"We partner with their school. Student exchanges and —"

Before she could finish, the gunman had reached the front of the car and kicked the grill. The message was clear. Surrender. When neither Teague nor Cecile complied, there was a gunshot, followed by a thump as the boy's body fell onto the car's hood.

Cecile screamed. So did the teenage girl until the arm around her neck tightened, cutting off her air. With his free hand, the gunman pressed the gun barrel against the girl's head. Teague stared into the panic-filled eyes of the teen. She was about the same age as his own daughter.

Cursing silently, Teague unlocked the car and stepped out. The gunmen were upon him instantly. They had Cecile's door open too, dragging her out of the car.

"You don't need her," Teague yelled to be heard. "She doesn't know anything."

Either they didn't understand him, or they didn't care. Then Teague and Cecile were shoved into the white van. The door slammed shut, and they were driven out of Leblon into the surrounding hills. Not one police car gave chase.

Seated on the van floor, surrounded by armed gunmen, Cecile was beginning to unravel.

"Cecile, look at me. Look at me!"

She did.

Keeping his eyes locked on hers, Teague said, "Ça va aller, Cecile." It will be okay. The kidnappers might understand English but would be unlikely to speak French.

"Je te promets que je vais t'en sortir sain et sauf."

"Comment?" How?

"Ils cherchent quelque chose. Ils pensent que je l'ai. Ils nous garderont en vie jusqu'à ce qu'ils l'obtiennent. Ils vont t'echangeront contre la carte mémoire."

What James Teague did not know was there could be no exchange. The memory card he was counting on using as a bargaining chip was gone. It was 30,000 feet in the air, over the Atlantic Ocean on its way to New York City, wrapped in Kleenex and tucked inside the bra of his seventeen-year-old daughter.

The last thing Teague remembered was the butt of an automatic gun striking the side of his head.

## 17.

---

# A BRUSH PASS,
# A FAKE PASSPORT & BAD NEWS

It was late when our plane landed in New York. Even at this time of night, the lines at customs and immigration were long and painfully slow.

"We've missed the last flight to London," Raphael said. "We'll have to get a hotel."

The idea of sleeping in a real bed held some appeal. It had been a long flight from Rio to New York and an even longer day. But there was something I needed to do first.

"May I use your phone?"

Raphael's brows arched in a question.

"I need to talk to my dad. I don't have a phone, remember?"

"Right. Sure."

He fished his phone from his pants pocket and powered it on. The screen lit up with a string of messages and alerts. Raphael's forehead cinched in a pucker. Something was wrong.

"Raphael, what is it?"

He looked at me with a tight smile that told me the next thing out of his mouth would be a lie.

"Nothing," Raphael said. "Everything's fine." He switched off his phone and slid it back into his pocket. "They don't like you to use cell phones in line."

That was true, but Raphael was hiding something.

"What were all those messages? Was it something about Marcos? Is Marcos okay?"

"There was nothing about Marcos."

I studied Raphael's face for signs of a lie. There weren't any. Good. That was good. Relieved it wasn't bad news about Marcos, I took three deep breaths. Still, it was obvious that something had happened back in Rio, and by the look on Raphael's face, that something wasn't good. If he didn't want to tell me now, in line, I could live with that, but once we were through passport control, I intended to make him talk. First though, I wanted to talk to my dad.

I really needed to hear his voice. Our goodbyes had been too quick. Too much had been left unsaid. Not to mention I had a growing list of questions. Like, why did Phil Millburn act as if he knew me? And how could Phil Millburn have met me in Berlin when we'd never been there? And then there was the *big* question, the crazy, impossible question ... who is Christine Louise Tyler, and how did I end up with an American passport issued in her name?

"We should split up." Raphael's voice jerked me back to the here and now.

Then, in a slick move I never saw coming, the selfsame American passport appeared in the palm of my hand as Raphael brushed past me.

"I'll meet you at the second baggage carousel," Raphael said and slipped away to join another line.

I was nervous. Holding a phony passport will do that to a girl, I thought grimly. But when it was my turn, I stepped up to the counter and presented it to the customs officer like I hadn't a care in the world. Just like I would my real passport. It was a measure of how much faith I had in my father that I could do that without collapsing into a puddle of tears and fears. It was because I trusted Dad would *never* do anything that would land me in trouble.

Minutes later, I'd made it through passport control without incident, so either my American passport was somehow genuine, or it was an excellent forgery. Either way, Dad had a lot of explaining to do.

When I arrived at the second baggage carousel, Raphael was staring at his phone, his forehead worry-puckered. He motioned me to follow him.

"Phone," I demanded.

"Not now."

"Why not?"

He ignored me and kept walking. I stepped in front of him, but his reflexes were quicker than I'd expected. He side-stepped me easily and continued walking. I scrambled to catch up, matching my pace to his.

"Talk to me, Raphael," I hissed.

He shook his head. "After."

"No. Tell me now."

Raphael tried to step around me again, but this time I was ready and planted my body firmly in front of his.

"I'll tell you later, Leah. Right now, we need to find a hotel."

I leaned in to look at his phone screen. He wasn't lying. He'd been searching for hotels.

"Fine," I said. "I know where to go. Dad and I always stay at the TWA if we have overnight connections at JFK. It's in Terminal 5. What terminal are we at now?" I asked, looking around. "Never mind. We'll just catch the AirTrain."

"You're not going to London, Leah."

"Not tonight. I get it. It's late and we missed the last flight. But if we stay at the TWA, it will be easier to get the first flight out tomorrow."

"You don't understand. You're not going to London at all."

"What? Why?" I was confused.

Dad's plan hinged on me staying with Uncle Wally while Dad sorted things out in Rio. How he was going to *sort things out*, I had no idea. But he'd promised, and I trusted that. I studied Raphael's face for answers, but there weren't any. Instead, his worry wrinkles had returned.

"There was a text from Dr. Masri," Raphael said.

"And?"

"He's been on a plane. That's why he hadn't answered any of the emails or texts."

"So Uncle Wally's been on a plane, so what? He's answered now, so his plane has obviously landed and he's back in London. What's the problem?"

"Palestine. Dr. Masri is in Palestine for a family funeral."

"Family? In Palestine?" I shook my head. "No, that can't be right. Uncle Wally doesn't have any relatives left there."

"He could have family you don't know about."

I shook my head. "I may not know much about Uncle Wally's background, but I know his whole family left during the Nakba — the catastrophe. His parents were the only ones from his family to settle in England, and they died before I was born. Uncle Wally has no family in the UK and no one in Palestine."

Raphael shrugged. "I don't know what to tell you, Leah."

"Who died, did he say?"

"His wife."

I snorted. Raphael obviously had his wires crossed.

"Uncle Wally's not married."

Raphael pulled up the message from Uncle Wally and held the screen up so I could read it.

I shook my head in disbelief. This made absolutely no sense. How could Uncle Wally be married? And if it was true, if he was married, how did I not know? How come I'd never heard about a wife even once in the last fourteen years?

"No," I said, shaking my head. "There's something wrong. Beyond the obvious, that Uncle Wally is Dad's *boy-friend*, I've spent every summer at his house in London. I know that place from the basement to the attic, and there's no evidence of a wife anywhere. No pictures. No clothes. No paperwork. Nothing. If there was, I'd have found it."

Raphael shrugged. "You saw the text."

"Give me your phone, Raphael," I demanded. "I need to talk to my dad."

Raphael tried to slip the phone back into his pocket, but I was quicker this time. I plucked the phone from his hands and hurried forward. He ran after me.

With Raphael's phone pressed flat against my chest between my breasts, I pivoted to face him. He started to reach for the phone, then stopped.

"Try it," I said, "and I'll scream so loud I'll have every passenger and every security person in this terminal running to rescue the *poor teenage girl* from the *big bad perve*."

Raphael's eyes narrowed. I bet he was trying to decide if I was bluffing.

"It already worked once today," I continued. "And if it worked in Rio, just imagine what would happen in a crowded New York City airport?"

"I don't need to imagine. I *know* what will happen. The authorities will find a teenage girl in possession of a phone that doesn't belong to her. Can *you* imagine what will happen when they ask for her ID? Christine?"

Crap on a cracker. He was right, and I hated that. People were starting to notice us. A few even paused as if deciding whether they should step in. I relaxed the death grip on Raphael's phone and held it part way out.

"Please, Raphael. I really need to talk to my dad. He'd want to know about Uncle Wally. And he needs to know that I can't go to London, right?"

Raphael muttered something in French under his breath before snatching the phone out of my hand and saying, "It's your dad."

"What about my dad?"

"He's been kidnapped."

I froze, then. My knees shook. My head swam. Like a boulder in a stream, eddies of grumbling people were forced to veer to the left and right of me. The raw current of my feelings threatened to drown me. Raphael grabbed my arm to keep me standing.

"Come on," he said. "Let's get to that hotel. We'll get some rooms, and I'll make some calls. I promise I'll find out what's happening. Can you hold it together until then?"

Stunned, I allowed myself to be pulled along zombie-like into the approaching AirTrain.

# 18.

## CALL "BIRTHDAY MAX"

I don't remember the AirTrain ride or checking in to the hotel. The word kidnapped strobed nonstop across my brain, neon and flashing. *Kidnapped. Kidnapped. Kidnapped.* I couldn't shut it out. I couldn't make it stop. By the time we reached our rooms, I was shaking so badly that I couldn't hold the keycard steady enough to unlock the door. Raphael had to open it for me.

"Leah? Leah, are you okay? What can I —"

I didn't let him finish. I pushed the door closed with Raphael on the outside, then searched for a kettle and the green tea and chocolate from my go bag. This wasn't the jangles. I knew that because I was wide awake, and the jangles only came from my nightmare. They woke me from sleep. *Hypnagogic hallucinations*, Dad called them. *Terrors of an unknown physiological root that happen between REM sleep and waking.*

This might not be the jangles, but I had to hope that the litany of things I did to manage the jangles might help quiet *this* growing panic — the fear that my dad might be hurt. Or worse.

"Deep breaths, Leah," I whispered to myself. "Deep breaths. If the tea doesn't help, there's a fitness center downstairs with a fleet of treadmills, and you can run till you drop. Just breathe. Breathe."

Some self-talk, breathing exercises, and a cup of green tea later, my panic had been dialed down, and I was knocking on Raphael's door. He may not be much more than a passing stranger, but I didn't want to be alone. And I wanted information.

Raphael was on his phone when he opened the door. I walked past him to the sofa, curled my legs up, and waited for him to finish his call. I tried to figure out who he was talking to, but the conversation was too one-sided, with Raphael mostly listening. Once, mid-call, he'd attempted to cover me in a blanket, but I shrugged it off. I didn't want a blanket; I wanted answers. When he finally hung up the phone, I swung my legs to the floor and stood up.

"Well? What's happening? Where's my dad? Do they have any news?"

"Leah," he said. The way his voice sounded, and how he looked at me when he said my name, sunk my stomach to my knees.

"Is he ...?" I couldn't bring myself to finish that sentence.

"No," Raphael answered quickly. "He's not dead. At least, they don't think so."

"What do you mean *they don't think so*?"

"There's been a demand."

That wasn't surprising. Dad warned me when we'd first moved to Rio that kidnapping-for-ransom was a growth industry there. It was why he'd bought *The Tank*. It was why he'd hired Raphael to replace Marcos. But I knew my dad.

*The Tank* and its driver would not be the only protection he'd arranged.

"Dad would have K&R."

Raphael's eyebrows raised upward. I guess he was surprised I'd know about *Kidnap and Ransom* insurance. He wouldn't be if he knew some of the places we'd lived.

"Leah," Raphael said, shaking his head.

"Look, I know my dad," I countered. "He was worried about Rio. I could have taken the school bus like the other kids, but he was worried enough to hire you to replace Marcos as my driver. And you've seen *The Tank*. I promise you that if my dad was worried enough about Rio to buy a car like that, he would have made sure we had K&R insurance."

Raphael looked like he was about to speak, but I was worked up and on a roll.

"And since we *clearly* have K&R," I added to seal the argument, "we can pay the ransom."

Raphael shook his head again. I wanted to shake *him* for not listening.

Then it hit me.

"They're not asking for money, are they?"

"They are not."

"The video?"

"The video. Cecile Plante, the woman who acted as your double, has been released. She's been instructed by the kidnappers to go to the consulate and retrieve the memory card."

It was my turn to shake my head. "Turn around," I said.

He didn't move, so I said it louder.

"Turn around!"

When his back was turned, I fished for the tissue-wrapped memory card hidden next to the underwire in my bra.

"Okay, you can turn back now."

I unwrapped the tissue and held it up for him to see.

"Merde," Raphael said. "Is this what I think it is?"

I nodded.

"Why would you do this? Do you know what you've done? Now Cecile will have nothing to trade for your father's life. Stupid, stupid girl!"

One thing I'm not is stupid.

"I checked before I took it. Dad uploaded a copy onto his hard drive. All they have to do is download the video onto another memory card. The kidnappers will never know it's not the original."

Raphael was still angry — that was clear from the tightness around his eyes and mouth and the pinching together of eyebrows that gave his forehead a bulldog-like wrinkle. But he *did* seem slightly assuaged.

"I'll let them know," he said.

"They'll need his computer password," I added. "I can give that to them too."

Raphael didn't ask how I knew my dad's password, and I didn't volunteer. He placed the memory card on the table between us, rubbed his temples as though I'd just given him a giant-sized headache, then began pacing and talking to himself.

"This was supposed to be a simple assignment," he muttered. "Drive a kid around for nine months. That's it. Nine months for the chance to work with James Teague."

When he stopped pacing, he turned to look at me. "The last instruction your father gave me was to deliver you to

London. But London is off the table now, and I don't know what to do," he admitted. "Family?"

"I'm adopted," I said, shaking my head. "And Dad's an only child. As far as I know, he has no living family. There's just Uncle Wally."

"Who is currently somewhere in Palestine and cannot leave. So what the hell am I supposed to do now? Merde."

Raphael wasn't talking to me. He'd started pacing again, talking to himself.

"Raphael?"

"What?"

"I want to talk to Uncle Wally."

"Go ahead."

I stuck my hand out. "I don't have a phone, remember?"

Raphael nodded and handed over his phone. I dialed. Uncle Wally answered right away.

"Raphael." Uncle Wally's voice was tight and anxious. I'd never heard him like that before. "Do you have news about James?"

"Uncle Wally, it's me. Leah. I'm using Raphael's phone."

I could hear Uncle Wally let out a small moan.

"Oh, habibti. Are you okay?"

I was *not* okay. Not even a little. I wanted to fall into Uncle Wally's familiar arms and cry against his shoulders like I'd done when I was a kid falling off his garden wall and banging my knees. This fear inside me was so large I didn't have words. And because it was so big and because the right words were so hard to find, I blurted out, "You're married?"

"Leah, is that *really* what you want to talk about now?"

"No. It's just ..."

I stopped then unsure what Uncle Wally knew.

"Do you know about Dad?"

"I do, Leah. The Consul General called me. I'm James's emergency contact person. Leah, I need you to listen very carefully to me. Can you do that?"

"Yes."

"First, are you with Raphael right now?"

"Yes."

"Then put me on speakerphone."

I did. I put the phone on the table between Raphael and me.

"Raphael, can you hear me?"

"Yes, Dr. Masri. I hear you."

"Good. Now Leah, this will not be easy to hear, but Raphael needs to return to Rio."

I wasn't looking forward to spending more time with Raphael. He was almost a stranger to me, but he was the stranger my dad had chosen, and if he left, I'd be alone. That might be worse.

"Why?"

"Raphael is a trained surveillance operative."

"My driver is *a trained surveillance operative?* Are you *kidding* me?" I looked up at Raphael. "Is this for real?"

Raphael nodded.

"Why would my dad want that? Wait, what about Marcos? Was he also ...?" I didn't finish that sentence. I couldn't. On top of everything else, this was too much to process.

"Marcos was ex-military," Raphael said. "He worked for your father privately. But to answer your question, Marcos had skills."

I hated being blindsided like this. I thought we had no secrets, Dad and I. What other bombshells were there, sitting around, waiting to blow up in my face? I looked up at Raphael.

"And you? Do you work for my dad *privately*?" I didn't even try to keep the vinegar from my voice.

"No. I work for a branch of government," Raphael said. "I've been temporarily assigned to drive and protect you during your senior year in Rio. After that, your father will mentor and train me."

"Train you to what? Be a cultural attaché?"

Raphael wouldn't meet my eyes, but I had more pressing problems than learning about Raphael's career aspirations.

"Leah," Uncle Wally interrupted. "I need you to listen to me. Sweet girl, you must have so many questions, and we have much to discuss. But this isn't the time. We must focus on getting James safely home. Do you understand that?"

He was right, of course.

"Yes," I said. "I understand"

"Good girl. Raphael is our best chance to locate and rescue James. He needs to return to Rio so we can get James back with us."

"Okay, but what do *I* do? If Raphael goes back to Rio, do I come to Palestine?"

"No. That would be a bad idea right now."

"Then what?"

"I think our best option is a boarding school."

Surprisingly, I didn't hate the idea.

"Where?" I asked.

"I think you should continue in an American curriculum, don't you? It would be the least disruptive. Do you know of any American boarding schools?"

I knew the big ones. The famous ones. Then I remembered Phil Millburn. He said his son Nick was at a boarding school on the east coast.

"Wentworth Academy. In Maine. But, Uncle Wally, Dad's always arranged schools for me. I don't know how to do that. And what if it's full? It's almost October. They'll be three weeks into their term by now. They might not even let me in."

"Leah, listen to me. You have three ICE numbers, yes?"

"Dad is ICE 1. ICE 2 used to be Marcos. I guess it's Raphael now, but if Raphael returns to Rio …?"

"And ICE 3?" Uncle Wally prodded me. "Who is ICE 3?"

"You mean Birthday Max?"

Uncle Wally chuckled, and right then I felt lighter. His musical laugh was a boon in the middle of all this chaos and worry.

"Quite so," Uncle Wally said. "Birthday Max is exactly who I mean."

"Who is Birthday Max?" Raphael asked.

"Max Klein. He's just someone I have to talk to once a year."

"On your birthday, I gather?"

"Yeah. He calls and asks me questions about my life, where we're living, school, my dad, Uncle Wally. Stuff like that."

Raphael raised his eyebrows.

"I know what you're thinking, Raphael, but you're wrong. Birthday Max is *not* my birth father."

"Are you sure?"

"Yes, I'm sure. I asked my dad the same thing when I was a kid. He explained that the calls were a condition of my adoption. A child welfare thing."

"I've never heard of that before."

"Yeah, well, how many kids are adopted and then immediately taken out of the country for fourteen years?"

Uncle Wally cut in. "Just call Max, Leah. He will take care of everything."

"It's after eleven o'clock, Uncle Wally. What if he's sleeping?"

"Leah, Max is an *emergency* contact. That means exactly what it says. You call when there is an emergency, any time of the day or night. Call him now, Leah. Tell him you want to go to Wentworth Academy as a boarding student. Tell him you need to start tomorrow."

"Okay, Uncle Wally."

"Good. Now, do you need anything else?"

"She needs a phone, computer, and tablet," Raphael said.

"And clothes," I added. All I have are the clothes I'm wearing and the sweater in my backpack.

"Make a list and be sure to tell Max. Max will make it happen. I guarantee."

⁓

Thirty minutes later, I hung up the phone with Birthday Max. My head was reeling. I'd read off a list of must-haves. He'd assured me everything on my list would arrive at the hotel at 0900 hours with a car that would drive me directly to Wentworth Academy, Maine. He told me I'd be there in time for dinner.

By the end of that call, I was spent. The day had held too much trauma, too many worries, and far, *far* too many questions, not the least of which were questions about Birthday Max — bringer of cars, clothes, and computers and the wrangler of school admissions. All I wanted to do was crawl into bed, turn on the television and fall asleep to some old, predictable reruns.

It was time to go back to my own room. I turned to leave, but Raphael grabbed my wrist. I tried to yank my arm back, but he was stronger. I glared at him.

Raphael only raised his eyebrows while at the same time rotating my arm until my hand faced palm up. In it, he placed the data card from my GoPro. Then he closed my fingers around it.

"You keep this, Leah."

"Why?"

"Insurance," he said.

"Insurance against what?"

"Call it a hunch."

"Not good enough. Explain."

"Pereira believes your father has the data card."

"But that's good, right? If Pereira thinks Dad still has the card, he'll keep Dad alive, and you can make a copy from Dad's computer for the exchange."

"Yes. We can do all that, but...."

"But what, Raphael?"

"Why would James sneak his daughter out of the country unless he'd seen the video?"

It hit me, then. "Dad's a witness now."

Raphael nodded. "Yes. So even if we hand them a data card, they won't let James go."

"They'll kill him?"

"I think so. Yes."

I didn't want to believe Raphael, but what he said made sense.

"Okay. Then *of course* I'll keep the video. But how will you get Dad back?"

"Have you ever played poker?" he asked.

I shook my head.

"Poker is a game of chance, strategy, and risk."

I was a fair hand at strategy games — Diplomacy, Off-world Trading Company, and Chess. And I was no stranger to risk-taking. "What do you have in mind?"

"I give Pereira a card but admit it's a copy. I tell him you have the original but that I can get it back. He will have to keep James alive until an exchange."

"How does that help?"

"It buys me time to locate James and put together an extraction team."

I nodded. "Okay. I'll keep the card. But..."

"But?"

I hesitated. "I want to help Dad. I'm going to help. It's just ... if you tell Pereira that I have it, won't he come looking for it? For *me*?"

Raphael shook his head. "There's no way he has that kind of reach, Leah. Pereira is a farmer. An obscenely rich farmer, to be sure. And one who is trying to use his wealth to buy his way into the presidency. And yes, he has managed to bribe some local police, even put them on his payroll perhaps, but he won't have anyone inside ABIN."

"ABIN? What's that?"

"Agência Brasileira de Inteligência. Think of it like Brasil's CIA. Look, if Pereira wins the election and gets sworn into office, this could change. His reach will expand. But I will have James out before then."

"So, I'm safe?"

"You're safe, Leah. I promise, you have nothing to worry about."

Wednesday, September 28th, 2022
Four days before Brasil's presidential election

# 19.

## THE REPORTER



*RIO DE JANEIRO, BRASIL*

Christina Ramos was stopped by security outside the US Consulate. After being made to check her computer bag and phone, she entered the building carrying only a clear plastic bag with her wallet ziplocked inside. Doing an alumni interview was *not* on her agenda for this trip, but Valerie Soto was an old friend who'd asked a favor, and it never hurt to be on the positive side of the favor-giving balance sheet. Especially when the other person was an extremely well-placed government contact.

"Good morning," Ramos said to a receptionist seated behind ballistic glass. "Valerie Soto asked me to come in this morning for an alumni interview with Leah Teague. My name is Christina Ramos."

Minutes later, Valerie Soto appeared, standing in an open doorway behind the fortified receptionist. Soto signaled to have Ramos let in.

When they were face to face, Ramos gave her former roommate a wry smile.

"I feel I can tell you this, Val, because we're old friends. You look a lot like you used to in college after pulling an all-nighter. But with better shoes," she added with a smirk.

Valerie Soto did not return the smile. "I am really sorry, Christina. Something's happened. I should have had some-one call you."

"What is it? What's up?" Ramos asked, always with a nose to a potential new story. This side trip to the consulate wouldn't be for nothing if she got a lead.

Valerie Soto ran her fingers through her hair.

"The girl you were supposed to interview, Leah Teague? She won't be coming in today. Her father was kidnapped yesterday, along with another Canadian consular employee."

"Jesus," Ramos exclaimed. "Hang on. I didn't see any-thing about that on the news?"

"They've been trying to keep it quiet — for negotiation purposes I suppose — but they won't be able to do that much longer. It should hit the local news outlets today. Look, Christina, I have to go. Something else has come up which needs my attention. Call me before you head back, okay? If things settle down here, maybe we can squeeze in dinner before you go."

"Sure. But you're buying the caipirinhas."

"Of course." Soto managed a weak smile. "I've really got to go, Christina. Sorry."

The door swung shut between them. The automatic lock clicked back on, leaving Ramos alone with the receptionist.

So James Teague had been kidnapped. Interesting. Teague was the man Valerie had asked her to investigate. If Ramos didn't want to interview his daughter Leah before, she certainly did now. There was a story there. Ramos could smell it. And there was something else too. Something about those two words strung together. Teague + kidnapped. Their sum felt significant. Added together, they triggered an itch, a distant memory that niggled her reporter's brain. It had to be an old story and not one she'd covered; she would have remembered that. Like a splinter lodged just under the skin, Ramos knew it would continue to irritate her until it was recovered. Her fingers itched for her smartphone, but it was outside, checked with her computer bag.

Ramos turned to the receptionist. "Excuse me. The high school student who was coming here for an alumni interview with me, Leah Teague, do you have a contact number for her?"

"I couldn't give that to you, even if I did."

"Of course," Ramos said, shaking her head. "I'm sorry. I just can't help thinking about what chaos that girl's life must be in now, with what's happened to her father. I don't want her to worry about college applications in the middle of it all. Maybe I could talk to her school and let them know I can make myself available once her father's safe and home. What do you think?"

"Oh." The receptionist actually smiled. "That would be nice."

"It's the least I can do, considering," Ramos said. "Do you have the name of her school?"

"Sure. One moment." The receptionist scribbled a name on a piece of paper and handed it to Ramos who nodded her thanks.

Outside the consulate, Ramos fetched her computer bag from the storage service, then hailed a cab. She handed the paper with the school's name and address to the driver. Once they were moving, Ramos pulled her phone from the bag and started a search. Before she reached the school, she found what she'd been looking for. An unsolved mystery from 2008. The accidental death of a Canadian student in Israel that had started a chain of events leading from Tel Aviv to London and Berlin. The story had piqued the world's interest and captured coveted front-page coverage for months alongside the Beijing Olympics, the election of Barak Obama, and even the Global Financial Crisis.

And James Teague had been part of it.

As her taxi pulled to a stop outside the school, Ramos felt that familiar thrill she experienced each time she was on the trail of something big. She paid the driver and walked to the gate. A guard approached.

"I'm here to talk to the principal," Ramos said. "Ms. Clease."

A further internet search during the cab ride had revealed the principal's name. Ramos handed her card to the guard. He read it and handed it straight back to her.

"No journalists," he said. "She will not talk to journalists about what happened yesterday."

Yesterday? Ramos didn't know what the guard was talking about, but she made a mental note to find out.

"I'm not here for an interview," she said. "I've come to offer my services. Will you tell Ms. Clease I'm here? Please."

Message delivered, Ramos stepped deferentially away from the gate and waited. As a print journalist, even one who'd won the coveted Pulitzer, her face was not instantly recognizable, but Ramos hoped her name and reputation would be enough to unlock the gate.

It was. Soon after, a woman emerged through the front doors, striding purposefully across the parking lot toward the gates, which Ramos noted, remained firmly closed.

The principal looked down at her phone, then looked up at Ramos.

"Ms. Ramos," the principal said, eyebrows raised. "It really *is* you. I must say, I am thrilled to meet you. Under any other circumstance and on any other day, I would be delighted to welcome you to our school. Unfortunately, today is not a good day."

"I understand, completely," Ramos said. "May I explain why I'm here?"

The principal checked her watch then nodded.

"I'll be quick. I'm in Rio for a story about João Matheus Pereira. My old roommate from Yale is the US Consul General here, and she asked me to do an alumni interview with Leah Teague. As a personal favor," Ramos added, watching for a reaction from the principal. Nothing. She'd be a helluva poker player, Ramos thought. "My interview with Leah was scheduled for this morning. She didn't make it, of course. Considering what happened with her father yesterday, I expect she's not even at school today."

Principal Clease continued to play poker.

That's fine, Ramos thought. I can play too.

"I remember senior year," Ramos said. "The worry about grades and college applications. Perhaps you would let Leah know that I'll be here in Rio through the weekend, if she feels up to an interview. I could even do it here, at school, if it helped her feel safe."

*That* got the reaction Ramos had been hoping for.

"Goodness! Thank you, Ms. Ramos."

"Christina, please."

"Thank you, Christina." The principal smiled. "That's very generous of you. But I'm afraid Leah is no longer a student here."

"What? Really? Do you know where she's gone?"

"I couldn't say."

Couldn't or wouldn't, Ramos wondered, but replied, "Of course. I understand."

When the principal reached through the iron grill to hand her card back, Ramos waved it off.

"Keep it. Please," Ramos said.

She made out like she was going to leave. Then she paused, turned back and, as if it was an afterthought said, "Look, I'd planned to do an alumni interview while I was here anyway, and now I have some unexpected free time. So if you have any other promising candidates applying to Yale ..."

She let that dangle for a moment. When she saw the interest spark in the principal's eyes, Ramos added, "I know alumni interviews can be difficult to arrange at international schools."

"That would be wonderful! Tyberius and Janneke, two of my top students, are applying to Yale for early decision. Do you have time now? I can pull them out of class."

"Of course."

Jackpot! One of those kids was bound to know something about Leah Teague.

## 20.

---

## MOSSAD

*TEL AVIV, ISRAEL*
*The Kirya, Mossad Headquarters*

Gabe Atir ignored the secretary's protests and walked straight into the office of the director of Mossad — Israel's national intelligence agency —waving a file. The director begged off his telephone call and motioned for Gabe to shut the door behind him. Few people could get away with this behavior, but Gabe and the director had a long friendship and an even longer history.

"What are you waving there, brother?" the director asked.

Gabe slapped the file down on the desk.

"I need you to sign off on this, Noam. I need to take a team to Rio."

"For?"

"An extraction."

"And who would you be extracting?"

"James Teague."

The director's eyes went wide, then he laughed. "Ahab, my old friend, you are still hunting your white whale, I see."

Gabe looked momentarily chastened, but recovered quickly and tapped his finger on the file folder.

"Read this."

"Are you commanding your commander?" The director eyed Gabe, but he opened the file nonetheless and scanned the contents. Finally, he closed the file and looked up.

"Let me understand this, Gabriel. James Teague has been kidnapped in Rio de Janeiro, but not for money."

"Correct. Our asset at the American Consulate tells us Teague has a video which, if revealed before Sunday's election, will ensure the current president, Emmanuel Santos, is reelected."

"You're telling me the Americans are not willing to assist with an extraction attempt to free Teague. Why?"

Gabe shook his head. "We don't have an answer yet. So far, we know only that the Canadians asked for help but were refused."

"Can you push your asset for more information?"

"Not without the risk of exposure."

"I see."

"Noam, the Canadians do not have the resources for a solo extraction. Without outside help, Teague will most likely die."

"Then that is very telling, is it not? Canada and America have a long and close alliance. One that exceeds even our own relationship with America."

Everything the director said was true, but Gabe had a different objective. He stood statue-still and waited.

"Yet you want me to grant you authorization to rescue Teague in direct opposition to the wishes of America, our strongest ally?"

"Yes."

"And why, brother, should I risk alienating the Americans for this?" he said, tapping his finger on the open file. "It was not too many years ago, I recall, that you advocated terminating both Teague and Masri."

"I admit I floated the idea. Teague was a problem for us then, and he is even more so now. For two decades, Teague has pulled the curtain back on things we never wanted the world to see."

"You are convinced of this, yet Teague has managed to satisfy the world of his professional detachment in this regard."

Gabe was about to protest when the director raised his hand.

"While we cannot draw a direct line between Teague and these ... these leaks, I concede you are correct, Gabriel. You have not found sufficient evidence to take your case to his government, but you have convinced me. Teague's relationship with Walid el Masri has created ... problems."

Sensing success, Gabe leaned forward and continued. "The tide has turned, Noam. The world increasingly embraces the Palestinian cause. Increasingly, we are seen as the villain."

"This is true." The director nodded again, more slowly this time as if deep in thought.

"Noam, we have an opportunity here. Help me put a cat among the pigeons."

"You have tried and failed before, old friend, or have you forgotten?"

"I have not forgotten. This time will be different."

"How? How will it be different?"

"For one, I know about the relationship between Teague and Masri now."

"Something you *should* have known the first time."

Gabe had the decency to look abashed.

"You are right. I should have had that information before inserting the asset. It was a calculated risk. Had it worked ..."

"But it did not. You saw only the goal line and did not take the time to know and understand the players. You put in a rookie to cover a seasoned player. She should never have been put in the field."

The director, a fan of American football, was known to use his favorite sport as metaphor.

"This is different, Noam. The child, Leah, is seventeen. We know that is a vulnerable age for recruitment. Let me take a team, a small team, to do what no one else will. Let us rescue Teague. Let Leah Teague see Israel as her champion. The child cannot help but be grateful."

"And how do we explain why Israel is extending help?"

"The girl is one of us. She's a Jew and her mother —"

"Stop right there, Gabe!" The director's face became stormy. "*Rebekah stays dead.* Understood?"

Gabe stayed silent, but his jaw tensed visibly.

"That is a contract we will not break, Gabriel," the director warned. Then he shook his head. "In any event, you and I would be severely sanctioned if that happened. You would never be operational again, and I would certainly be sent home, forced to spend the remainder of my days tending my olive trees."

Gabe looked about to protest when the director stopped him.

"On this point, be very, *very* clear, Gabriel. Rebekah's skills make her more valuable to Israel than either of us could ever hope to be. You know this, old friend. Deep down, you *know* this."

"Fine," Gabe conceded. "Then we do not explain, we just act. Rescuing Teague will make the child grateful. And through the child ..." He let the sentence dangle like bait on a fish on a hook.

The director took a deep breath and stared out his office window before speaking.

"I believe this is naive," he said finally. "The father's rescue does not assure the girl would ever agree to become an asset. You know as well as I do that gratitude does not burn as hot as revenge, or as solid as ideology. Thankfully for us, Rebekah was an ideologue. But the child? She has no religion or politics, am I right?"

"Correct."

The director waved a hand dismissively. "I do not accept that this effort would be effective."

"If the father dies, the girl believes she will be an orphan."

The director stared over his glasses at Gabe. "And so she must continue to believe," he warned. "But I have another option."

"What is it?"

"Let the Americans have their way. Let Teague die. He will be replaced with someone new. With luck and a little nudge from a well-placed Sayam in Ottawa, the replacement will be better disposed toward Israel's position."

Gabe lowered his head. "I admit, I made mistakes as Rebekah's *katsas*. As her case worker, I pushed her too hard and too fast. I won't make the same mistakes with the girl, Noam."

The director stood up and began pacing. When he finally spoke, it was with his trademark summary of events, a sign he was considering Gabe's request. He stopped behind his desk, resting both hands on the back of his chair.

"Israel needs the world's support, yet each day we grow closer to an impasse with the international community. To his employers, Teague appears neutral and unbiased, refusing all postings within our arena, claiming his relationships with Masri as the reason. But we know differently. Teague doesn't need to be in the region to have influence. What you seek would be a good outcome, yet I believe you are whistling into the wind, my old friend."

Gabe began to protest, but the director frowned and raised a hand. "But ..."

"But?"

"Masri is in Palestine."

"What? When?"

"Since Tuesday. His entry was flagged; I got the report yesterday. We suspect something is stirring, but as of yet, we don't know what."

Gabe held his breath and his tongue and waited.

"So you may have your team, Gabriel. It is a long shot, or as our American friends would say, a Hail Mary pass, but you may try."

"Thank you, Noam."

"Go gently with the girl when the time comes. Do not push her — or your agenda. Understood?"

"Yes."

"And Gabe?"

Gabe met the director's stare.

"There can be no hints or suggestions to the child that her mother lives. Understood?"

"Understood."

"No mistakes this time, Gabriel. No backfires. If Rebekah discovers what you're doing, we *all* suffer."

**21.**

______________

# WENTWORTH ACADEMY

After the hare-like speed of Tuesday's events, Wednesday moved like the proverbial tortoise. A car and driver were waiting outside the hotel for me, just like Birthday Max said they'd be. Also waiting for me in the car were three boxes of electronic equipment: a computer, a tablet, and a new phone. Raphael instructed the driver to wait while he unboxed the phone and, keeping his promise to my dad, entered three ICE numbers. Then he handed the phone back to me. I barely knew Raphael, but at that moment, I was very reluctant to leave him behind.

"Raphael?"

"You've got to go, Leah. Me too. I have a plane to catch."

I knew he was right, but my feet stayed rooted to the sidewalk. I didn't want to be alone.

"Go to your new school. Get settled in and try not to worry. I'll let you know as soon as I have your father."

Feeling helpless and out of control wasn't something I handled particularly well. But Uncle Wally said Raphael was

164

our best chance to get Dad back, so I squished my jitters into a tight ball, buried them someplace deep, deep inside me, then climbed into the car's back seat.

"At least it looks comfortable," Raphael said as I buckled the seatbelt.

"Better than our last car ride," I replied, pointing to the footwell. That got a small smile from Raphael. He held out my navy backpack cum go bag. I didn't reach for it at first; I had no use for a go bag anymore. Then I remembered. In my hurry to create a shopping list for Birthday Max, I hadn't included a book bag. The navy backpack, plain as it was, would be useful for school. I took it, noting it was slightly heavier than yesterday.

"Keep it safe," Raphael said. The look on his face and the tone of his voice turned those three small words into a warning.

I would have questioned him — "keep *what* safe and *why*?" — but Raphael gave his head the barest shake and closed the door. Then he slapped his hand on the roof twice for the driver to move.

As we pulled away from the TWA, I unzipped the bag and looked inside. Next to the box of green tea was the manilla envelope Dad had retrieved from the consulate safe back in Rio. The same envelope that held my phony American passport.

Damn you, Raphael, I don't want this! *Keep it safe?* I wanted to burn it! I had no idea what the penalty was for using a fake passport to enter the US, but I'd be willing to bet it was right up there with smuggling drugs. I didn't know what to do, but whatever I decided would have to wait until I got to Wentworth. I zipped the backpack closed and tried not to think about it.

It was a long drive from JFK to New Rye, Maine. Too much time alone to think and worry. I could feel my control slip. Part of me wanted to curl into a ball, cover my eyes and make the world disappear. But another part of me, a bigger part, was a survivor. It was how Dad raised me. He'd want me to fight. He'd want me to succeed. I could almost hear him quoting Confucius.

*When it is obvious that the goals cannot be reached, don't adjust the goals; adjust the action steps.*

Okay, Dad. This one's for you.

Action Step 1: Find out about Wentworth Academy. The more I know going in, the easier it will be to figure the place out.

I picked up my new phone and began searching for info. According to its website, Wentworth Academy was a New England landmark. Set on three hundred and sixty-seven acres of manicured lawns, playing fields, and even a nine-hole golf course, Wentworth Academy bordered the Atlantic coastline. It began life as the home of a wealthy 19th-century industrialist and was named after the family's ancestral home in Surrey, England. If the pictures on the website were any indication, the place reeked of money and old-world aristocratic charm. I read on and learned that the original owners had been forced to abandon it during the Great Depression. Since then, the estate had been a convent, an art gallery, a residential care home, and, very briefly, a wedding venue. In 2008, the Wentworth Estate was bought and converted into a school. Fourteen years later, it was flush with the children of tech billionaires, movie stars, and oil magnates. With a few diplomats' children sprinkled in for gravitas.

I stopped reading and put down my phone. Is that how Birthday Max got me into Wentworth? Gravitas? I was too prideful to let that stand. I made myself a promise. Birthday Max may have used Dad's consular job to get me admitted, but if I *had* to go to Wentworth, I intended to prove that I deserved the place.

With Wentworth researched, I needed something else to do. The car had a video screen, but I wasn't interested in watching a movie. It did, however, remind me that I had a movie of my own that needed attention.

Action Step 2: Unbox the computer, load the Rocinha video and make a video file of the footage Janneke needed to complete our documentary.

I thought watching the video again would be difficult, but it was okay. All the good favela footage happened before the shootings. I forced myself to stay ultra-focused and on-task, and before long, I had a file for Janneke that she was going to love! It was too big to send by email, but that wasn't a big deal. The first chance I got, I'd figure out a way to send it to her. Fresh out of Action Steps after that, I split the rest of the ride between sleep and obsessively checking my phone for news from Rio.

I arrived at Wentworth late afternoon and was personally met by a grinning Headmaster Mitchell. Clearly, Birthday Max hadn't told him about my dad's kidnapping. That was okay by me. It's not like it was a secret, but I'd rather be the one to tell people, and only when I was ready.

The day was sunny and cool but not so cold that I needed more than the sweater from my go bag. Which was good because I hadn't checked out the small suitcase of clothes that magically arrived with the car that had ferried me from New York to Maine.

Headmaster Mitchell insisted on giving me a campus tour and escorting me to my dorm. Partway through the tour, he stopped in front of an ultra-modern building. It looked out of place among the original mansion house, staff quarters, and converted stables.

"The computer lab is housed here," the headmaster said. "I cannot tell you how delighted I am that we're now able to upgrade and expand the facility. This investment is exactly what Wentworth needs to stay competitive."

He smiled at me as if waiting for my response. I had none. He continued.

"Would you like to see the lab?"

I liked computers — I couldn't imagine life without one — but after a butt-flattening, seven-plus-hour drive to get here, touring the computer lab was definitely *not* something I wanted to do. Still, once a diplomat's daughter, always a diplomat's daughter. Even now.

"It looks wonderful," I said with my best crafted smile. "But it's been a long day, Headmaster Mitchell, and a very long drive from JFK. Would you mind if I went straight to the dorm?"

"Of course, of course," he said. "This way."

He seemed weirdly eager to please. He steered me onto a paved path that wound into the distance. One side of the path was punctuated by old-world lampposts, and the other was bordered by a high hedge of lilacs. The whole place looked so much like a Victorian movie set that I could easily imagine women in bustled skirts strolling past.

As we walked east toward Yew Tree Cottage, we passed signs for other dormitories, some old and some new. Headmaster Mitchell pointed out each one as we approached. As we got closer to the coast, the manicured lawns and playing fields disappeared. Dirt footpaths emerged, weaving vein-like through tall grasses. I suspected they'd been pounded into the ground by a decade of boarding students taking shortcuts from dorm to dorm. One path caught my attention. It seemed to head directly east toward the ocean. I'd learned during my backseat-research that this part of Maine had sea cliffs. One of the first things I intended to do was to check out those cliffs to see if they'd be any good for climbing. If the jangles returned, I may need them.

"Here we are," Headmaster Mitchell said. The lamppost-and-lilac path ended, leaving us standing at the front door of an attractive Victorian-era brick building. "Yew Tree Cottage is the dormitory all our senior girls aspire to. Dormitory places here are awarded based on grades and stewardship. The residents of Yew Tree Cottage represent Wentworth Academy's best and brightest."

If that were really true, why put *me* here? Sure, I was a good student, good enough under normal circumstances to at least have a shot at an Oxbridge or Ivy League school. Still, the headmaster couldn't know how I'd stack up against Wentworth kids. Not yet. I hadn't been in Rio long enough to get a report card.

Headmaster Mitchell held the door open for me. "Welcome to Yew Tree Cottage. Your home for the school year."

A year? I'd agreed when Uncle Wally suggested boarding school; I even liked the idea. But a year? I didn't have the heart to tell Headmaster Mitchell this wasn't permanent. Once Dad was safe, or Uncle Wally was back in London, I'd likely be moving on.

"Leah?" Headmaster Mitchell interrupted my thoughts. "You don't like our dorm?"

I quickly marshaled my face and squeezed out a second feigned smile.

"It's very beautiful, sir. I'm just nervous. I've never been a boarding student before. Or had a roommate."

"You're in good hands. Your roommate, Breine Berenson, is an exceptional young woman. She's not only a top student academically, she's also a faith leader here at Wentworth. Breine runs the JSU on campus — that's the Jewish Student Union — as well as co-founding our Multi-Faith Collaborative. We are especially proud of that organization. Follow me. Your room is on the top floor," he said and began to climb. "You'll love the views."

I collapsed the handle on my suitcase and followed Headmaster Mitchell up the stairs. I would have liked a little help carrying everything, but I didn't need it. My arms were officially guns from years of wall and rock climbing.

There was only one door off the top landing, and it was closed. The headmaster knocked.

"Breine, it's Headmaster Mitchell."

"Come on in. It's open."

The headmaster turned the handle and held the door open for me. Taking a deep breath, I stepped inside.

# 22.

## YEW TREE COTTAGE

My dorm room in Yew Tree Cottage turned out to be a large, repurposed attic. What it lacked in ceiling height, it made up for in floor space. Single beds sat against opposing walls, tented beneath steeply slanted ceilings which mirrored the roof's pitch. It was clear that the second bed, desk, and dresser had been hastily added. The tightly made bed and the pattern of dust on the floor gave that away. It seems my last-minute arrival had allowed enough time to carry in furniture but not enough time to clean. My roommate — Headmaster Mitchell had called her Breine — had made the place her own. She'd wallpapered the lower vertical walls and even parts of the sloped ceilings with posters.

Breine, who'd been typing on her phone when we came in, quickly finished what she was writing and hit send. She put her phone face down on her bed, stood up, and smiled.

Breine was about my height and build. She had smoke-brown, chin-length hair and baby bangs that looked like she cut them herself.

"Leah," the headmaster said. "This is Breine Berenson. We have a proctor system here at Wentworth Academy, and

Breine earned the top spot. This room in Yew Tree Cottage is one of the privileges of being selected Senior Proctor."

"I bet that didn't include having a roommate, did it?"

Breine's head tipped to one side, and her eyebrows pinched slightly. She was curious now; I could tell.

The headmaster cleared his throat. "That is true. The Senior Girls Proctor generally has the suite to herself. But Breine is pleased to share her room with you." He looked pointedly at my new roommate.

"Of course I am," she answered.

I studied her face for signs of sarcasm. I couldn't find any.

"Welcome to Wentworth, Leah."

Hearing the answer he'd wanted, Headmaster Mitchell relaxed.

"Breine will take you to the refectory for dinner and later to Study Hall. She'll also be your guide during your first week here. I'm sure you two will get along beautifully. Wentworth will feel like home in no time."

I very much doubted that but smiled a *thank you,* anyway.

"This is me?" I asked, pointing to the side of the room with the newly installed bed.

Breine nodded. I wheeled my suitcase across and lifted it onto the bed. This close, I could see that the posters, at least the ones over my bed, came from different Jewish organizations — IfNotNow, J Street, Jewish Voice for Peace, and the New Israel Fund. Interesting. I knew those groups from Uncle Wally. It seemed my new roommate wasn't just the organizer of the Jewish Student Union on campus; she was an activist. She was Jewish, and sympathetic to the Palestinian cause — Uncle Wally would *definitely* approve.

"Good. Then I'll leave you two to get to know one another." Headmaster Mitchell checked his watch. "You should have time to unpack before dinner."

He glanced toward a closet still full of Breine's clothes. A thin slice of space held a few empty hangers and two conspicuously new uniforms. A pair of black, Oxford-style shoes sat on the floor beneath.

"Breine," Headmaster Mitchell said with a hint of a frown. "That won't do. You need to make more room for Leah's clothes." For the first time, I heard a touch of irritation in his voice. "And your posters too. I think you should limit them to your half. Leah may want to decorate her side of the room her own way."

"The posters are fine," I said. "They're great, actually. And the closet is just fine for now too. I don't have much. I didn't know what to expect weather-wise so ..." I pointed at my small carry-on suitcase. "I'll buy whatever else I need online."

"That's right, of course," Headmaster Mitchell said. "You came from Rio de Janeiro. After all that sunshine, I expect you'll find our New England winters a bit of a shock. That reminds me. We have another student from Rio. His father is also in the diplomatic corps, and I believe he's from the same international school as you. Nicholas Millburn. Do you know him?"

Did I know Nick Millburn? Technically, I did not. I *did* know his girlfriend *and* his dad. Phil Millburn was the reason I landed here at Wentworth. It was because of his casual mention of the school's name on our drive to Galeão Airport that Wentworth Academy was front and center in my brain when Uncle Wally asked about boarding schools. But I didn't tell the headmaster that. I shook my head.

"No, Sir. I've never met Nick. I was only in Rio for eight weeks."

"Still," Headmaster Mitchell said, "since you both came from the same school, you may discover that you have people in common. Breine, I believe Nick is part of your group of friends?"

"Yes, sir, he is. He's rooming with Bas."

I'm not sure why that was important, but the answer seemed to satisfy Headmaster Mitchell.

"That reminds me of another important detail," Headmaster Mitchell said. "Nick Millburn is applying to Yale. I was informed by Mr. Maxwell Klein that you would also be applying to Yale."

"That's right," I answered, wondering how Birthday Max knew that. But I was careful to keep the surprise from my face.

"Wentworth has an excellent record of admitting students to Ivy League schools. In fact, we have a campus tour scheduled two weeks from now. October 14, 15, and 16. Make sure you sign up soon so we can schedule either a student or an alumni interview for you."

"An interview would be great! Thank you," I said. Privately, I noted how ironic it was that his offer came on the very day I *should* have been sitting across a table from Christina Ramos.

"Good, well ... I'll be looking out for you, Leah. And Breine, take very good care of our newest student."

With that, Headmaster Mitchell left, and Breine's smile left with him.

"Are you sure you're okay with the posters?" she asked, with a testing look.

"I'm positive," I said.

I opened my suitcase. There wasn't much inside. Since Wentworth students wore uniforms to class five days a week, I wouldn't need much. And, if I'm honest, the clothes Birthday Max had arranged for me didn't totally suck. As I put everything into the drawers, I noticed Breine watching me.

"Sorry about the closet space," she said. "This was all kind of last minute. I had nowhere to put anything. I've asked for another set of drawers, but they said it would be Friday before they could get one up here. If you want, you can borrow any of my stuff. I think we're pretty much the same size."

"I should be okay, but thanks," I said as I put my new clothes away, their price tags still conspicuously attached. I'd deal with that later.

Breine flopped down onto her bed and reached for her phone.

"Hungry?"

"Sure, I could eat."

"We'll go once you're done unpacking. Am I spelling your last name, right? T-E-A-G-U-E?"

"Why?"

"I thought maybe the office had it wrong on your class schedule," she said, pointing to the papers on my desk beside a tall stack of textbooks.

"Why do you say that?"

"Because I can't find you on any socials. No one can."

What did she mean, *no one*? I tried to shrug it off.

"You won't find anything because there's nothing to find. I don't use social media."

"Really? Nothing? How come?"

"I'm just too busy, I guess," I answered while I unboxed my new computer and tablet, then plugged each one in to charge.

Being busy wasn't the reason I didn't have any social media. It's not like I hadn't tried creating accounts on the sly. Of course, I had. But Dad somehow discovered each one within hours. It was almost creepy how quickly he found them. Then he'd supervise me while I shut them down, all the while spewing warnings about the dangers of digital footprints. *Don't draw attention to yourself, Leah* and *Nothing online ever disappears.*

I always figured it was his age. I had an old dad. He looked great, but he was pushing sixty, and old people just didn't get social media and what it could do. It bugged me sometimes. Sometimes it even made me a little nuts, but I'd learned to accept it. Obviously, I was no saint. I'm the same girl who lied to get her dad off her back about college and careers, but even a liar like me could see how much Dad agonized over my safety. I suppose it's because his work took us to some pretty risky places, and social media was the one thing he could control. So if staying off all socials kept him from losing sleep, getting an ulcer, or having a stroke, I'd do it. He'd earned at least that much. And anyway, it was like Hunter S. Thompson wrote, right? *You can't miss what you never had.*

"It's not just socials, though," Breine said. "We can't find you at all."

There it was again. The collective *we.*

"Show me anyone our age that doesn't have a digital footprint. Even if it's only from photos their mothers and grandmothers post on Facebook."

"Well, I don't have a mother, Breine. Or a grandmother. At least, none that I know of. I'm adopted, and my dad's gay. In fact," I said and pointed to one of the posters that hung over my bed. It announced a speaker series at Cornell University.

"See that?"

"What?"

"This guy here, the one presenting at this speakers' series?"

"Dr. Walid Masri? What about him?"

"He's my dad's boyfriend," I said without thinking. But was he really? Raphael had shown me Uncle Wally's text. It said he was in Palestine at his wife's funeral. I thought 'wife' must be some stupid autocorrect thing, but when I asked Uncle Wally about being married, he didn't deny it. He'd said, "Leah, is that really what you want to talk about now?" Still, the more I thought about it, the more I figured it had to be a mistake or misunderstanding because Dad wouldn't have sent me to stay with Uncle Wally in London if they weren't still together, right? I shook my head. None of this made sense.

"Get out!" Breine exclaimed. "Dr. Walid Masri is your dad's boyfriend?"

"I call him Uncle Wally, but yeah."

Her forehead puckered, and her mouth twisted to one side.

"Interesting."

Then she shook her head.

"Still, a teenager with no social media is not exactly normal, is it?"

Maybe she was right. Maybe I wasn't normal. Normal kids didn't have drivers who got injured protecting them.

Normal kids don't have kidnapped dads. And normal kids certainly didn't have fake passports with fake names. Breine was right about social media too. It *was* weird to be seventeen with no digital footprint and no socials. Dad claimed it attracted unwanted scrutiny. Turns out, the opposite was true. It was *because* I had no social media that my roommate was raising a red flag.

I looked over at Breine. My gut told me she was nice, *really* nice, but her questions set me on edge and there was one more thing I had to do that I didn't want an audience for.

"So is there a room key for me?"

Breine nodded and went to her desk to get me the key. When her back was turned, I took the memory card from my computer and slipped it into a zippered compartment in my wallet. Then I stuffed the wallet deep into the belly of my go bag, my fingers brushing the corners of the manilla envelope. I shuddered. I'd have to deal with that later.

"You okay, Leah?"

I marshaled my face, then nodded. She held out the room key. When I reached for it, she pulled it back.

"I get that Rio's tropical, and you needed new stuff for Maine, but everything? Even your socks and underwear have the sales tags still attached. What's up with that?"

"Seriously?"

She raised her eyebrows and cocked her head.

"It's just a fresh start," I said, grabbing the key and slipping it into my pocket.

"If you say so. Come on. I want to introduce you to the rest of the gang. I have a feeling byou're going to fit right in."

Breine headed for the door, and I followed.

# 23.

## THE INTERROGATION

"We're here," Breine said.

It was the first words she'd spoken since we'd left the dorm. To be fair, I'd spent the entire walk glued to my phone, writing Raphael and compulsively checking every news outlet I could find for info about my dad.

"Is everything okay back home?"

"Why do you ask?'

"You've been staring at that thing the whole walk here."

"Sorry, Breine."

I put my phone in my pocket, looked up, and saw that, sure enough, we'd arrived at a set of double doors. The sign over them said *refectory*. Not cafeteria, not dining hall. Refectory. I'd gone to a lot of different schools all over the world and met lots of American kids. If I had one consistent observation as an outsider, it was the irony that America had fought a war of independence from England yet seemed to revere all things British.

I don't just mean those British Royals — Queens and Kings, Princes and Princesses, Dukes and Duchesses, and on and on down the royal line — though Americans did seem more starstruck by royalty than most. Maybe that was because their own hierarchy wasn't codified, based instead on wealth and power. For me, it was how they spoke. All over the world, the American kids in my classes said aunt and pasta like they'd inherited a seat in Britain's House of Lords or gone to Eton, like Uncle Wally. For Dad, Marcos, and I, it was the plain old, short-a vowel *Eat pasta; run faster.*

Titled or just entitled, refectory or just a plain old cafeteria, students at Wentworth still had to serve their own meals. Breine took a tray and slid it along the rails. I followed behind, each of us choosing the lesser evils from the vats of food sitting in warming trays. Breine loaded her plate with a confusing combo of healthy salad, steamed broccoli, and greasy fries while I was more curious. After fourteen years of living in different countries, I knew how much school food varied from place to place. I made my choices, relieved not to see any black beans. After only eight weeks in Rio, I was sick of the sight of them.

"No meat?"

"Ethical vegan," Breine answered. "At least, I'm trying to be. It's hard sometimes."

With dinner chosen and tray in hand, I followed Breine as she wound her way between tables.

Wentworth's refectory was a large sunny room paneled with half-walls of golden oak. One entire wall was a row of windows that overlooked playing fields. These were clearly the best seats in the place, reserved, I guessed, for ranking seniors. Breine headed straight for one, which, if she was welcomed, would make her some measure of Wentworth royalty.

Three people sat guarding three empty chairs. Breine claimed the one empty chair that faced the window. As I circled the table to find a seat on the far side, conversations stopped, and four sets of eyes followed me.

"Here she is," Breine said, with a smile and a head tilt in my direction.

"Excellent! Fresh meat."

I looked across the table and glared at the boy who'd just labeled me *meat*, but my glare quickly turned into a gawk. He was gorgeous. *If* you liked the well-muscled, broad-shouldered, square-jawed jock type. I could go on ... his eyes, his skin, his lips ... but I knew I shouldn't objectify his many, *many* attributes or his cocky smile or ... I looked away.

Sitting between the boy and Breine was a willowy, fresh-faced girl with honey-blonde hair. She *had* to be his girl-friend; she was equally gorgeous. The girl looked like she'd stepped off the cover of one of Uncle Wally's glossy British magazines. I could easily picture her posed in hunting pinks and surrounded by hounds, or inside the Manor House, elegant in a cashmere twin set and pearls.

I tugged at my own top, immediately self-conscious. It was the same one I'd worn leaving Rio yesterday. The one from my go bag.

"Bas, darlin'," the cover girl admonished. "Remember what Margaret Walker said? *Friends and good manners will carry you where money won't go.* We need to be polite. In-troductions first."

Then the girl turned to me and smiled. "I'm Avery."

Turns out Avery was not an English rose after all. There was more than a hint of the American south in her vowels. Avery was a true southern beauty who also seemed to be channeling my quote-of-the-day dad. I couldn't resist adding a quote of my own.

"Hi, Avery. It's nice to meet you. But I believe Mary Wilson Little said, *Politeness is half good manners and half good lying.* So I have to wonder," I said, biting back a grin of my own and tossing in a southern pronoun borrowed from movies and tv, "Are y'all as good liars as you are well-mannered?"

Avery burst out laughing. Even her laughter was beautiful. Like bells.

"Well, color me impressed, Leah Teague. Either you're a fan of southern writers, or you have a sticky flypaper brain like me."

I returned her smile. "More like I have a dad who is overly fond of sharing quotes."

"Well, either way, welcome to Wentworth Academy. You already know Breine. That's Evie," she said, indicating the girl sitting next to me.

Evie had short, almost black hair swept back with a healthy dose of product and eyes heavily circled with thick black eyeliner. Not thick enough apparently to violate the school dress code, but enough to make a statement. I'd gone to private schools the world over and recognized the type. Five US dollars said this girl was rebelling, probably against her parents, and would have a *take-that-Mom* tattoo hidden somewhere out of sight. In the small of her back or on a butt cheek. Another five dollars said it would have Japanese or Chinese characters that she believed said something profound, but for a subtle brushstroke or because of a smirking tattoo artist, said something else entirely. Just the thought had me biting back a grin.

Avery continued with the introductions.

"And this rude boy beside me, staring at you like you're Mamie Eisenhower's famous chocolate fudge is Evie's twin brother and all-round troublemaker, Bas."

"Short for Sebastian," Bas said, leaning forward, placing his chiseled jaw (chiseled really *was* the only word for it) in the palms of his hands and batting his eyelids at me. He *actually* batted his eyelids.

"And before you ask, yes. I am currently single *and* available, you lucky lady." Then, holding his thumb and pinky finger to his ear, he mouthed, "Call me," and winked. Not a small, intended-to-be-flirty-but-comes-out-creepy kind of a wink, but a full-faced, open-mouthed, slapstick comedy wink.

I laughed. He was so over-the-top I couldn't help it.

"Hi, Bas. Evie. Avery. It's nice to meet all of you."

"Not quite all of us," Bas said. "Nick, my roommate, isn't here yet."

"Where *is* Nick?" Breine asked.

"Surprise call from the girlfriend in Rio."

"It couldn't wait until their nighttime smoochie-smoochie session?" Evie grumbled.

I bit back a grin. Not that many weeks ago, Nick Millburn had been the *fresh meat*, and Evie clearly didn't like that he was off the menu.

Breine was more compassionate than me. She reached across the table and squeezed Evie's hand. "Sorry, Evie."

After that, things at the table got quiet. I didn't know if their silence was pity or compassion. I only knew that if I was in Evie's place, I'd be really uncomfortable, and even though I didn't know Evie from Adam, I wanted to rescue her and get the conversation started again. So I blurted, "I know Nick's girlfriend. She's a good friend of mine. Her name's Janneke."

"Hold on a sec. You know Janneke?" Bas said. His forehead furrowed and his eyebrows pinched together making the cutest little wrinkle between his eyes. When I nodded, he shook his head.

"What?" I asked. "What is it?"

"That's weird, is all."

"Why is that weird?"

"Because we asked Nick if he knew you, and he said you'd never met."

"He's right. We haven't met, but what's weird is why you'd even ask him that in the first place. Nick didn't know I was coming to Wentworth. And you couldn't have known. I didn't even know until last night!"

"The whole school knew you were coming, Leah. They announced it during homeroom this morning. A new kid from Rio and partway through term? That's big news around here."

Before I could figure out how to react, Evie cocked her head, narrowed her eyes, and said, "Wait a minute. Backup. You didn't know you were coming here until last night? What's that about? I bet I know. You messed up big, didn't you?"

I sat there like an idiot, gaping at Evie.

"Yeah, you did," Evie said with a wry smile. "You messed up. My money's on you got kicked-out of school. I just can't decide what you got kicked out for. Cheating? Drugs? Did you get arrested? Wait, are you childing?"

"What?"

"You know ... preggers, knocked up, enceinte?"

"No!"

"Dial it back a notch, sis," Bas said. "This is Wentworth Academy, not some CIA black site. Not everyone is miscreant like you and me. And anyway, Breine says she belongs, right? She's one of us."

Evie shrugged. "Yeah, well I still have questions."

My head ping-ponged between them as they talked about me. Evie may have issues, and given time, maybe I could learn to be more understanding. But right then, I didn't appreciate Evie taking whatever hurt she was dealing with out on me with her third degree. I didn't want anyone to think I'd been forced to leave a school because I'd lied, cheated, taken drugs, been arrested or that other thing. Private schools are like small towns, or expat communities. They're a petri dish for rumors. For a brief moment, I considered telling them everything. It might shock Evie into silence and put an end to her wild speculations.

Four sets of eyes stared at me, waiting for my answer. I settled on a compromise.

"It's okay, Bas. Evie, I didn't get kicked out of school. Stuff happened with my dad's job, and he ... he couldn't look after me."

"What about your mom?"

"I don't have one, I'm adopted."

"You could still have a mom."

"But I don't," I countered. "My dad's gay. He has a boyfriend. Not a wife."

"Why couldn't his boyfriend look after you?"

Evie was a scrapper. Generally, I liked that quality in a friend. Janneke was like that — forceful and direct. But I didn't particularly appreciate having Evie's interrogation bright-lights aimed at me. I pushed back.

"Dad's boyfriend doesn't live with us. Their jobs don't let them live together for now. Satisfied?"

Breine stepped in then. "Call off the dogs, Evie. Leah's okay. She'll tell us her story when she's ready. When she trusts us. Right, Leah?"

"Maybe, maybe not," I said. Fitting in was important, but so was setting boundaries. "I think it's my turn to ask questions. You say I'm *one of you*. What are you, exactly? What is it you've been screening me for?"

It was Avery who answered.

"To see if you're a *Disappointment*, of course."

# 24.

## THE DISAPPOINTMENTS

"A disappointment?"

"Disappointments to our parents, each and every one of us," said Avery. "Bas, Evie, and Breine are the originals. I joined partway through ninth grade, and we found Nick when he became Bas's roommate. Now there's you. The Disappointments are a family. Not the one we were born to. The one we chose."

"Okay. Well, thank you, I guess? But what makes you think I disappointed my dad?"

"Didn't you?" Evie asked.

I wasn't ready to admit it to them, but Evie was right. Dad *must* be disappointed in me.

"Allow me to present the evidence," Evie said. She held up her index finger. "Point one. No senior, especially one with Ivy League ambitions, would willingly leave their school eight weeks into term. Ergo, you got kicked out or, anticipating getting kicked out, you chose to leave so it wouldn't be on your record."

"I did *not* get kicked out of school, Evie."

She ignored me and held up a second finger. It made a peace sign, but this felt anything but peace-like.

"Point two. Wentworth's boarding program is maxed out. We are literally packed to the rafters with a long waiting list that includes the kids of some big-name box-office Hollywood types. Yet here you are."

"Evie," Breine said, "maybe it would help if you told Leah what you heard this morning."

"Yeah, okay." Evie nodded, then turned to me. "I volunteer in the administration office. Community service hours," she shrugged. "This morning, I overhead Headmaster Mitchell saying someone pledged to donate enough money for the school to expand and refit the computer lab with new, state-of-the-art *everything* if, *and only if*, Wentworth found a spot for their kid today. It had to be today. And here you are."

"That's not me," I said, shaking my head. "Headmaster Mitchell had to be talking about someone else."

"You, Leah Teague, are the only new student arriving at Wentworth today."

"Then whoever Mitchell was talking about must be arriving later today or not coming at all because it's definitely not me. The whole idea is nuts," I said, shaking my head. "It's more than nuts, it's not possible. My dad doesn't have that kind of money. He's a cultural attaché, for crying out loud. He works for the Canadian Foreign Service. Yeah, I go to private schools, and yes, they're expensive, but we don't pay the tuition. The government does."

"I know what I heard. And what I heard was that someone is willing to spend big bucks, really big bucks, to buy a spot at Wentworth and here you are. Case closed."

Evie was sticking to her story like a conspiracy theorist who thought the moon landing was staged or the 2020 election was — air quotes — stolen.

The idea that my dad bought my way into Wentworth was ridiculous on so many levels. For one, he didn't even know I was here. And even if Dad knew I'd chosen Wentworth, he was in no position to do anything about anything. He was in the hands of kidnappers, probably bound and gagged. Birthday Max and his mysterious connections did all the heavy lifting on this one. Which reminded me ... once this João Matheus Pereira stuff was over, and Dad and I were together again, I intended to make Dad tell me more about Birthday Max. If Max was connected enough to get me admitted to Wentworth last minute, then he was obviously much more than a simple adoption lawyer. There had to be a helluva story there! For now, I could only shake my head as Evie leaned back in her chair and folded her arms across her chest.

Bas called his twin down with a look, then jumped in. "Our working theory is that you screwed the pooch big time. It would explain why you left Rio so fast and why you didn't know you were coming here until yesterday. Face it, Leah. You're one of us."

I couldn't roll my eyes back far enough. It was like I'd already told them. Dad's job afforded us privileges most people don't have, like school, housing, and travel allowances, but we definitely did not have the kind of money that would let us buy our way into a place like Wentworth Academy.

"We're not rich. We're expats. There's a difference. A *huge* difference."

There was a protracted silence. Four pairs of eyes stared at me. It had been an excruciating two days, and I was rapidly reaching the limits of my ability to deal. My frustration must have been visible because Avery said, "Leah, honey, just hear us out, okay? Breine?"

Breine held up three fingers. "Point number three. You don't exist. Digitally, that is. We've had our best people on it," she said, indicating Evie and Bas, "and they can't find a trace of you anywhere online."

"We already talked about this, Breine."

"But did we really? All you said was that you were too busy to bother with social media. The bottom line is you don't just have a *minimal* footprint, Leah. You have a *zero* footprint. And that tells us that someone has gone to great pains to erase you and whatever happened that got you sent here."

I opened my mouth to object, but Breine's fourth finger popped up.

"And finally, four. Everything you own — your suitcase, computer, phone, tablet, and clothes — is brand new. Even your socks and underwear still have the price tags attached. I'm not sure what that means exactly, but you have to agree, it's not normal."

I didn't have an explanation for that last one. Not being able to talk my way out of something made me feel trapped, and that made me feel combative. Avery noticed because she leaned forward and patted my hand.

"We get it, honey. Something happened that made your daddy feel he had to send you away. That's a hard thing to talk about. I know all about that. Those words stick in your throat like a hair in a biscuit, don't they? But girl, we've all been where you are. And *that*, darlin', is what makes you one of us. A Disappointment."

# 25.

## TIKKUN OLAM

Avery was right. I was a disappointment. I hadn't cheated on a test or showed up to school wasted. I'd never been in a fight, and I most definitely had not, nor would I ever, take drugs. But I was one of them all the same. A disappointment. Not only because of the Big Lie I'd told Dad back in Istanbul, the lie about wanting to be a journalist like Christina Ramos. My class got shot at because of me, Marcos was in the hospital, and my dad had been kidnapped. All because of me. I'd screwed up so colossally that deep down I worried my dad would never look at me the same way again.

I reeked with self-loathing right then. My face must have given that away because Avery chimed in. "Leah, no one here wants to lick the red off your candy."

Avery was trying to be nice, but right then I didn't feel like I deserved nice. Dropping my eyes, I stood up, grabbed my dinner tray, and made to leave.

"Please don't go, Leah," Bas added. "Evie shouldn't have pressed you so hard." He turned to his sister. "Remember what it was like when we first got here, Ev?"

Evie scrunched her eyes shut, then after a stretched-out second, she said, "Yeah, I remember. Sorry, Leah."

I nodded, but I didn't sit down. Not yet.

"Please stay, Leah," Bas said, locking his eyes to mine. "Please?"

He wasn't being cocky or flirty now. His face oozed kindness. I may not think I deserved their friendship, but I knew I needed it. I put my tray down on the table and sat down.

"Thank you," Bas said. "And Leah, what Avery said about being a disappointment to our parents ... it's true for all of us. Take Evie and me," he said, turning back to his sister. The look that passed between them right then was heartbreaking.

"Before work took over their lives, our parents would actually play with us."

"It wasn't play, Bas," Evie said, her voice laced with vinegar. "They were teaching us to code, for shit's sake. Before we could even read!"

Evie turned to me. "Our parents are software engineers. They have a company that does AI, machine learning, and all that crap. That's all they care about. The company and its precious proprietary code."

"Come on, Evie," Bas said. "You're only remembering the bad stuff. They made learning-to-code into a game. It was good times, right?"

Evie glared at him.

Bas took a deep breath, then blew it out between pursed lips. "Yeah, okay. Evie's right. All the good times happened *before* they started the company. Once we moved to the valley, all they ever did was work, and by the time Evie and I were in middle school, we never saw them anymore."

"We *literally* never saw them," Evie said. "We were shuffled off to sitters, after-school programs, and summer camps. We're their blood-and-bones babies, but their real baby, the only one they truly love, is their company. Long story short, Bas and I didn't appreciate being tossed aside like an old toy. So we found *creative* ways to get their attention."

"Creative?"

"Very creative," Evie said with a wry smile. "After the — what was it, Bas, the third ride home in a squad car —?"

"Fourth. We got the social worker after the third time."

"Right. The same social worker who suggested our parents send us to a treatment facility. Puuhlease! We were a couple of lonely twelve-year-old kids desperately trying to get our parents to act like parents." Evie shook her head.

"At least they sent us here, Ev."

"My baby brother of nineteen minutes is annoyingly optimistic about good old mom and dad. He wants to believe that sending us to Wentworth means they cared about us. Personally, I think they would have happily locked us away if they weren't worried people might find out their kids were at some private rehab for junior criminals. But here's the kicker. We didn't know it then, but Wentworth required *an extra incentive* to accept us as students. Like you, Leah, money changed hands."

I wanted to correct her again, but what was the point? Evie had made it clear she believed everything Headmaster Mitchell had said was about me and some ludicrous *quid pro quo* donation.

All that money nonsense aside, I felt terrible for Bas. Evie too. This break with their parents may have happened four long years ago, but Bas's pain and Evie's anger were still swimming dangerously close to the surface. It had to hurt. And I got that. I'm still hurt that my birth mom gave me up. The difference is my birth mom was probably some scared teenager. Not a parent who decided they were done with parenting. I don't know how I would have handled that kind of rejection.

"But it's all good," Bas said. He really *was* an optimist. "We came here, met Breine, and made a family we can depend on."

"Okay, my turn," Breine said. "Before Bas gets too mushy. I also got sent away by my parents, Leah. I'm a third-generation American Jew and great-granddaughter of German Jews who escaped Nazi Germany in 1942 with three small kids in tow."

"Wow. Really?"

"I know. Crazy, right? They got out just as Hitler intensified his 'Final Solution' — his plan to kill all the Jews. It wasn't easy, but the family made it to America and settled in Oklahoma. Great grandad got work on the oil rigs. He worked hard and eventually started his own company, Berenson Petroleum, which my grandad took over and grew until he retired. Now my dad runs the show, and his parents — my grandparents — live with us.

"The Berenson family believes in the State of Israel. It's how I was raised. To believe that also. After everything that's happened, not just to my family but to Jews throughout the centuries — we need somewhere safe. A home. A homeland."

This did not sound like the same girl who plastered her dorm walls with posters of Jewish organizations that supported Palestine and who looked genuinely excited when I'd told her Dr. Walid Masri was my dad's boyfriend. As much as I did not want to get dragged into some political-religious discussion, I needed to know … had I read her wrong? Was I losing my touch? I waded in.

"I hear you, Breine. Six million Jews in four years. It's… it's almost impossible to wrap your head around something like that."

"And that's just World War 2. Recent history. Jewish persecution has been going on for centuries."

I was quickly becoming confused by my new roommate. It must have shown on my face because she asked, "What is it, Leah?"

"I mean … well … it's just that Israel was formed when? Around 1950?"

"1948. May 14."

"Okay, right. But in 1948, weren't people already living there? You know, where they *suddenly decided* to put Israel?"

"Of course, there were people already living there. More than half a million of those people were Jews. Did you know that?"

I did not. I shook my head.

"In 1948, in Jerusalem alone, there were more than 100,000 Jews. Leah, Jews have lived in that area of the Middle East for centuries."

"So … uh …I didn't know that. It's just … what about all those posters in our room? They're all from organizations that support Palestine."

"So?"

"So? Come on, Breine. Why plaster the walls with those posters if it's not something you believe in?"

"But I do. I *do* believe in them."

"Look, I really don't want to wade into any political or religious argument here. I don't have an opinion. I don't *want* to have an opinion. I work hard at staying out of these sorts of discussions at home. All I'm trying to do here, is get a read on things."

"Fair enough. But is it okay if I explain?"

I nodded.

"I told you that the Berensens believe in Israel. What I didn't tell you was that it was my grandparents' dream to make Aliyah."

"Aliyah?"

"That means moving to Israel and becoming Israeli. For as long as I can remember, Opa, my grandfather, has talked about the day my dad would take over the company. Then Opa and Oma — that's my grandmother —could finally make Aliyah and move to Israel. But before that happened, Oma developed dementia. It was pretty bad. Moving her to a strange place in a strange new country wasn't a good idea. They ended up moving in with us. I was twelve and in the middle of preparing for my Bat Mitzvah, which I took seriously. Even back then, I knew I wanted to be a Rabbi.

"I was reading more, paying attention to the news. I discussed things with my Rabbi, who gave me stuff to read. The more I read, the more questions I had about Israel and what was happening there."

Breine paused and pulled her lower lip between her teeth. After a moment, she continued. "Jews have a phrase," she said. "Tikkun olam. Should the world need fixing, it's our duty to fix it. It's the Jewish principle of improving the world through actions."

"Tikkun olam," I repeated. "That's beautiful, Breine."

"Yes, it is. It really is. And I thought talking about tikkun olam and Israel and Palestine could help my grandfather. He'd worked hard his whole life for their dream of Aliya — he couldn't stop talking about how disappointed he was. I thought if I shared what I was learning, he might not be so upset about what he was missing and be happy they were staying here in America with us.

"Stuff like, did Opa know that Palestinians were being excluded and discriminated against based on their religion? How did he feel about that as a Jew? Because that's what had happened to us? Right?

"But he wouldn't talk about it. *I was just a kid. What did I know?* When I told him about all the Jewish organizations in America that were raising the same concerns I was and that I planned to join one of these groups once I left for college, Opa got so angry and upset that my dad was worried he was going to have a heart attack or stroke.

"Looking back now, I get it. Opa felt like the world — and worse, his very own granddaughter — was whitewashing over everything his parents had experienced. You said it yourself, Leah. Six million Jews in four years."

And here, Briene placed a clenched hand over her heart and said, "But I believed in tikkun olam with all my heart. I wanted to fix the world, to make things right. And I wanted my family with me.

"My dad said it was no good trying to fix the world if, in the process, I broke my grandfather's heart. They decided it was best if I went away to school for a while and let things settle down at home. So they sent me here, and in protest, I took every penny of my Bat Mitzvah money and donated it to Jewish Voice for Peace."

I didn't know what to say. My dad was fiercely overprotective and demanded a lot of me — too much sometimes — but there wasn't a day I hadn't felt his love. Even if that love felt a little suffocating.

"Now me," Avery said. "My daddy is Scott Lascelles," she announced, her southern drawl deepening.

She said his name as if I should know it. I didn't. I shook my head and shrugged my shoulders.

"Scott Lascelles. From Houston?"

I shook my head again.

"You really don't know who he is, Leah?"

"No, Avery, I really don't. Who is he?"

"My daddy is the pastor of the Hillforest Church in Houston," she said. "The biggest megachurch in America. You must have seen him on TV or in the papers. Those New York-type papers are always writing things about Daddy. About how he's more interested in people's money than their souls, and about how he comes to church each Sunday in God's Chariot."

I shook my head.

"God's Chariot? It's Daddy's trademark. A baby blue helicopter with clouds painted on the sides and yellow cross on the helicopter's belly."

I drew a blank on all of it.

"Goodness, you really don't know who my daddy is, do you, Leah?"

"Avery, I came from Rio, remember? Before Rio, we were in Belarus. And before that, it was Hong Kong, Turkey, the Netherlands, Moscow, and more. I've never heard of your father or his helicopter."

"Well, all right then. Cliff Notes version. Daddy is a rather famous Texas preacher who is loudly on record saying it's a sin to be homo-*sex*-ual."

Avery's accent was in full force now. She said homo-*sex*-ual with a long, drawn-out drawl and the heaviest emphasis on "sex." She smiled, then leaned over, hooked a finger under Breine's chin, turned it to face her, and planted a full kiss on Breine's lips.

Bas and Avery weren't a couple; Breine and Avery were.

"Okay. I get it," I chuckled.

Breine blushed. Avery planted a second kiss on Breine's cheek, then continued.

"I came out to my parents around Christmas of ninth grade. They did *not* take it well, let me tell you. Momma was all in a tizzy about what people would think. Her friends and committees and such. But Daddy, well, he might preach Christian values of love, peace, and truth, but he's a big ole bigot who's none too fond of Jews, Muslims, and any of the letters LGBT or Q. Daddy was worried that donations might dry up if anyone found out his precious daughter liked kissing girls.

"I could hardly believe they'd do such a thing to me, but in January of ninth grade, they up and sent their little embarrassment away. When I arrived at Wentworth, I was as lost as last year's Easter egg. Until Breine found me. My darlin' Breine cannot stand to see a creature in pain or abide an injustice. She swooped in, scooped me up, and brought me into the fold. You didn't expect to fall in love, though. Did you, honey?"

"I did not," Breine said, reaching for Avery's hand while Avery finished her tale.

"We became a family. We had a synergy that made us better together, and soon it was Breine, Bas, Evie, and me twenty-four-seven. One Friday night, we snuck out and built a bonfire on the beach under the cliffs. I said how I thought it was funny how four kids who were such disappointments to their respective parents could have found so much happiness, friendship, and success in the very place they'd been banished to. The name stuck, and we became The Disappointments. So Leah, whatever you did that got you sent away, darlin' girl ... we've all been there."

"No. No you haven't," I said. "Not like this."

For the first time since Rocinha, I felt tears form and fall. I wiped them away with the back of my hand until both Breine and Avery reached across the table taking my hand in theirs.

Everything spilled out then. Almost everything. I kept Pereira's name secret, but I told them about the favela, the drugs, the shootings and the attack outside the school. I told them about the video I'd made and how Dad had sent me out of the country to keep me safe and how, since they couldn't get to me, they'd kidnapped my dad and were holding him for ransom.

It was a relief to talk about it. Like the valve on a pressure cooker that popped open to let off steam.

"It's okay," I said, looking across the table at Breine. She hadn't let go of my hand the whole time. "I'm okay."

She squeezed my hand. "We've got you, Leah. Whatever you need."

Then Bas's phone beeped.

"It's Nick," Bas said. "He's on his way. He'll be here soon."

By the time Nick Millburn arrived, I was more or less dry-eyed and composed.

I knew it was Nick. I recognized him from pictures on Janneke's phone. Nick Millburn was tall, long-limbed, and lean. He still had sun streaks in his hair and a tan that was baked layers deep into his skin. He put his tray down next to mine.

"You must be Leah."

"And you're Nick. Janneke talks about you all the time."

"Yeah, crazy coincidence, us both being here at Wentworth, right?"

"Sure. Sort of."

"I just got off the phone with Janneke. She says to say hi and that you better call her. She was pretty upset when she learned you'd left Rio."

"Things ... things happened fast. I didn't have time to let her know."

Nick nodded his understanding. "Yeah. Janneke told me what happened to your driver. I'm really sorry."

"Thanks, Nick. I hate that Marcos was hurt protecting me, but it's all good. We got him to the hospital quickly, and Rio has excellent medical care," I said, parroting my dad's words. "Marcos is strong. By now, he's probably driving the nurses crazy."

Nick's face clouded.

"What? What is it?"

"Your driver," Nick said. "Marcos?"

"What about him?"

"I'm sorry, Leah. He didn't make it."

## 26.

# YOU'RE GOING TO BE THE DEATH OF ME

*He didn't make it.*

Nick Millburn said Marcos didn't make it.

That couldn't be true. Marcos couldn't be dead. *He couldn't be!*

I heard a collective gasp come from The Disappointments, followed by the sound of chairs scraping. Still, I clung to my denial. Breine ran around the table and wrapped her arms around me. They all did. Avery and Evie. Even Bas and Nick. I've got to admit, it felt good. But I didn't want *them*. I wanted Marcos.

Raphael must have known about Marcos. Why hadn't he told me?

Why hadn't I asked?

*Oh, Marcos. We were both supposed to be moving on —* *me to college and you to Poland to marry Basia. I was ready* *for you to leave. I was happy for you. But this? I'm not ready* *for this. I'm not ready for a world without you in it.*

I needed ... I needed ...

I needed to run.

Tears streaming down my face, I wriggled and twisted out of their hugs until I was free, then I ran for the door. In a fog, I sprinted toward the lamppost-and-lilac path, then kept running, my feet pounding the pavement harder and faster. I didn't stop when the path ended at Yew Tree Cottage. I headed for the water. Only an ocean would be large enough to hold my grief. I ran as fast as the rough dirt path would allow.

Running was something Marcos and I did together. We'd run together so many times, I half expected to hear his footfalls beside me and feel his shoulder next to mine. I don't think I'd ever be able to run, look at a map, board a plane, or speak another language ever again without thinking of him.

*Oh, Marcos.*

As my feet pounded the ground, memories of Marcos pummeled my brain. At first, all I could see were the memories from yesterday — Marcos lying face down on the road, his body leaching blood onto a starched white shirt. I wanted — no, I *needed* — to remember a different Marcos. I forced that image out and replaced it with happier times. When we first became a family.

Mumbai. To a four-year-old, that city was magical — a bright box of crayons and a full orchestra of sounds with Marcos as its daily conductor. From the start, Marcos collected words like some people collect coffee spoons. He insisted I learn the names of everything around us. He began with the trees. Jacaranda. Frangipani. Pichkari. And my favorite tree, the one that grew right below my bedroom window, the naag-keshar. In the summer, its leaves turned soft pink, and its flowers made me hungry for breakfast because they looked like eggs cooked sunny-side-up. But the best part of the naag-keshar tree was the smell. To me, it was nicer even than jasmine.

After trees, Marcos taught me the names of birds. The backyard of our house was filled with birds. In my memory, those birds sang from morning to night. My dad warned me not to feed them, worried that if I did, more and more birds would come, and our back garden would be overrun. But I didn't listen. I thought the birds were beautiful. Marcos introduced them all to me.

There were parakeets and golden orioles. A brilliant turquoise bird visited now and then with a white throat and bib and a long red beak. Marcos said it was a white-throated kingfisher. It was beautiful, but my favorite bird, the ones I hoped would fill the garden, were the hummingbirds. Purple-rumped sunbirds, Marcos called them. Lemon-chested and plain until the sun shone, then their feathers would dance with iridescent colors: blues, greens, purples, like so many sparkling jewels.

Out of nowhere, a memory slapped me upside the head. It happened one morning after Dad had left for work. Four-year-old me smuggled a roti up to my room. I tore off small bits of the illicit flatbread and threw them from my bedroom window, watching enchanted as the birds swooped down with all their bird aunties, uncles, and cousins to feast on my leftover bits of breakfast until there were only scraps left. As they fought for food, their screeches grew and grew. I loved the theater playing out below so much that I joined in by screeching back at them. The next thing I knew, Marcos burst through my door, holding a whole roti in one hand and a kitchen knife in the other as though my screams had caught him mid-chop.

"Bread!" I said, oblivious to his fear and delighted to have more food for my hummingbirds. I snatched the flatbread from him and tossed it, whole, out the window. A bird war ensued, and our yard became so noisy it sounded like the bird seller's stall in Mumbai's Crawford Market.

"Oh, little girl," Marcos said, laughing. "You're going to be the death of me."

Those were his exact words.

Not long after, Dad complained that the birds were getting worse by the day and asked Marcos to *take care of them*.

I knew Marcos would never kill my birds. With a sideways wink to me, Marcos replied, "Yes, sir."

And every morning after Dad left for work, Marcos was right there beside me, feeding the birds.

Yew Tree Cottage was far behind me now. I'd reached the ocean. Almost reached the ocean. I was cut short by a chin-high chain-link fence. Fingers clenching wire, I howled my grief at the top of my lungs, but the wind and the pounding surf swallowed my screams.

Once purged, I found a seed of resolve. A flimsy wire fence was not going to stop me. Sticking the toe of my Vivobarefoots into the chain-link, I pulled myself up and over. From there, it was only a few short strides to the edge and a wild coastline of zigzag cliffs and tumbled rock. I sat down on the grass, hung my legs over the cliff edge, and stared out over the vast Atlantic.

Marcos had always been here for me. My whole life, he'd kept me safe. I hadn't made it easy for him. I constantly tested the limits, even when I was little. When I'd jump out of a too-tall tree, ride a bike too fast down a steep hill, or try a route up a climbing wall that exceeded my skills, Marcos was always there. Each time he would pick me up, and with a smile and shake of his head, he'd say, "You're going to be the death of me."

And in the end, I was.

My back heaved up and down in uncontrollable sobs. I was crying so hard, I didn't hear Nick. I didn't know he was there until I felt his hand on my shoulder and heard him speaking into his phone.

"I've got her. Take the footpath from Yew Tree Cottage. We're just over the coast fence."

# 27.

## SHE SAID IT WAS VREEMD

"Hang in there, Leah," Nick said. "Everyone's coming. They'll be here soon."

The combination of Nick's voice and his hand squeezing my shoulder brought me back from the edge. Gulping large swallows of air, I steadied my breathing, wiped my eyes, and looked at him.

"I'm so sorry, Leah," Nick said. "I figured you already knew about your driver. Why didn't anyone tell you?"

"There's no one left to tell me." I swallowed a sob.

"Right. Because your dad's been ..."

He knew. He didn't want to say kidnapped, but Nick knew even though he wasn't in the refectory when I'd told everyone.

"How did you find out? From Janneke?"

He nodded. "Leah, can we move back to the fence? I'm really not good with heights." Nick was already edging backward away from the cliff edge.

"How did she find out?" I asked. "When I looked online, I couldn't find anything."

"She heard about it from a reporter. Christina Ramos."

I sprang to my feet. "Ramos?" I'd almost forgotten about Christina Ramos and the college interview Dad had pulled strings to arrange. How was it that Janneke talked to Ramos on the very same day I was supposed to?

"Leah, can you *please* move away from the edge?"

I looked down. I was not afraid of heights — too many years spent rock climbing — but I was as close to the edge as you could get without going over. The iodine smell of the ocean, the slap of waves, and the barest touch of sea spray lifted and carried by the wind were all things that soothed me, but clearly not Nick. At least, not at this height. I nodded, stepped away, and joined him at the fence. We sat together, backs leaning on the chain-link, staring out over the ocean.

"Better?" I asked.

Nick slowed his breathing and nodded. "Thanks. You?"

"A little. Thank you for coming to look for me. But Nick, how did Janneke meet Christina Ramos?"

My dad had pulled strings to get me an interview with Ramos. I knew Janneke's parents wouldn't be able to do that, even if they'd wanted to.

"Ramos showed up at school this morning."

"Why? Was she planning to write about what happened there? What happened to Marcos?"

"Ever read her stuff?"

I had, thanks to Marcos who would cut out her articles for me. I'd read them just often enough to keep Dad convinced that I was an earnest student with journalistic aspirations.

I nodded.

"It was awful what happened to your driver, but don't you think it's too small a story for the New Yorker or the New York Times? And not just because you're Canadian," he added.

Now that he'd said it, it did seem unlikely. Foreigners are killed every day all over the world, but unless those foreigners were American or someone famous or important, it's not the kind of story the New York Times would carry. So what was Ramos doing?

"So Ramos just showed up out of the blue offering alumni interviews for kids applying to Yale?"

"According to Janneke, yeah. And it's a big deal, right? You know what it's like for international students. How often do we get a shot at alumni interviews, especially since the pandemic? Scoring one, particularly with a famous Yale alum, was huge for Janneke. Teebo too, I guess, but even more so for Janneke. If she doesn't get accepted at Yale, her parents say she's got to go back to the Netherlands for university. They have great universities, but we want to be together."

"*And* she wants to study film in the US," I added.

"Yeah, that too," he admitted. "I don't want to lose her, Leah. We've *both* got to get into Yale. I'll get an interview. You know that Wentworth arranges them for us during our campus visit, right?"

I nodded. Headmaster Mitchell had told me as much. But Nick was getting off track. I needed to steer him back.

"Janneke and Ramos?"

"Right. Sorry. The interview was important for Janneke, but ..." Nick let his voice trail off.

"But what?"

"She said the whole interview was vreemd. That's Dutch," he added.

"I know what it is. We were posted to the Netherlands. Why did Janneke think it was strange?"

"The interview began like you'd expect — normal stuff about Janneke, school, and why she wanted to go to Yale.

But then things changed course pretty quick. Ramos started asking about your dad and you."

"It makes sense Ramos would ask about my dad if she'd heard about the kidnapping."

"Except the Rio police told Ramos it was an *express kidnapping*. You know what they are, right?"

I did. Dad made sure of it. I answered, "It's when they grab you off the street, take your phone and wallet and make you give them your pin so they can take money out of your account at an ATM."

"Basically, yeah," Nick said. "But kidnappers have also been using an app that lets the victim wire-transfer larger amounts. The thing is, when Janneke heard about your dad, she was upset, right? She was worried about you and your father, so she asked Ramos if she'd heard anything because, you know, reporters can find stuff out."

"Did she? Did Ramos learn something?"

"Ramos told Janneke that she'd checked with the police, and they told her not to worry. Express kidnappings happen all the time, and once the kidnappers got their money your dad would be released."

I knew that wasn't true. Money was not going to buy my dad's freedom. I held my lower lip firmly between my teeth to let Nick finish his story.

"According to the Rio police, your dad's kidnapping would sort itself once the kidnappers got their money. So Ramos probably wasn't at school because of him, right?"

I nodded.

"And we already agreed she wasn't there because of what happened to your driver. Both stories are too small, localized, and, well, too Canadian for a big New York paper, right?"

"I guess." I was still trying to process why Ramos was really there and what she might know. "So what did Ramos want to know about me and my dad?"

"Stuff like where else you'd lived and did other kids at school have personal drivers. Janneke called her on it. She's Dutch, right, so she's direct." Nick mimicked Janneke's accent. '*Why are you asking about all that? This is my interview. You are supposed to be asking about me, not my friend*'."

Nick smiled and shook his head. He obviously admired his girlfriend's tell-it-like-it-is quality. I was a little in awe of it as well.

"What did Ramos say to that?"

"A lot of bullshit, frankly. Stuff she expected Janneke to swallow. But she's seventeen. Not stupid."

"Anything else?"

"Yeah. Ramos already knew you'd left the country."

"How?"

"I dunno. The police, maybe? She didn't say, but she asked Janneke if you two were in touch. Leah, Ramos wanted to know where you were. Does that make sense to you?"

It didn't. And the look on Nick's face and the edge in his voice told me he also thought it was strange.

"It's okay, Nick. It's not like Janneke could have told Ramos anything; she didn't know where I was. And you couldn't have told her because you two only talked minutes ago — just before you came to the refectory — right?"

Nick's face puckered. "That's not exactly true. We found out you were coming this morning, remember? They announced it in homeroom. As soon as I heard the new kid was from Rio, I texted Janneke to see if she recognized your name. Leah, she knew you were here at Wentworth *before* she met with Ramos."

I let that sink in. Then I asked, "Did she tell Ramos I was here?"

"It slipped out. She's really sorry, Leah. But hey, maybe it doesn't matter. It's not like it was a targeted kidnapping where they hit up relatives for ransom money. The police said your dad will be released soon."

I shook my head.

"What? What is it?"

Dad always said that *a problem shared was a problem halved,* and I desperately needed to halve the weight of everything I was carrying — grieving for Marcos and being crazy worried that Raphael wouldn't be able to save my dad.

"You can't trust the police, Nick. They're part of it."

"Part of what?"

I told Nick everything then. About João Matheus Pereira, the video, everything. Nick's eyes widened.

"That's the real reason I came to Wentworth. The police — at least some of them — are working for Pereira. Dad worried he couldn't protect me from them, so he sent me out of the country. When Pereira couldn't get to me, they took my dad, but I didn't find that out until late last night. I was supposed to go to London and stay with Dad's boyfriend, but that didn't work out, and I had nowhere to go. I remembered your dad saying you were at Wentworth Academy, and since I had to go somewhere, Wentworth seemed like as good a place as any."

"Wait," Nick said, head shaking, his forehead wrinkled with questions. "When did you talk to my dad?"

"Yesterday. He smuggled me out of the Canadian Consulate and drove me to the airport. Our dads know each other, Nick. They're old friends."

"How do our dads know each other?"

"I assume it's work. Your dad is with the State Department, right?"

"Yeah. He's a cultural attaché."

"That's it then. My dad is a cultural attaché too. Nick, do you think maybe your dad could help?"

Nick looked flummoxed. "What could *he* do?"

"Not him exactly, but he's been in Rio a while. He might know people that could help?"

I could almost hear the gears grinding in Nick's brain as he tried to find a way to fit the pieces together. It was obvious that Nick had more questions, but voices sounded above and behind us. I turned and looked. Evie, Bas, Avery, and Breine had arrived at the other side of the fence.

"Are you okay, Leah?" Breine asked, worry written across her face.

I nodded. I might not be one hundred percent fine, but I was a whole lot better for being part of The Disappointments.

"Then we should move," Evie piped in. "Sunset was ten minutes ago, and we have Study Hall soon."

Nick and I stood up and climbed across the fence. Bas handed me my go bag. I'd left it in the refectory. That was colossally stupid. My fake American passport was inside. I couldn't afford to be that careless again.

Slinging my bag over my shoulder, the six of us jogged toward campus and our dorms. When we reached Yew Tree Cottage, I turned to Nick.

"Nick, something your dad said yesterday has been bugging me."

"What?"

"He said we'd met before, but I don't remember him at all."

He shrugged. "I don't remember most of my parents' friends either."

"No, it's more than that," I said, shaking my head. "At Galeão, I asked him where we'd met. He said Berlin. But I've never lived there. I've never even been to Germany."

Nick stopped on a dime and stared at me. His jaw went slack. I wanted to ask him about it but didn't get a chance because Avery and Breine had linked their arms through mine and were pulling me inside Yew Tree Cottage.

"Study Hall calls," Avery said. "And you, Leah Teague, need to get cleaned up."

"Cleaned up?"

Avery drew a pretend circle around her own eye. "Your mascara," she said.

"Yeah," said Evie. "You look like a raccoon."

"Fun fact," Avery said. "Did you know that President Coolidge had a pet raccoon? Her name was Rebecca. He built her a house and visited her every day. He even walked her around the White House on a leash."

"I definitely did not know that, Avery."

She laughed. "You'll get used to me, Leah. It's just my sticky fly-paper brain. Breine says I have a ridiculous memory for trivia. She calls it my superpower."

As the three girls pulled and pushed me through the dormitory door, my eyes darted toward Nick.

Something I'd said about Berlin had landed Nick Millburn a gut punch. We needed to talk. I'd hoped we'd get a chance that night at Study Hall, but I had to wait until the next day, after our Contemporary World Issues class.

**28.**

## IT FELT LIKE THE JANGLES, BUT …

I couldn't sleep. At first, all I could think about was Marcos. Then, as I lay in the dark staring at a strange ceiling, worries about my dad crept in, took over, and began running frantic loops inside my brain. Where are you, Dad? Are you hurt? What are they doing to you? Are you even alive? At night, in the dark, I couldn't make the questions stop or turn my imagination off. Fear kept me awake and checking my phone for messages, emails, news, anything. More than once, Breine stirred in tandem with the sudden glow from my phone screen. I turned the screen brightness as low as it would go.

I kept picturing Dad in the hands of kidnappers. I never thought I had a particularly vivid imagination, but lying there, I conjured image after awful image. And smells. I could almost swear I smelled stale cigarettes and body odor. I couldn't shake these thoughts. I couldn't turn them off. Soon, an old familiar feeling began to take hold. My heart beat faster, and my breath quickened.

"Please, please, please," I mouthed silently. "Not now. Not here."

This felt like the jangles. But it couldn't be. The jangles came from nightmares. The terrors that happened between REM sleep and waking.

I forced myself to breathe in through my nose ... one, two, three, four. Hold it ... one, two, three, four, five, six, seven. Exhale through the mouth ... one, two, three, four, five, six, seven, eight. I repeated my pranayama breathing over and over and over until I could feel my heart rate settle and my breaths lengthen and deepen.

I *should* have asked myself what triggered this jangle-like incident. I *should* have been more suspicious. Instead, I returned to the business of checking the news apps in the dark.

The last time I remember looking at my phone was just before three.

Three and a half hours later, it happened again. My nightmare.

*A gray day, heavy with clouds and cold. A tire swing and my small hands in red wool mittens struggling to hold onto the swing chains. A woman screams. Or is it me? The feeling of being lifted off the swing and pinioned against a rough wool coat rank with the stink of cigarette smoke. A gloved hand presses too hard over my mouth, mashing lips against teeth, then the salt-penny taste of blood touching my tongue. A struggle, a muffled sob — mine? — and one red mitten lying on snow-dusted ground before everything becomes suddenly dark.*

Thursday, September 29th, 2022
Three days before Brasil's presidential election

# 29.

## YOU THINK HE'S GHOSTING YOU?

My first day of classes at Wentworth Academy was almost over, and I still hadn't heard from Raphael. I'd had an email from my dad's boss, Jerome Hutchins, the consul general in Rio, but all it said was they were doing all they could. There was no new information. If it weren't for a new slate of classes, classmates, and teachers, I might have spent the entire day in a fetal curl, worrying. Instead, I was so busy that I didn't have a moment to think about anything but school. Until later in the day. Until Contemporary World Issues.

Wentworth didn't offer AP Human Geography, so they'd put me in a class they thought was the most comparable. It meant losing an AP credit, but I still had four APs on my college application. I hoped that would be enough.

Classes at Wentworth were small. Contemporary World Issues had a dozen kids, thirteen including me. The full cast of The Disappointments was there. Bas waved me over, patting the empty chair beside him. He'd returned to the funny flirty self I'd first met in the refectory and gave me another comical wink.

"I see we have our new student. Welcome. I'm Dr. McConnell."

"Thank you, Dr. McConnell," I said, hoping she'd move quickly past me to the lesson. No such luck.

"Tell us a little about yourself, Leah. Aside from your rather impressive transcripts, which I've only just received this morning, all I know about you is that your father works for State, and you've just come from Rio. Like Nick here," she said, gesturing across the room to where Nick Millburn sat watching me. The crease between his eyebrows reminded me we needed to have a chat about Berlin.

"Not the State Department, Dr. McConnell," I said, a cardboard smile pasted across my face. "My dad works for the Canadian Foreign Service as a cultural attaché."

I resisted looking at Nick, but I could feel him staring holes in the back of my head.

"I stand corrected. Most of our students here at Wentworth are very well-traveled, but only a few have lived outside America. Perhaps you'd tell us about some other places you've lived, Leah. Perspectives like yours and Nick's can add to our understanding of other parts of the world."

"Okay," I said reluctantly. "What would you like to know?"

"Start with the most recent."

"Rio? I was only there eight weeks, so I can't tell you too much about the city."

"Then where did you live before Rio?" Dr. McConnell asked. She was annoyingly persistent. I was beginning to think she didn't have a lesson plan; I was it.

"Before Rio, we were in Belarus."

"Belarus? Goodness. When were you there?"

"From June last year to July this year."

"What an interesting time to be in Belarus," Dr. McConnell said. "You were there for the Slipper Revolution Protests then?"

I nodded. There had been lots of protests, though I never saw Tikhanovsky or his famous car with the giant slipper on the roof. When we arrived in Minsk, he was already in jail on a trumped-up charge. Belarus wasn't the only place we'd lived where there were protests or troubles either, but I always tried to tune out the political stuff.

"Before Belarus, we lived in Hong Kong. I was fifteen when we arrived and sixteen when we left. And before that, it was Istanbul, Turkey."

Dr. McConnell's eyebrow pinched. "Interesting. Were you in Hong Kong during the protests over the Anti-Extradition Law Amendment?"

"Yes," I replied. "And we arrived in Istanbul just after Jamal Khashoggi was murdered. My dad's a cultural attaché. He says that countries in turmoil are generative places for the arts and that some of the most interesting art is a response to events like these."

Hoping to end the interrogation and turn the spotlight away from me, I quickly listed the rest of our postings in reverse order: The Netherlands, Moscow, Myanmar, and Mumbai.

"My goodness. I didn't realize that consular life was quite so peripatetic. Do you have a favorite, Leah?"

"Mumbai," I said, thinking of Marcos. "Definitely. But I loved the Netherlands too."

"Well, Leah," Dr. McConnell said, "That's quite a remarkable collection of postings. Between you and Nick here, you have experienced some of the most dramatic political events of the last decade. I expect both of you will have a lot to contribute to class discussions and projects. And speaking of projects ..." she said, turning to the SMART board.

A collective groan emerged from the class.

A newsreel beamed across the screen. Footage from an incident on the disputed lands between Israel and Palestine. After the reporting was done and the on-screen pundits had finished their analysis, Dr. McConnell said, "As you all should know by now, Contemporary World Issues examines resource distribution, globalization, human rights, and democracy. Focusing on any or all of those issues, this class will participate in a series of debates. We will split into teams. One side will represent Israel, and the other will argue Palestine's position."

Dr. McConnell turned to me. "Leah, in your file, Dr. Walid Masri is listed as a contact."

"Yes?" I said, suspicious.

"Masri is an Arabic name, I believe. Do you know its provenance?"

"His family's from Palestine," I said, but I didn't like where this was heading. I certainly wasn't going to tell her that Uncle Wally was in Palestine this very minute for the funeral of ... someone.

"Did Dr. Masri's family leave during the great diaspora?"

"The Nakba — the catastrophe — yes. But that's all I really know."

It was true. I'd heard him talk over the years, but I'd never asked him about his family or his work. He was just — Uncle Wally. I knew he taught at SOAS at the Centre for Palestine Studies, and I definitely knew how he felt about the Israel-Palestine conflict. It was his and Dad's favorite postprandial topic of conversation, especially when we were at Uncle Wally's house, where those discussions were usually paired with a fire in the hearth and a snifter of brandy. They'd tried to engage me many times, but I always begged off. To me, it was just one more attempt by my dad to drag me prematurely into adulthood. As important as the issue was — and I did know it was important — the Israel-Palestine situation was also pretty intense stuff. It was the business of foreign ministers and Secretaries of State. Not some teenager.

"Leah, perhaps you should captain the Palestinian position," Dr. McConnell said.

"Me? But, I don't know much of anything about what's going on in Israel or Palestine."

Dr. McConnell raised her eyebrows. I don't think she believed me.

I added, "I've heard my dad and Uncle Wally talking about stuff, sure, but ..."

"Then consider this a good opportunity to learn, Leah."

Breine's hand shot up. "Dr. McConnell?"

"Yes, Breine."

"Could I co-captain with Leah?"

"No. I'd like you to head up the other side. You'll argue the Israeli position."

"Why, because I'm Jewish?" Breine bristled. "I can't argue a pro-Israel position, Dr. McConnell. I don't support what the Israeli government is doing in Palestine!"

"Everyone at Wentworth is aware of your position, Breine. That's not the point of this exercise. Look, class ..."

Dr. McConnell stood up, walked around the front of her desk, and laced her fingers together.

"We live in an era of great political division; a division which is only growing wider. We need to acquire tools to help us bridge that gap. Standing on one side of that chasm, arguing your personal beliefs, does not help."

"Then why debate?" Breine argued. "Debates have winners and losers."

"Winning a debate doesn't mean you're right, Breine. It simply means you've done a better job of preparing and presenting. Class, you will need to do substantial research and then synthesize that information. You will need to think critically and be able to express those thoughts concisely when challenged. And to get that coveted A-grade, I'll be looking for indications that you have genuinely connected with the position you're assigned to defend."

"Connect with Israel's treatment of Palestinians?" Breine looked incredulous.

"Yes, Breine. I could have just as easily chosen any other controversial issue. Roe v Wade. Climate migration. The Second Amendment. The rise of nationalist movements in Europe or here in the US. I chose this event because it's fresh. It appeared on this morning's news.

"Class, the debate topic is secondary. It's about learning strategies to better resist rhetoric, propaganda, and the ocean of misleading information the world is awash in. And it's very much about empathy. Standing on one side of a fence shouting your position will never change hearts and minds. Communication — real communication — might. And class, if you remember one thing, remember this — effective communication always stems from empathy."

Breine looked about to interrupt again, but Dr. McConnell wouldn't let her.

"Breine, we've discussed this before, you and I. I know that you believe Israel has a right to exist."

"Of course I do. After everything our people have suffered, I believe Jews need a homeland. What I *don't* believe is that Israel has the right to expand into Palestinian territory. I categorically oppose settler colonialism!"

"It is precisely because you disagree with Israel's expansion, Breine, that you need to take the pro-Israeli position in this assignment."

Dr. McConnell turned away from a visibly annoyed Breine to address the entire class.

"It's my hope that your generation can be the one to find the way through the morass. God knows my generation has left things in a mess." Dr. McConnell paused, took a deep breath, then asked, "Class, does anyone know what Confucius said on the topic?"

My hand went up. No surprise there. It had been one of Dad's Post-it Notes.

"Leah?"

"*Real knowledge is to know the extent of one's ignorance.*"

"Very good, Leah," Dr. McConnell said. "And with that, you've earned first pick."

We choose our teams. Mine included Avery and Bas. Breine got Evie and Nick. Bas, it turned out, was whip-smart and a stellar organizer, and soon we each had research tasks assigned and were working hard. The bell rang before I knew it, and everyone packed up and left. Everyone except Nick.

"Is this a good time to talk, Leah?" he asked.

I nodded. As I followed Nick out of the classroom, my phone vibrated, and the screen lit up. It was Raphael. Finally!

"Sorry, Nick," I said. "I have to take this. It's about my dad. Can you give me ten minutes?"

"Yeah. Sure. I'll wait for you at the tables outside the student center," he said and walked away before I could ask where that was. I'd figure it out later. I answered the phone and headed outside. The wind had picked up, bringing cold air from the north.

"I got your messages, Leah," Raphael said. "*All* of them. Are you alright?"

Cupping my hand over the phone to cut out the wind noise, I said, "No, I'm not alright. What's happening? Have you found my dad?"

"There's no news, Leah."

"None?"

"Not yet."

"Can't the consulate do something? Mr. Hutchins wrote me this morning. He said they're trying."

"He is, at a diplomatic level. But Leah, we need people with a certain skill set."

"Isn't that why you're there?"

"Yes, Leah. But this isn't something I can do alone. I need help."

"What about Phil Millburn? He knows Rio. Maybe he knows the right people? You were going to ask him for help."

"Phil Millburn is not answering my calls."

"I don't understand. Is he in Rio?"

"Yes. That much I know."

"So, what ...? You think he's ghosting you?"

"It seems that way."

"That makes no sense, Raphael. He and Dad are friends. He helped us get out of the country, remember? Have you tried calling their consulate?"

"Of course, I have."

"And?"

"They tell me he's not there."

"That's ... that's weird. So what are you going to do?"

"Millburn was my best shot. I'll have to look elsewhere now."

"Where?"

"Leah, I have to go. I have a meeting with Jerome Hutchins now. Trust me, I am doing everything I can to help James. I'll call you when I know more."

"I want to help, Raphael."

"There is nothing you can do, Leah. Let the professionals handle this. And now, I really have to go. I'm late."

And with that, Raphael hung up. I stared at my phone screen. Raphael was wrong. There was something I could do. Mr. Millburn might be ghosting Raphael, but I was positive he would pick up for his son. I hurried to find the student center and Nick.

## 30.

———————

## BERLIN

I found Nick right where he said he'd be, straddling a picnic table bench outside the student center. I sat down, side-saddle, and twisted to face him. The wind was even stronger now, promising a real nor'easter. I wrapped my arms around myself and hugged them to my body. Nick offered me his jacket. I declined.

"That phone call," Nick said. "It looked like it might have been important. Everything okay?"

"Not really, but it can wait."

That wasn't exactly true. I needed to ask Nick for a favor — I needed him to call his dad for me — and I was impatient for that to happen. But Nick was the one who'd approached *me* after class. As I watched him sitting there on that picnic table bench, I could tell by the way his eyes searched mine that he was really struggling with something. Whatever it was, I figured it would be better to let him get it off his chest first. Then, I could have his full attention.

"So, Nick, you wanted to talk to me about something?"

"I didn't want to come to Wentworth, you know."

That was *not* what I expected him to say. After yesterday and the expression on his face when I mentioned Berlin, I figured *that's* what he wanted to talk about. Berlin. That, and our dads knowing each other.

"I thought the idea was to come here so you'd have a better chance to get into Yale. That's what your dad said."

Nick's forehead wrinkled. He had that concerned eyebrow-pinch thing again. He looked at me like I was a puzzle that needed solving. Finally, he spoke.

"Yale was how they sold me on the idea. By last spring, my parents were fighting all the time. I think it was Rio. I love Rio, but the place triggered something in my mom. Like when we first got there, and she learned we needed an armor-plated car. She freaked out and screamed at my dad for moving us there. Every time she'd see a story in the news about a shooting or drugs or a kidnapping — and there are always a lot of those — she'd threaten to take me and leave. Then pandemic hit, and she came unglued. That's when things really started to go down the shitter."

"Why didn't she go back to the States? At least for a while?"

"The pandemic didn't just hit Rio, Leah. Everyone was getting slammed." Nick shrugged his shoulders, then continued.

"I think Yale was an excuse to get me out of the way because they're, you know, probably going to split up, and they don't want me around while they're figuring things out."

I could see the naked pain on his face. For all that adults wax on about teenagers being happier once fighting parents split, or about divorce being the new norm, or the really big one, that teenagers are old enough to understand and accept a parental break-up, it always seemed to me that deep down, kids — at least the ones I knew — wanted their parents together. Except for me, of course. I only had my dad, and that was fine by me.

"Last spring, things were so bad it was getting hard to concentrate on school. My grades started to slip. Janneke was worried I wouldn't get the marks to get into Yale, then my mom suggested Wentworth. Janneke and I talked about it and decided that being away from my parents and their fights could make it easier for me to focus on school."

"But?" I could see there was something else. Nick hadn't asked me here to tell me about his messy home life. He nodded and continued.

"When my parents argue, it's loud. I could be in the furthest corner of the apartment with the doors closed, and I'd still hear them."

"Do you think things are better at home now that you're here in Maine, and your mom knows you're safe?" I asked.

"I dunno. Maybe she'll relax, and the two of them can figure things out. But that's not why I brought it up. The thing about their screaming matches is that sure as the sun rises in the east, if my mom feels like she's losing the fight, she brings up Berlin."

"Okay, I get it now. That's where you're going with this. Because your dad said he met me in Berlin."

"We used to live there," Nick said. "I was three years old."

"Do you remember something? Something that involves me? Because I saw your face when I mentioned Berlin."

That wrinkle between his eyes deepened. "It doesn't make sense, but yeah." Then he shook his head. "I dunno, Leah. Maybe? It's just ... it's strange."

I didn't think it qualified as strange, but it might explain what Phil Millburn had said at Galeão airport. And who knows, maybe Dad and I had passed through Germany when I was too young to remember. On our way to Mumbai, maybe.

Nick continued. "Stuff happened in Berlin that messed my mom up pretty bad. I was too little to remember much, but every time my parents fight about something big, and that's happened a lot since we moved to Rio, it's Berlin, Berlin, Berlin."

"I'm sorry, Nick. That must be really hard, having parents who argue."

He closed his eyes like he was lost in a memory. Or a nightmare? I understood nightmares.

I felt bad for Nick. I did. It sucked to have parents who fought. Maybe I'm a rotten person, but all I could think of was that I didn't have time for this. If you put each of our problems on a scale — fighting, possibly divorcing parents vs. a kidnapped dad — there was no contest whose problem was weightier. Still, Nick had shown himself to be kind and a good friend, and both those things were important to me. He'd earned my attention. I dug deep to find an ounce of patience I didn't feel, tossed it on the scale for balance, and waited for him to continue.

"Berlin was my mom's trump card. I figure I've heard the Berlin story easily a hundred times."

"The *Berlin* story?"

Nick nodded. "My dad had a friend who'd just arrived in Berlin. He had a kid with him. A little girl, three-years-old like me, and he needed someone to watch the kid for a few days."

"Okay. I get it now. You're thinking I was that kid, right?"

"Maybe. None of this sounds familiar?"

"Nope."

"Really? Nothing?"

"Nothing. But Nick, even if it's true and we have met before, that was fourteen or fifteen years ago? It's like you said, we were too little to remember."

"Yeah, well. I remember some things about that day, and my parents' arguments colored in the rest."

Nick took a deep breath before continuing.

"Mom agreed to babysit the kid, this daughter of my dad's friend, but back then, Dad's job only rated a small apartment. My mom thought we needed to run around and tire ourselves out. It was November and cold, and for some reason, the kid didn't have warm enough clothes. So, my mom dressed her in some of my winter stuff, then we walked to the park. It couldn't have been too far from our apartment because my mom was five months pregnant and tired all the time. And because we only had one car. She brings that up a lot," Nick said with a shake of his head. "Anyway, I was on one swing, and the girl was on the other."

A swing? Goosebumps pimpled my arm.

"Was it a tire swing?" I asked.

"Yeah."

My goosebumps became goosehills, and a shiver ran the length of my spine.

"Why do you ask?"

I shook my head and Nick continued. "I was only three, but I still remember those tire swings. I think Mom and I must have gone there a lot. Anyway, two men came up to us. One man grabbed the girl off the swing, and one grabbed me. They started ripping off our hats and snowsuits."

"Why?"

"They wanted the girl. But it was November and cold, and she was wearing my clothes. Boy's clothes."

"So, they didn't know which one she was," I said aloud. I still had not conceded I was that little girl.

"Exactly. So they grabbed us both. My mom ran at them, trying to get me back, and they knocked her down. But she got up and went at them again. I guess she fought like a tiger. She clawed and kicked and grabbed at them, but they were ..."

Nick took a deep breath and dropped his eyes.

"They were rough," he continued. "Once the hats were off, and they saw the military short-back-and-sides haircut that Dad always insisted I get, they dropped me on the ground and left me there. Mom too. But she was five months pregnant, and like I said, they were rough."

"Oh, God! She lost the baby, didn't she?"

Nick nodded. "She would have been my little sister. Mom even had a name picked out."

"Those men? They took the girl?"

Nick nodded.

"Was it ... was it snowing?"

"I don't remember. It's not a detail mom tosses into their arguments."

"Was the girl wearing red mittens?"

"Why? Do you remember something?"

This was my nightmare. The same nightmare that triggered the jangles. If it had happened, then Dad was wrong; my nightmare wasn't physiological.

I stood up. Then I sat right back down again. There would be no answers if I left.

"I think I'm that little girl from the park."

"That's what I thought too, but ..."

"But what?"

"That's what's so confusing. You can't be."

"Why not?" My nightmare twinned Nick's story of what happened in Berlin. "For freak's sake, Nick. You're the one that brought this up!"

"I know. It's just ... the girl's name wasn't Leah."

"Are you sure?"

"Positive. I've heard my mom scream her name."

My heart was racing. What I was feeling right then might not be the jangles, but it was awfully close.

"It had to be me," I said. "It's not a stretch to think that one friend would ask another for a babysitting favor."

"Except," Nick shook his head. "Leah, it can't have been you."

"Why? Because of the different name?"

"That. And because the kid my mom was babysitting was famous."

"Famous, how?"

"I dunno."

"You didn't look it up?"

"They only ever used her first name."

"What was it?"

"Naomi."

I sank, realizing how much I wanted this to be true. I wanted to be that little girl. If I was her, there would be an explanation for my nightmares. It would mean that I wasn't some freak. It would mean that the jangles — all those years of panic wakings — weren't some garbage genetics I'd inherited from my birth parents. It meant I wasn't having hypnagogic hallucinations that I'd spent a lifetime worrying were precursors to Parkinson's or schizophrenia. I really, *really* wanted my nightmares to be plain old PTSD.

"Here," Nick said. He handed me a handkerchief. "It's clean."

When I didn't take it, he reached across and wiped my cheeks. I hadn't even realized I'd been crying. Nick placed the white cotton hanky on my lap and left it there.

"What you described, Nick ... the park, the swings ... it's my nightmare. I've had it as long as I can remember."

Nick's forehead creased. "So you *do* think it's a memory?"

"It makes sense, yeah? In the dream, I'm in a park. The grass is brown with just a little snow, like ... like icing sugar on a chocolate cake. It's cold, and the sky is gray. There's a playground with tire swings, and I'm holding a metal chain."

I lifted my hand, reenacting what always happened in my dream.

"No. Wait!" There was something else. I squeezed my eyes shut. "I'm trying to hold onto the chain, but it's too hard to get a good grip through my mittens, so I shake them off onto the ground. In my nightmare, I can feel a chain dragging across my palm. Like I'm being pulled off!"

"Anything else?" Nick asked.

"Someone screams, and I see a red mitten lying on the ground. The nightmare usually stops there."

As soon as I said those words out loud, there was more. A new memory. A small room with no windows, a man with sour breath, body odor, and cigarette-infused clothes.

I shook the image out of my head, at least for now. I had bigger problems. What I needed most was to get my dad back, and for that, I needed Nick's help.

"I really need to talk to your dad, Nick. Right away. Will you call him for me?"

"Sure. But why?"

"Raphael needs to talk to him."

"Wait. Back up, Leah. Who's Raphael?"

After quickly explaining who Raphael was, and that he'd gone back to Rio to find and rescue my dad, I said, "Raphael's been trying to call your father, but he's not picking up. It's like your dad's ghosting him."

"I don't get it, Leah. Why does your new driver think my dad can help?"

"Raphael only arrived in Rio a few days ago. He needs contacts."

"And he thinks my dad might have the kind of contacts he needs?"

"He's been there a few years, so yeah. Don't all your consulates have, like, guards and stuff?"

"Yeah, I guess. There's the Marines and the SCS."

"What's that?"

"The SCS? The Special Collection Service. It's kind of a mash-up of the CIA and the NSA."

"That's perfect! They've got to have the kind of people who can help, right?"

"Okay," Nick nodded. "Sure. Whatever you need, Leah."

I waited and watched as Nick pulled out his phone and dialed. He put it on speaker. My legs jiggled up and down while I waited for Phil Millburn to answer, but after only two rings, it went straight to voicemail.

"Where is he? Why doesn't he pick up?"

"At work," Nick said. "He can't always pick up when he's working. If it's important, I'm supposed to call my mom."

"But your mom can't help me."

"Yeah, I know. And I *definitely* don't want to tell her about this, whatever *this* is. She'll lose it. Look, Leah, I'll call my dad back and leave a message this time. Okay?"

"Please! Tell him ... tell him Leah Teague needs to speak with him. Your dad doesn't know I'm here at Wentworth, Nick. He thinks I'm in London, so hearing that I'm here with you should get his attention."

Nick nodded. He was about to call his dad when his phone rang.

"It's Janneke," Nick said. "I have to take this."

"Wait." Hearing Janneke's name reminded me of something. I pulled a flash drive from my blazer pocket. "Can you send this file to Janneke for me? I haven't got my internet account here yet and Janneke needs it to finish the project we've been working on."

He nodded, pocketed the drive, then answered his phone. I headed for Yew Tree Cottage.

# 31.

## SHALOM, RAPHAEL



*RIO DE JANEIRO, BRASIL*

In Rio de Janeiro, Raphael was rapidly running out of options and time. Since returning to Rio late Wednesday evening, he'd tried to convince his counterparts at other local missions to help him assemble an HRT — a Hostage Rescue Team — but none of the FVEY countries would stand up. Not Australia, New Zealand, the United Kingdom, or the United States. He thought he could count on Phil Millburn for help, but Millburn had gone to ground. With time running out for James, Raphael turned to Jerome Hutchins, his consul general, for help.

"Sir, I need your help," Raphael said. "I need to contact a friend of James at the American Consulate. Phil Millburn. He's not returning any of my calls, but I think if you asked their CG —"

Hutchins interrupted. "Sit down, Raphael." Once Raphael was seated, Hutchins continued. "Phil Millburn was here yesterday. He was sent to collect the data card with the video James's daughter made."

Hutchins fixed Raphael with a hard stare. Other than a blink-and-you'd-miss-it tightening around the eyes, Raphael was stony-faced.

"I take it that you won't be surprised to learn that James's computer had no data card. Do you have it, Raphael?"

"No. But I know where it is. Sir, what happened when Millburn couldn't find the card?"

"He made a copy from a file on James's hard drive, then he deleted the file."

"Deleted? Sir, I needed that file! I need to make a copy to trade for James. Millburn *must* have known that."

"There are many things in life we take on faith, Raphael, from our belief in God to our willingness to follow a chain of command because we trust that those above us have good reasons for asking us to do what we do, even when we aren't privy to those reasons. Phil Millburn had orders to get that file, and unfortunately, I was ordered to let him. But I guarantee Millburn understood what was at stake for his old friend."

Consul General Jerome Hutchins pulled a small note from his desk drawer and handed it to Raphael.

*Bruno Silva Investigador Policial Polícia Civil*

"Millburn insisted the only way to ensure James' kidnappers keep him alive in the short term was to make Pereira aware that the original data card was *not* in the hands of the Americans. And I should use Detective Silva to relay that message."

"Did you?"

"Yes. Quietly."

Raphael tried to process what this meant. "Sir, why do you think the Americans want that video?"

"Unless it's to stop Pereira from being elected, I don't know. But they haven't released it, so ..." Hutchins shrugged his shoulders up and down. "I *did* speak with their CG, Valerie Soto. She wouldn't tell me anything, of course, but I got the sense that she was almost as far out of the loop as me. She mentioned something about the video containing CUI-level information. Do you know what that means?"

"CUI. Controlled Unclassified Information. That's smoke. There is nothing on that video that merits a CUI label."

The CG sat back in his chair, drumming his fingers on the desk blotter.

"I might have an idea," Hutchins said at last. "More like a germ of an idea. Back in the spring, there was a delegation of sorts from the US. It happened before James arrived. It wasn't a CODEL — an official congressional member delegation — but it included two congressmen and Oren Glass."

Raphael shook his head. Oren Glass wasn't a name he knew.

"Glass is a kingmaker. They call him the Wizard of Washington. He's been described as the man behind the curtain pulling all the levers to ensure certain people get placed into specific political positions curtain — including presidents. Glass is a political animal, which is why his trip here was noteworthy."

"Do you know why Oren Glass came to Rio?"

"Not Rio. Mato Grasso."

"Mato Grasso? Pereira owns half the state!"

When Hutchins raised his eyebrows questioningly, Raphael shrugged. "I've been reading about Pereira. New York to Rio is a long flight."

"Then you may have also read that vast deposits of rare earth elements were recently discovered on Pereira's land. Neodymium and terbium."

Raphael didn't know what that was, but he filed the information away. "Do you think that's what's behind all this?"

"I honestly don't know. From what I've heard, the Chinese have those rights all but sewn up. And it doesn't explain why Glass was here. It certainly wasn't to negotiate some mining contract. That's not what he does. Still, Glass being in Brasil is noteworthy."

Hutchins shook his head. "Our focus needs to stay on James. I tried contacting our allies in FVEY for assistance. Against orders from Ottawa, I might add."

"I also tried them," Raphael said. "MI6, ASIS, and NZSIS all said no. And Phil Millburn isn't taking my calls. I don't know why."

"The Americans have asked all FVEY countries to stand down."

"All?"

Hutchins nodded. "Including us."

"Merde!" Raphael muttered. "Where does that leave James?"

"It leaves him out in the cold, I'm afraid. Unless ..."

"Unless?"

"Unless you're willing to try an end-run around our FVEY partners. Assuming, of course, that you haven't received any orders yourself?"

"I have not. Not yet."

"Good," Hutchins said. "I know this is your first posting, Raphael, but can you find a way to backchannel with other agencies?"

"I've been trying, sir, but I haven't had any luck. I don't have many contacts yet. I was counting on Phil Millburn's help."

Jerome Hutchins stood up, walked around his desk, and extended his hand to Raphael.

"This is a helluva thing," he said. "I never thought I'd see the day we would treat our own like this. It's challenged my faith, I don't mind telling you. Just do your best, Raphael. It's all any of us can do."

"Before I go, sir, I'd like to talk to the woman who acted as a stand-in for Leah."

"Cecile Plante? I'm sorry, Raphael. She's gone. Once she was released from the hospital, I sent her home to recover."

Raphael stood up. "Then I better get started. James is running out of time."

⌁

Raphael sat at a table in the crowded Bar de Lado, nursing a drink and staring out across the ocean. It had been a long and fruitless day. He'd exhausted every avenue he could think of. He was out of options. Worse, his phone was blowing up with calls from Ottawa. Worried he was being ordered home, he left anything with a 613-area code unanswered.

Raphael had faith. Faith in God, country, his agency, and the chain of command. But he'd never once imagined that the agency he'd pledged to serve and the country he vowed to protect would knowingly leave a man out there. Not like this.

Deep in thought and nursing a drink, Raphael didn't notice when someone approached his table.

"Well, hello. Funny to run into you here. I thought you were heading back home to Canada?"

It was Phil Millburn. Seeing him here was a shock, especially after his recent meeting with Consul General Hutchins. Raphael adjusted quickly to the charade.

"I'm leaving soon. I have a few things to wrap up first. Join me for a drink?"

Millburn made a show of checking his watch, but he was, Raphael knew, taking careful stock of his surroundings. If Millburn sat down, they were clear. If he declined, he was being surveilled. Millburn slid into the chair across from him.

"You haven't returned my calls."

"I've been looking for answers," Millburn replied. "You?"

"Time is running out. I'm dodging calls from Ottawa, but I won't be able to do that much longer. I need help, Phil. Everyone I've approached has been asked to stand down."

Millburn's eyebrows pinched together. He looked down at the liquid in his glass, swirling it around before taking a long drink. "The irony of all this kills me," he said.

"Irony?"

"FVEY countries have been sharing signals intelligence since the Second World War. But it was James who spearheaded more direct inter-agency cooperation. I can't tell you how many times we've called on each other for help over the years. And now, when James needs that cooperation, no one will lift a finger."

"Do you know why? Is there any angle here I can use?"

"Use to do what? Change minds?" Millburn shook his head. "Forget that. You and I, we're just little fish. This stand-down order came from high up the food chain."

"How high? Do you know?"

Millburn shook his head. "I don't know. Our CG is toeing the line, but I'm pretty sure she isn't happy about it."

"Do you think this is coming from your State Department?"

"Not from our seventh floor." Millburn shook his head again. "At least, I don't think so. If I had to guess, I'd say it's coming from inside my shop. We've had some bad apples in the barrel recently. I'm sure you've seen the news. Even if that's true, I don't know if someone there is pulling the strings or having their strings pulled."

"Siphonaptera," Raphael mumbled.

"What?"

"The poem. Siphonaptera. *Great fleas have little fleas upon their backs to bite them. And little fleas have lesser fleas, and so ad infinitum.*"

Millburn let out a snort. "Something like that. Look, I want answers. I want to find which fleas are doing the biting. I especially want to find out if I need to bring in an exterminator to clean my own house. But I have to be careful. I don't know how far I can push. What will you do, Raphael?"

"I'll stay as long as I can."

"Good," Millburn nodded. "I was hoping you'd say that. I'll give you whatever help I can. Quietly, of course. For now, though, the best I can do is introduce you to some friends of mine. They've recently arrived from Tel Aviv via Spain."

And with that, Millburn stood up to leave. He pushed his chair tight against the table and then wrapped his knuckles twice on the tabletop. It was a signal.

Just before he left, Millburn whispered sotto voce, "Tell her to keep it safe."

"Osti!" Raphael muttered. Phil Millburn had figured out that Leah had the data card.

At that moment, a man pulled out the chair recently vacated by Phil Millburn and sat down.

"Shalom, ma nishma, Raphael."

# 32.

# THE REPORTER

*RIO DE JANEIRO, BRASIL*

Christina Ramos was both sleep-deprived and exhila-rated. She hadn't managed more than a head-on-desk catnap since leaving the US Consulate early Wednesday morning when the news of Teague's kidnapping had triggered the memory of a sensational news story from a decade and a half earlier. That sort of thing was fresh-blood-in-the-water to a shark like Ramos. In the hours since leaving her consulate, the story had mushroomed, gaining momentum with each new piece of evidence she uncovered.

Ramos was relentless. She chased down leads. She scoured the internet for fourteen-year-old news articles making pages of notes. She called in markers and promised favors. She made phone call after phone call throughout the evening, the small hours of the morning, and the entire next day without any regard for time zones until she'd constructed a timeline that led her to an audacious assumption. Then, convinced her assumption was correct, Ramos set out to gather enough proof to satisfy her editor. She saw herself as one of the three princes of Serendip; through luck and her own sagacity, she and she alone had solved the mystery. And it felt fantastic! This was the ride she spent her career chasing. Once this story hit the web, other reporters would scramble to climb aboard, but what mattered was that she, Christina Ramos, was driving the train.

It was time to talk to her editor.

Tyrell Washington had been her editor at the New York Times for eight years. Tyrell was a good man, a rock-solid editor, and a formidable gatekeeper. Ramos knew he wouldn't let any story through that couldn't be independently verified. She also knew she didn't have everything, but she believed the facts she *did* have would be enough for Tyrell to run the piece. He was careful, but he was also hungry. It had been a while since her paper had pipped the Washington Post with a breaking front-page story of this magnitude. She dialed.

"Let me get this straight," Tyrell said, dispensing with polite greetings. "I send you to Rio to interview Pereira. Instead, you potentially crack one of the biggest unsolved mysteries of this century?"

"Not instead, in addition to. And not potentially, definitely. Did you look at what I sent you?"

"I did. It's ... good," he conceded.

"So are you going to run it?"

"Slow your roll, Christina. I have some questions first."

"What questions?" she snapped.

"Take a breath, for chrissake. You sound like you've been slamming double espressos with Red Bull chasers."

He wasn't wrong. She was, in a word, wired. She'd barely slept in the past thirty-six hours.

"I agree that you have enough direct evidence for the inferences you've made," Tyrell said.

"But? I hear a "but," Tyrell."

"Yes, you do. Look, Christina, this story is huge. The number of uniques we're going to get on this will have advertisers beating down our doors. But I have some concerns."

"Like what?"

"Like the girl. Leah. How much do you think she knows?"

"I'm not sure," Ramos admitted. "My gut says Teague has kept her in the dark, but ..."

"But?"

"Okay. There is a 'but' — something I can't wrap my head around."

"And that is?"

"Social media. The girl doesn't seem to have any social media accounts. I couldn't even find a photograph of her online. She's seventeen, Tyrell. You've got teenagers. Don't you find that strange?"

"Very strange. I could build a credible map of my kids' entire day by tracking their social media. Where they are, where they're going, who they're with. Even what they're eating."

"Exactly. But not Leah Teague. Online, she's a ghost. It's as if she doesn't exist."

"Why do you think that is?"

"I have to assume Teague recognized how potentially dangerous social media could be for her and warned her off. But cards on the table, Tyrell, that bugs me too. I don't have kids, but I can remember being a teenager. I have a helluva hard time believing any teenager would blindly accept a parental edict like that without first being given a compelling reason."

"Yet your gut tells you she doesn't know?"

"Does that even matter to the story, Tyrell?"

"It might."

There was a protracted silence while the editor and journalist stared at one another through their phone screens. Ramos broke that silence. "My position, for now," she said, "is that Leah doesn't know. My opinion may change once I interview her, but there's a bigger issue, Tyrell."

"And that is?"

"There's only a very slim chance James Teague is still alive. Kidnappers took him on Tuesday. It's Thursday night now."

"And you're certain his kidnapping has nothing to do with the daughter?"

Arrogant about the correctness of her research, Ramos answered. "One hundred percent! Other than me and now you, no one knows who Leah Teague really is. Detective Silva of the Rio police told me he's certain Teague's already dead. They're looking for a body."

"Shit. That's too bad. But why does he think that?"

"In Silva's words, the time between snatch and ransom in an express kidnapping is usually very short. Teague's kidnap length is already far, *far* outside the normal window. Silva said the kidnappers likely had no idea who Teague was when they took him. And when they realized they'd grabbed a foreign diplomat by mistake, they panicked, killed Teague, and dumped the body. The police say everything points to Teague being dead already. And if they're right, if Teague is dead, the kid's an orphan again. She deserves to know who she really is; don't you think? There's a helluva lot at stake for her."

"You're right about that. What a thing," Tyrell said, shaking his head. "Remind me why you think Leah is somewhere in the US?"

"One of her classmates, Janneke Van-der-something."

"She told you where Leah was?"

"She did. This Janneke has a boyfriend at boarding school in the US where Leah Teague apparently showed up yesterday."

"Damn, Christina. Good work. Where exactly is this school?"

"Wentworth Academy, Maine. I want to head there on Monday after the elections are over, and I have my victory interview with Pereira."

"You're that sure he's going to win?"

"Good question. If you ask anyone here in Leblon, they'd tell you the only way Emmanuel Santos could be reelected is if he's the one counting the ballots. I agree that Pereira will probably win, but I suspect it will be a tight race, despite all the money Pereira's been throwing around."

"Understood. Okay, so then let's focus on the girl. I want you to head to Maine tomorrow. Find Leah Teague. Get an interview. Get her on record."

"Can't it wait until after the election?"

"You're not the only reporter who's been in the game long enough to remember that old story from Berlin. It won't be long before someone catches up to you, and I don't just want to break this story, Christina. I want us to get in front of it. All of it. Understood?"

"Understood."

"In the meantime, give me five hundred words on Leah Teague. I'll run it tomorrow morning."

"How about seven fifty? It's worth the inches."

"Fine."

After she hung up, Christina Ramos hit send on the seven-hundred-and-fifty-word article she'd already penned before the call, then leaned back in her chair, triumphant. She was willing to bet her apartment in Brooklyn that this story would be more widely read and translated than any other she'd ever written. She poured herself a hefty three-finger drink and went out to her hotel balcony. Feet on the railing, Ramos lifted her glass in a toast.

"To Valerie Soto, my old college roommate, for guilting me into an alumni interview I didn't want to do. And to all those friends, colleagues, and contacts I hit up for information and favors. This one's for all of you."

She lifted the glass higher, held it a respectful moment longer, then took a long, generous drink. Sinking back into her chair, she gazed out over the ocean and began composing the speech for her next Pulitzer.

Friday, September 30th, 2022
Two days before Brasil's presidential election

# 33.

## PASSPORTS & LIZARD BRAINS

*NEW RYE, MAINE*

I woke up to sunshine beating through the window and into my eyes. I closed my eyes and rolled over. A third straight night of tossing and turning had left me tired, frazzled, and more sleep deprived than I could ever remember.

My brain wouldn't shut off. When I was in class or study hall or with The Disappointments, I was too busy to obsess about what was happening back in Rio. But at night, in the dark, things got bad. I kept seeing the Rocinha shootings and the attack on Marcos playing in my head like a looped video with no off switch. When I wasn't seeing bloody reruns, I was worrying about my dad — Was he okay? Was he hurt? Was he still alive? — or worrying about what would happen if the authorities found out I'd entered the US on a fake passport. That could send me to jail for twenty years; I'd looked it up.

Then it hit me. The passport! What if it wasn't a fake? What if Christine Louise Tyler was the name I was born with, and Dad had somehow kept my identity alive? I didn't get how anyone could do that, but it made a lot more sense than my strait-laced dad skulking around back alleys arranging forged documents. And if Christine Tyler was my birth name, maybe I could use that to find out about my parents, or at least my birth mother.

Galvanized, I threw back the covers and sat up. I squealed when I saw Breine leaning over me. Where did she come from?

"I didn't mean to scare you," she said. "You're white as a sheet. Wait, are you shaking? Leah? Did you have the nightmare again?"

"No nightmare. It's ... everything else," I said, rubbing my eyes. That's when I noticed. Breine was dressed in her school uniform with a book bag slung across her shoulders.

"Did I sleep in? Am I late for class?"

"It's Friday. You don't have a class first period, remember?"

"Thank God," I said and flopped back down onto the bed, head on my pillow, shutting my eyes against the sunlight streaming through the windows.

"I've got to go, Leah. I have bio first period. It's a lab. I can't be late. I just came back to the room to warn you that the refectory kitchen closes in thirty minutes, so if you want to grab something to eat ..." She let the sentence drift off unfinished.

"Thanks, Breine."

"Okay then. Well, you've been warned."

My eyes might be closed, but I could hear the smile in her voice. It met an answering smile on my face. I lay there for a while thinking about how lucky I was to have landed here, with Breine as my roommate and The Disappointments as friends.

I heard her footsteps on the stairs and the heavy front door as it dropped closed. With Breine gone, Yew Tree

Cottage was silent. A reminder that classes were about to begin. Forcing myself to get up, I quickly put on my uniform. Then I grabbed my go bag and slung it over my shoulder, hyper-conscious of that manilla envelope at the bottom of the bag that may hold answers to my identity. Sometime today, I'd find a quiet, out-of-the-way corner on campus where I could be alone and take a good long look at that US passport. Right now, I needed coffee.

I'd almost reached the refectory and the coffee I so badly needed when I ran smack into a group of students filling the entire width of the hall. First-years and sophomores, by the look of them. They looked like a rugby scrum, all leaning over each other trying to see something in the scrum's center. I admit, I was curious about what could have drawn such a crowd, but I was also dangerously close to having the refectory doors shut in my face. If I was going to get through Day Two at my new school, this body required caffeine. Plus, my belly was nauseous from lack of sleep — it needed carbs in the worst way. Moving to the wall, to the thin edge of the pack, I tried to squeeze past.

"Excuse me."

No one even looked up. I didn't have time for this. I tapped the shoulder of the boy closest to me.

"Let me through, please."

Without so much as a glance my way, the boy waggled his shoulder like I was a bug he was trying to shake off.

"Please," I said, more insistent this time. "I need to get past."

He turned toward me; his mouth crooked up at the corner like he was preparing some choice four-letter words.

Instead, his sneer disappeared, his mouth dropped open, and his eyes widened.

"Hey, you're her! You're that new kid, right? I've seen you with Breine Berenson. Guys, it's Leah Teague!"

Like a practiced set piece, all heads in the scrum swerved at once to look straight at me. Unnerved, I took a step backward.

"Are you her? Are you Leah Teague?" a disembodied voice asked.

I strained to see who spoke. Leaning around the many heads and shoulders, I saw a girl standing in the center — if this was rugby, she'd be the scrum-half — holding up a tablet.

"You're the new kid from Rio, right? The senior?"

"Why?" I asked. "Why do you want to know?"

"Because of this," she said and turned the tablet to face me.

Even from this distance, I recognized the format displayed on the screen. It was a news article. Thinking only that here, at last, was information about my dad's kidnapping, I shouldered my way through the bodies and plucked the tablet from the girl's hands.

## Kidnapping in Rio Linked to the Disappearance of Textile Heiress?
By Christina Ramos
Reporting from Rio de Janeiro

Sept. 29, 2022  Updated 06:25 a.m. UTC+2

In 2008, one of the year's biggest stories was the kidnapping of three-year-old Naomi Nowack. Even at that young age, little Naomi had a tragic family history. In 1940, her grandfather

Jakob's family lived in Nazi-occupied Poland. Everyone but Jakob was killed when the family tried to escape the Holocaust. Jakob was smuggled out of the country and eventually ended up in Canada, where, as an adult, he established a textile company known today as Settler Holdings LLC. Tragedy struck the Nowak family once again when Naomi's parents, Esther and Edward Nowak, perished in an avalanche while skiing in Switzerland, leaving their teenage daughter, Rebecca, orphaned— and the heir to Settler Holdings, now a billion-dollar company. At 21, Rebecca Nowak, by all accounts a brilliant computer science student, moved to London, England to continue her studies at Imperial College. One month into term, she became pregnant. Enter family friend James Teague.

Teague was a cultural attaché at the Canadian High Commission in London. According to a consular source who worked with Teague at the time, Teague had been a close friend of Esther and Edward Nowak, Rebecca's parents. Because of that decades-long friendship, Teague invited Rebecca to move into his flat so she could more easily continue her studies. After the birth of her baby in June 2005, Rebecca Nowak and baby Naomi continued to live with Teague. Statements from friends and neighbors confirm that Teague, then 42 years old and a confirmed bachelor, doted on the child, Naomi, and considered himself her grandfather. Three years later, in 2008, Nowak completed her studies. She left Naomi with Teague for a doctoral studies interview in Tel Aviv, Israel. While there, she was in a car crash and died instantly from her injuries. Now it was Naomi, who was the orphan and heir to the family fortune that had only grown in the years since her parents died.

According to a statement issued at the time by the Canadian High Commission, Teague was instructed to bring the child to Berlin for DNA testing to see if she had relatives in Europe. But in a shocking turn of events, Naomi Nowak was kidnapped from a Berlin park and held for ransom. In what has remained a mystery, though the German authorities reported a successful rescue, Naomi Nowak has not been seen since. There are reports she went to live, covertly, with distant relatives in Germany or Poland. Some have speculated the rescue was not as successful as the authorities claimed, and the child did not survive. But now, with a second kidnapping, the story may be taking a more clarifying shape.

I stopped reading. Here, in black and white pixels, was the story Nick told me yesterday. A story that was disturbingly close to my nightmare. Standing there, surrounded by so many sharp-eyed students, I felt my breath quicken. I forced myself to ignore the rapid rise and fall of my chest and the stares from the underclassmen who pressed too close. Clutching the tablet in a death grip, I continued reading.

Teague, currently stationed in Rio Di Jannero, was kidnapped Tuesday afternoon. Teague and a fellow consular employee were forced from their car in Leblon, an affluent district in Rio's South Zone. According to police, express or flash kidnapping is on the rise in Rio. Wealthy individuals are forced at gunpoint to withdraw funds in person or electronically.

As Teague's kidnapping was being reported on, some interesting details about his personal life began to surface. Immediately following the reported 2008 rescue of Naomi, Teague returned to Canada, reportedly for cancer treatments. During his recovery, he adopted a child, Leah. This, despite the fact it seems dubious that an adoption agency would permit a newly recovered cancer patient and single parent to adopt. Leah's adoption records are sealed, but several intriguing facts have come to light. Leah Teague's place of birth is listed as London, Ontario, Canada.

Naomi Nowak was born in London, England. Both Leah Teague and Naomi Nowak share the exact birthdate.

It is not unreasonable that Teague, if permitted, would have adopted young Naomi Nowak. Teague was an old family friend who had known the child since birth and who, by all accounts, adored the child like a grandfather. It is also reasonable to assume Teague would have changed the child's name to protect her from further incidents like the one in Berlin in 2008.

Until recently, Leah Teague was a senior at a top international school in Rio de Janeiro. She withdrew from school the same day her adoptive father was kidnapped. Sources say Leah Teague has since transferred to a prestigious private school in New England. It is unclear at this time whether Leah Teague is aware that she may be the missing heiress, Naomi Nowak.


"Is it true?"

The floodgates opened then, and I was swamped by a torrent of questions. I looked around at the sea of faces staring at me. I tried to back away, but their questions kept coming, and the circle of people tightened, pressing closer and closer. Then cell phones appeared, and people began taking pictures.

Covering my face with my forearm — a reflex — I pushed and shoved my way through the pack. I needed to get out. I needed to move. When I reached the perimeter of the pack, I ran. I ran through the halls and outside onto the lilac-and-lamppost path. With each step came questions.

Was Ramos right? I didn't want to believe it, but the similarities between Naomi Nowak and me were impossible to ignore. So much for my brilliant theory that I'd been born Christine Louise Tyler! But if I was Naomi Nowak, that meant my dad had known all along who my mother was.

Why would he lie about that? And why would he have made such a big deal about my adoption papers being sealed? None of this made sense.

I raced for Yew Tree Cottage and my dorm room, desperately trying to erase the memory of the Ramos article (and all those camera phones pointed in my direction). Breathing heavily, more heavily than I should be for how far and fast I'd run, I dropped my backpack onto the bed.

I had no plan; my brain was roiling with everything I'd just read. I was trying to figure out what to do about it all when I spotted my workout clothes on top of my dresser and decided to do the one thing that always made me feel better. Climb.

I tore off my uniform, leaving it in a crumpled pile on the floor. Then I pulled on my leggings, a lightweight hoodie, and runners. I didn't have proper climbing shoes yet, but my Vivobarefoots were light and flexible, and if the cliff was climbable, they'd do.

I shot a quick glance at my go bag *cum* backpack. The only thing inside was my phone, wallet, and the manila envelope with my American passport. I trusted Breine wouldn't snoop, and I definitely did *not* want to climb wearing a pack. Not today. I was already too distracted by what I'd read. I couldn't process one more thing.

Leaving my go bag behind, I bolted out of my room and down the stairs. My lizard brain was telling me to run. So I did. Feet pounding against the hard-packed earth, I ran as hard and as fast as I could, straight for the cliffs.

**34.**

---

## YOU HAVE AN HOUR, TOPS

Nick Millburn was in the middle of a biology lab when his phone rang. He'd forgotten to turn off the ringer.

"No phones, Mr. Millburn!"

"Yes, ma'am. Sorry, Ms. Fletcher."

He switched it to silent mode, but not before checking who the caller was. His mom. Nick turned the phone face down on the table and tried to concentrate on the lab, but between the unprecedented middle-of-the-school-day call from his mother, and every disturbing thing he and Leah talked about yesterday, Nick was worried.

His dad knew Leah's dad.

His dad had smuggled Leah out of the Canadian Consulate then drove her to the airport.

His dad told Leah that he'd met her before. In Berlin. *Berlin!*

Then there was the video. His dad had seen it too, and if Pereira was intent on leaving no witnesses, could the same thing that happened to Leah's dad happen to his father? Nick slid the phone off the table and onto his lap. As he did, his phone screen lit up with another text message, then another.

*Call me!!*

He stood up and walked to the front of the class, bringing his phone.

"Yes, Nick?" Ms. Fletcher said.

"I'm sorry, Ms. Fletcher, but it's my mom in Rio. I think something's wrong."

As he held out his phone to show her, a third panicked message arrived.

"Go on. You better call your mother."

Anxious, Nick stepped out into the hall and dialed.

"Nicky!" his mother's voice cracked. It sounded like she'd been crying.

"What's wrong, Mom? Is it Dad?"

"What? No. Your father is fine, but you have to leave Wentworth, Nicky. Now!"

Nick sucked in a big breath. His dad was okay. That was all that mattered.

"I'm fine, Mom. Are *you* okay?"

"Nicky, you're not listening to me!"

His mother's voice edged higher and higher into what Nick privately referred to as *the screech zone.*

"It's not safe there!"

Nick bit back the retort that nowhere would be safe enough for his mother. She was the Sikorsky Super Stallion of helicopter moms.

"Wentworth is in the middle of nowhere, Mom. You don't have to worry. The biggest danger here is that someone gets their hands on a bottle, gets wasted, and tumbles over the cliff."

"You don't understand, Nicky. She's there," his mother said. "I saw the Ramos article."

"Who's here? The journalist from the New York Times?"

"No! The Nowak girl. She's there at Wentworth. She's pretending to be someone else, but it's her. And if she's there, you can't be. It's not safe to be anywhere near her. You have to leave. Now!"

Nick was used to his mother's histrionics, but this was over the top, even for her.

"Maybe I should talk to Dad. Where is he?"

The next voice Nick heard was his father's.

"Nick, it's dad. Your mother and I saw the Ramos article in the Times this morning. It mentioned that Leah Teague was at a boarding school in New England. Nick, did she show up at Wentworth? She'd be a senior, like you."

"Yeah. Leah came Wednesday."

"So you know her?"

"She's my friend's roommate, so yeah. She sits at our table in the refectory, and she's in my Contemporary World Issues class. Dad, Leah is the reason I left you all those messages yesterday."

"Christ! She's supposed to be in London."

"Yeah, well that fell through. She had nowhere to go and apparently you told her about Wentworth so ..."

From five thousand miles away, Nick heard his father's sharp intake of breath.

"Dad, what's going on?"

"I don't want to do this on the phone, Nick. We'll talk tonight when I see you."

"You're coming here?"

"Not Wentworth. I'll meet you in Boston. Nick, I need you to pack an overnight bag, take a cab to the bus station in New Rye then get on the next bus to Boston. Don't go all the way to the city center. Get off at Logan Airport. Your mother will book you a room at an airport hotel and text you which one, the address, and a confirmation number. That's where I'll meet you. Understood?"

"No. I don't understand. Why do I have to leave?"

There was a pause, some chatter in the background, then his dad said. "Okay, your mother is in the other room now making your bookings, so we've got a few minutes. Nick, they're saying Leah stole a data card with sensitive government documents."

"That's crazy, Dad."

"I know. Leah didn't steal anything. I don't have an explanation for this yet, but we have to play the cards we've been dealt, and it's a lousy hand. Nick, Leah's father and I are old friends. I helped her leave Brasil. And now she magically ends up at the same school as my son? It's not a big leap for the Company —"

"Wait, the Company? You mean the CIA?"

"Yes, Nick. The CIA. They will conclude that I arranged for Leah to go to Wentworth to hide her. From there, it's a very *very* short step for them to infer I was complicit in what they're calling *the theft*. And once someone at the Company makes the connection that my son attends the same school ...? Nick, you could be swept up in this. Maybe even taken in for questioning."

"So what do I do?"

"We're lucky your mother's worry-radar led us to Leah's location first. We can still get ahead of this. But this is very important. They must not find *either of you* on campus when they arrive. *Do you understand what I'm telling you, son?*"

"Yes, sir. I think so."

"Good. Then I'm going to hang up now. Look for your mother's texts. And Nick, now that Ramos has pointed the CIA toward schools in New England, it won't take them long to learn she's at Wentworth. *At most,* you and Leah have a few hours before they figure out where she is and show up with a warrant."

With that, the call disconnected. Nick looked up to see Breine standing just outside the classroom door.

"Are you okay?" she asked.

Nick shook his head.

"It's Leah," he said. "The CIA is coming for her. Do you know where she is?"

"Last time I saw her was before bio. She might be in the refectory now."

"Can you check, Breine?"

"Of course. And I'll call Avery to help look. You call Bas and Evie?"

"I will. But hurry. We've got to find Leah before the CIA does."

## 35.

---

## WHO AM I?

The ground was slick from last night's wind and rain. Directly in front of me, the sea roiled. Yesterday's promised nor'easter hadn't arrived yet, but the sky was heavy, and in the distance a bank of gunmetal gray clouds was moving in. If I was going to climb the cliffs — and right then I needed to climb — I'd have to hurry. Which meant I had to find a way down.

I knew there was one — Avery's story of The Disappointments' bonfire on the beach told me so. Sure enough, a thin, footworn path paralleled the chain-link fence in both directions. I hesitated. Which way should I go? To the left, I could see where the school grounds ended. To the right, Wentworth's property seemed to go on and on. I went left, north, toward the oncoming storm.

I ran hard, pushing myself faster and faster until I came to the end of the chain-link fence. Its last post butted up against an elaborate border wall belonging to the neighboring estate. Here, the school's chain-link had been detached from the post and its spiny edges sausage-rolled, leaving a gap just big enough to slip through. And I did.

There were no cliffs at the north end of the school grounds, only large rocks that had been tumbled haphazardly by weather and time. I picked out the best route and scrabbled down to the shore. Then, ignoring the angry sea, I doubled back in the direction I'd come from, south, toward the cliff I'd dangled my legs over just days ago.

The tide was out, but the shingle it left behind wasn't firm enough for a hard run, so I slowed to a jog. At this pace, it was impossible to keep my thoughts at bay. Memories and questions crashed into my brain like the waves on the shore.

Was Christina Ramos right? Was I really Naomi Nowak? It would mean that my birth mother hadn't abandoned me. But if Ramos was right, it also meant that Dad knew who my birth mother was. Yet, he'd presented me with sealed adoption papers as evidence that I would never be able to learn her identity. How messed up is that?

And what about my nightmare? Dad *had to know* where it came from, but he let me think it was the result of some junk genetics.

Then there's the whole heiress thing which, of all Ramos's claims, is the craziest. If I'd inherited a whack of money, how come Dad made me jump through hoops each time I wanted to buy something fun? Like the Chuck Taylors that Kamala Harris wore on the campaign trail? Seriously, they were only a hundred bucks! And what about those inspirational Post-it Notes and speechifying? *Climbing, running, and hanging out with your friends doesn't count, Leah. You can't pay rent and buy food doing those things.* Why did I need to be worried about paying rent if I had all that money? None of this made sense. Either Dad had lied to me my whole life, or Ramos had it wrong.

Right then, standing alone at the bottom of the sea cliff, I don't know if any of that mattered. Whether I was Naomi or Leah, orphaned or abandoned, the singular truth was I'd been alone in the world without parents or family until Dad adopted me. Dad *chose* me. So if it turns out that Ramos was right and Dad lied, I'll be crazy mad at him. But I'll still love him. And even though Dad doesn't go to church like Avery, to synagogue like Breine, or to mosque like Uncle Wally, he's still the most moral person I know.

Standing there, staring at the cliff wall, I decided that the only thing that truly mattered was that Raphael find a way to rescue my dad. If he didn't, history would repeat itself, and I'd be an orphan. Again.

I shook my head. This was all too much. I needed to climb.

I tested the cliff rock by pulling myself up and hanging from my fingers. If the rock was friable, if it crumbled or broke off under my weight, I'd have to abandon my plan and find another way to clear my head. But the rock held. Dropping to the beach shingle, I stepped back as far as possible, almost into the surf, then I looked up.

Marcos would not have approved of me doing this without ropes or, at the very least, a climbing buddy. But it's not like I was free climbing El Capitan. This cliff wasn't that much higher than the bouldering wall at my old school. It was twenty feet, tops. Granted, that was five feet more than the tallest bouldering wall I'd ever tried, *and* there were no crash mats here to cushion a fall. Shingle was definitely not a great surface to fall on, but it wasn't the worst either. Anyway, I wasn't planning to fall. And I *needed* this. I needed to do nothing else except focus on my next handhold and foothold. Every second spent concentrating, each vertical inch earned, was time I could defer thinking about Dad and that stupid Christina Ramos article.

Turning my back to the cliff face, I walked to the water's edge and wet my hands. I didn't have a chalk bag, and even though my hands rarely got sweaty when I climbed, salt water would help remove whatever oils were there. Then I stepped up to the cliff wall and began to climb.

## 36.

# WARRANTS, ANAGRAMS & ESCAPES

The climb started well. Then, the wind picked up. In no time, my backside was covered in sticky salt spray. The rain came next, making it hard — a whole lot harder than I'd banked on — to find handholds and footholds. It took everything I had to keep my grip on the increasingly slippery rock. My fingers ached with the effort. Then, five feet from the cliff top — five feet from safety — my concentration was pierced by a scream, and my foot slipped. Suddenly, I was splayed against the cliff wall, fifteen feet above the beach below, hanging only by my fingers.

Trying to ignore the voice screaming my name above, I frantically probed the cliff wall for a foothold. Something strong enough to hold my weight. Dangling from my arms was causing a wicked lactic acid build-up in my biceps, triceps, shoulders, and even my hands. I knew that the longer I free-hung, the worse it would get. Soon, I wouldn't be able to hang on anymore.

You can't get rid of lactic acid the same way you clear out catecholamines — the panic hormones. Rest is the only thing that reduces lactic acid; for that, I needed to let my legs bear most of my body's weight. I needed toe holds. A fifteen-foot drop doesn't sound like much, and I'm confident I would have survived the fall, but it would probably hurt. A lot.

Hyper-focused now, I continued to test the rock face with my toes inch by rocky inch until I found a decent toe hold. Weight on one leg bought me time to find a second toe hold. Once both quads were engaged, and after some pranayama breathing to help slow my racing heart, my shoulders and arms got the rest they desperately needed. Only then, splayed like a spider against the cliff wall, did I dare look up to the source of the screams.

It was Avery, lying on her belly with her head stuck out over the cliff edge.

"Don't jump, Leah," Avery called, her beautiful face distorted by worry. "I mean Naomi. I mean ... oh, whoever you are. It doesn't matter, okay? Just don't jump! You have friends who care about you."

Breine's head appeared. She took a hard look at me. Her lips pursed, then her mouth ticked up at the corners.

"Leah's not suicidal, Ave. She's climbing up, not jumping down."

Avery's head swiveled to look up at Breine.

"You mean she's hanging there on purpose?"

Breine nodded at Avery then she turned to me. "It makes sense now — the calluses on your hands, the muscle definition in your forearms. At first, I thought you might be a rower, but that didn't track. You're way too short."

"Gee, thanks," I called back up.

"So you're really okay, Leah?" Avery asked. "You're not fixin' to jump?"

"No, Avery. I'm not going to jump. I'm climbing."

"Enough chitchat," Breine said. "Leah, you need to move. Now! Those clouds are coming in fast. The storm will be on us any minute."

I didn't have to look. I could feel the wind and rain getting stronger by the second.

As I climbed the last five feet, the wind really began to howl, and with it came the hard, horizontal rain. The moment my head breached the surface, Avery grabbed one of my arms. Breine grabbed the other, and I felt myself being hauled over the cliff edge to the grass. The next thing I knew, Avery was flinging her arms around me.

"Don't you scare us like that again, you hear?"

I was touched they cared enough to come looking for me, especially since it was clear they'd seen the Ramos article — Avery had called me Naomi. I was about to say thank you when Breine tugged Avery out of the hug.

"Later," she said. "We need to get away from this cliff edge before the storm gets any closer, and we need to get you out of sight. Are you okay to move, Leah? Can you run?"

I nodded.

"Good. Then follow me."

Breine and Avery climbed back over the fence, their school-issued leather Oxfords all the worse for being jammed into the metal diamonds of a chain-link. I had a much easier time of it. By the time we landed on the other side, we were all soaked to the skin. Then we started to run — not toward Yew Tree Cottage, where I assumed we'd go, but toward Wentworth's distant southern bjørder. Avery set the pace, and it was quick. I wondered why we weren't going to the dorm, but we were running flat out, far beyond talking pace. My questions would have to wait.

We arrived at a large stand of trees, wide across, deep, and densely packed. It completely blocked any view of the school. As soon as we got there, Avery cupped her hands around her mouth and called, "We're here!"

Moments later, Nick emerged from between two trees.

Like me, Nick wasn't wearing his uniform. He was carrying a duffel and had a pack slung across one shoulder. Unlike me, Nick was dry.

"Hurry up. Get in here," he said. Then he turned and headed back into the grove.

I had no idea what was going on, but before I could even think of what questions to ask, Avery took my hand and tried to pull me forward. Despite the driving rain that had already flattened my clothes to my body and my hair to my head, I hesitated until Breine gently pushed me from behind and said, "We'll be safer in here. Go!"

I let Avery lead me. Soon, we were a line of Disappointments, forcing our way between some shadbush and holly.

One by one, we stepped into the heart of the grove, entering a cave-like space. Pine, birch, maple, and trees I couldn't name formed a ceiling above us. Their branches wove together like lovers' interlaced fingers, creating a room below easily large enough for the four of us to lie down side by side. Best of all, it was dry. With each step, the packed blanket of pine needles and fallen leaves crackled like candy wrappers beneath our feet. Despite the beauty of the place and the respite from the weather, my wet clothes stuck to me like second skin. I was cold, uncomfortable, and confused.

I looked from Breine to Avery to Nick. "Will someone please tell me what's going on?"

"I suppose we've got a minute or three," Avery said. "What do you think, Nick?"

He checked the time. "Yeah, okay. But five minutes tops. We have a bus to catch."

"Who's we?"

"You and me," Nick said.

In tandem, Breine and Avery crossed their legs and sat down in one smooth move that suggested both girls were very familiar with yoga. I chose to stand. Nick dropped his duffel to the ground, then slid the backpack off his shoulder and handed it to me.

"Hey, that's mine!" I said, recognizing the navy backpack *cum* go bag I'd left on my bed.

"I gave it to him, Leah," Breine said. "I wanted to get it out before ..." She didn't finish her sentence.

"Before what?"

"There's not much time, darlin'," Avery said. "You need to let Nick explain."

"Then explain!" I was wet, tired and I'd had one too many shocks already today.

"The CIA is after you," Nick blurted.

"What?"

"They say you stole a data card with sensitive government documents."

"That's nuts! It's *my* card! All you'd have to do is look at the video to know it's mine. You can hear my voice and see my classmates. Janneke's on there, Nick."

"We believe you, Leah. So does my dad. That's why he warned me. He said we need to get you off campus before the CIA arrives. Well, not the CIA exactly because they can't arrest people, but some kind of federal agents are coming for you."

Just then, all three Disappointments' cell phones pinged. Mine was silent, still in my backpack, and still with only three ICE numbers in my contacts.

"Too late," Avery stared at her phone screen. "They're here. They're in your room. Evie sent a video. See?"

Avery held up her phone. I watched open-mouthed as two agents rifled through drawers and upended mattresses while Evie yelled at them to stop. Then the door slammed, and Evie's video ended.

"Was the data card in your room?" Nick asked.

I shook my head. "It's in my wallet, in my backpack."

"Good."

"Here's an idea," Breine said. "If it's obviously just a student video on that card, why not give it to them? They'll see it for what it is, and poof, problem gone. Right?"

"I can't risk it. If the video leaks while my dad's still a hostage, there'll be no reason for the kidnappers to keep him alive."

"Why would the CIA leak the video?"

"Think about it," Nick said. "The CIA is famous for planning coups and regime changes in foreign countries, right? And Brasil has an election on Sunday. With only two days left before the election, releasing the video is going to be the only way to make sure Pereira doesn't become president."

"*If* that's their agenda," I added.

"Whether it is or it isn't, it still doesn't make sense. Why issue an arrest warrant for Leah like she's some criminal?" Breine countered. "A search warrant would be all they need, right? I don't know. This all feels ... off."

Breine was right, but the *why* didn't matter.

"I can't let them have the video, at least not until Raphael can free my dad."

"Okay," Breine said.

"Okay?"

She nodded. "We'll help. Won't we?"

"Of course we will," Avery added. "Why else would we be here, hunkered down inside these trees? But at the risk of being the gal that starts an argument in an empty house, you've got to know that they're gonna find you eventually, Leah. Between all us Disappointments, we're clever enough to get you out of here today and maybe even hide you for a time or two, but we're no match for real spies. And girl, when you can't run with the big dogs, you best stay under the porch."

"Ave's right," Breine said. "You may outrun them for a few days. But that's it. You're seventeen. They're professionals. They *will* find you. If you want to protect the data card, you have to hide it."

"I'd help," Nick said, "but they'll be looking at me because of our parents."

"I'll take it," said Breine.

"Uh uh. No, honey." Avery shook her head. "You saw Evie's video; they're tearing apart your side of the room too. You're the roommate. After Nick, you're the next logical choice to be questioned and searched. I'll take it."

Breine started to object, but Avery stopped her dead. "It has to be me. It certainly can't be Evie or Bas. Not with their history with the police. And besides," she said, her accent suddenly thicker, "I am the good Christian daughter of Pastor Scott Lascelles. The rightest right-wing Republican in Houston."

With a honeyed smile, Avery folded her fingers together and lifted them under her chin like she was saying her prayers. She was the very picture of daddy's-little-girl sweetness.

I nodded. Fishing the data card from the zippered container in my wallet, I handed it to Avery, still wrapped in the tissue from my dad's desk. Avery took it and tucked it into her bra, just as I'd done only three days earlier.

Three phones pinged once more with the latest search update from Bas.

"That reminds me. Give me your phone," Breine said.

"Why? What are you doing?"

"We won't be able to contact you by email. Obviously." Her fingers flew over the phone's keyboard. "I'm making you a Twitter account. They won't expect that. It's mostly old people on Twitter. Later, when the dust settles, Bas will add you to our Signal chat so we can safely stay in touch."

I was about to protest. Despite spending years wishing for social media, avoiding it was as deeply ingrained in me as the church was for Avery or being Jewish was for Breine.

"You need this, Leah. You'll need a way to contact Avery when you're ready to do something with that video. Don't worry. I've given you an obscure handle. See?" she said, turning the screen to face me.

MontKulaki

"Sounds Hawaiian."

"It's an anagram for Tikkun Olam."

Tikkun Olam. Repairing the world. Keeping Pereira from becoming president would be a good mending action. Still, I had to choose — stop Pereira or save my dad. It didn't look like I could do both.

Breine said, "We'll send you a DM when we have news, but don't follow anyone, not even us. Okay?"

"You sound like my dad."

"I like him already," Breine said. "And when I meet him, I'll tell him so."

*When* she meets him. Not *if*. When.

"Thank you, Breine."

"We're out of time," Nick said. "We've got to go, Leah. Now."

"How? I can't just walk back through Wentworth if the CIA is looking for me."

"You don't have to," Breine said. "This grove isn't that far from the south edge of campus. Just follow the coastline until you hit a fence."

"What's on the other side of the fence?" I asked, remembering the large wall at the north end of the school grounds that protected the neighboring estate from wandering Wentworth students. Estates have security cameras. Maybe even dogs.

"A public park. On a nice day you might run into someone walking their dog, but today, in this weather, there won't be anyone there."

"Okay. Then what?"

Nick answered. "Then we head to the road. There's a convenience store there. I'll call for a ride, and you can stock up on supplies."

"Supplies?"

"We're taking the bus to Boston. It's a long ride. After that ..."

I understood. After that, I'd be on my own.

"I'll need clothes."

"You'll have to buy them. Sorry," Breine said. "I only had time to grab your bag."

"That reminds me," said Avery, fishing a roll of bills from her pocket. "Here. All those spy shows say you shouldn't use credit cards when you're on the run. You're going to need cash money. There's six hundred dollars there. It's everything The Disappointments could cobble together real quick. Take it."

I gave them hugs; Avery, then Breine.

"Thank you," I said. It wasn't enough, but it was all I had to give right then.

"Shalom haver," Breine said. "Try and get this all figured out soon, okay? I need my co-captain back in Contemporary World Issues before the debate."

Confused, I shook my head. "Co-captain?"

"Why is Dr. McConnell making me represent Israel?"

"Because you're Jewish?" I said.

"So are you, Leah."

"I'm not, though."

"I know you read the Ramos article. Your mom was a Jew."

"My dad is a lapsed Catholic, and his boyfriend's a Muslim. What's that got to do with anything?"

"Roommate, you have a lot to learn. You're Jewish because your mom was Jewish. It's Halakha. It's our law. *Your* law. Just promise me you'll come back when this is all over, okay? Debate aside, I'm dying to hear all about your Uncle Wally. You have *got* to introduce us."

Then Avery took Breine by the hand, and together they headed out of the grove and back to main campus. Pulling my hoodie up over my head, I hurried to follow Nick, who was already heading south at a fast clip. I had no idea what I was walking into right then. Only what I was running away from.

# 37.

## WHEN MOSSAD MEETS CSIS



*While Leah was on a bus to Boston with Nick Millburn, Raphael, was walking across the Praia do Arpoador to meet Gabriel Atir, the man from Mossad. New to CSIS — a spy at the start of his working life — Raphael was hungry to learn. In contrast, Gabriel Atir was at the apogee of his career and more determined than ever. He'd waited almost twenty years for another chance to put eyes inside James Teague's world and now that goal seemed tantalizingly close.*

The beach at Arpoador was a mecca for surfers and the Mossad agent did not look out of place. At fifty-something, tanned and fit with intense eyes and a shaved head, he bore more than a passing resemblance to world champion surfer Kelly Slater. Enough to garner stares from people wondering, could it really be? Gabe sat bum on the sand, knees tented, arms wrapped around his knees. While he waited for

Raphael, he stared out over the Atlantic as though he was studying the crowded water and considering whether the surf was worth his effort.

"You wanted to meet?" Raphael said, sitting down on the sand next to Gabe.

"Yes, my young Canadian friend. We move tonight."

"You found James? How?"

"For that, we have the reporter Christina Ramos to thank. After her article came out, Pereira traveled to the hold site."

"Wasn't that risky for him so close to the election? He must have reporters following him all the time."

"Oh yes, very risky. But not as risky as leaving his hostage in the hands of thugs who, thanks to this morning's article in the New York Times, now know who Teague's daughter is and how much she is able to pay for her father's return. Pereira was worried, and rightly so, that money could make his men forget who they worked for. He went to the site to make sure they understood what he would do to them if they tried to move ... independently."

"So where are they holding James?"

"Vila Cruziero."

"I think I've heard of that. It's in São Paulo? Brasilia?"

"Rio. It is Pereira's old favela, the place he grew up."

"But the papers said Pereira was north on his final campaign push before Sunday's election."

"He was," Gabe nodded. "He returned to Rio quite suddenly yesterday for a meeting at the American Consulate. Which, my friend, is something else we must discuss. I would not normally do this, but here our interests align. What I am about to tell you comes from an asset within the American Consulate."

Raphael's eyebrows knit together.

"The story begins Tuesday after Millburn saw the girl's video. He returned to his consulate and reported what he had seen. That resulted in a flurry of calls to both Washington and Langley."

"Langley?"

Gabe nodded. "The phone calls shifted to a SCIF. You know this word?"

"Of course. A Sensitive Compartmented Information Facility."

"Yes. The meetings ran late into the night. In the end, a decision was reached; Soto would officially request the Canadians to surrender the data card, citing a need to protect a field operative. A lie, of course. I'm told Soto agreed but was not happy. Once her part was done, she kicked the football back to the CIA, who sent Millburn to your consulate on Wednesday with orders to retrieve the video. Our asset heard little more until yesterday, Thursday, when a man from Washington arrived. Oren Glass. Do you know him?"

Before yesterday, Raphael had never heard the name Oren Glass. Now, he'd heard it twice in as many days.

Raphael nodded.

"Then perhaps later you will tell me about him," Gabe said. "For now, I will continue my tale. A meeting room was prepared for Glass, complete with a video screen. Contracts and pens were set out across the conference table by Glass himself. Pereira arrived, and the doors were shut. No aides were allowed inside. The meeting lasted only minutes. Then Pereira left, followed by a furious Oren Glass."

"Blackmail?" said Raphael.

"Attempted blackmail. That is my assessment," Gabe said. "But it clearly failed. What we do not know is *why* it failed."

Raphael had the answer. "Glass came to show Pereira the favela video, but Pereira knew it was a copy. He knew the original was still out there."

"And how, my young Canadian friend, did Pereira know that?"

"We leaked it to Pereira via one of his people. A policeman in Rio. We thought — we hoped — it would protect James."

"Interesting," Gabe said. "Do you also know the end goal of this attempted blackmail?"

Raphael shared what his CG had told him, including Hutchins' assessment that Oren Glass would not have made the trip simply to negotiate a mining contract. Glass was a dealmaker who solely trafficked in political manipulations.

"Interesting. It makes one very curious, yes? Something to follow up on, perhaps? But back to what is important for you and for me. After the failed meeting between Pereira and Glass, Millburn was called in and instructions were issued. Find Leah Teague."

"Leah?"

Gabe nodded. "Yesterday, the CIA searches were directed at Canada, England, and the Netherlands. Yet this morning's article in the New York Times claims the girl is in New England. Curious, is it not, that there is no record of her passport being used to enter America?"

Raphael kept silent.

The Mossad agent shrugged. "I would have expected no less from James Teague. Unfortunately, the same Ramos article that led us to Teague's hold site will also lead the CIA to the girl. If it hasn't already done so. And this, my young Canadian friend, is where our interests align. You are tasked with protecting the girl, yes?"

"Yes, but I don't know for how long. I've been ducking calls from Ottawa. I think I'm being pulled off her detail."

"What will happen to the girl?"

Raphael shook his head. "I don't know."

"Call her."

Raphael hesitated.

"The CIA is looking for her. After what I have told you, do you think their objective is to protect her?" Gabe shook his head. "No. There is some … relationship between this man Glass and the CIA that we do not understand. It has put the girl in the CIA's crosshairs."

"What do you suggest I do?" Raphael asked. "Even if I wanted to help, if they pull me from her detail, I'll no longer have access to the resources I'd need to keep her safe."

"I have resources," Gabe said.

"What can you do?"

"To begin, I will arrange a safe house."

When Raphael hesitated, Gabe said, "Contact the girl, Raphael. Tell her about me. Most importantly, tell her to leave her school immediately. She must leave right away and do it quietly."

"Quietly? How? She's only seventeen. She's a kid."

"Instruct her," Gabe said. "The girl is clever, yes? And courageous. She climbs mountains and swims with sharks. I believe she can do this. She has to. Make her understand that."

Raphael arched his eyebrows, but before he could respond Gabe added, "The girl needs protection. You cannot offer that. I can."

"And James?" Raphael asked. "You will get him out tonight?"

"What's left of him."

Raphael stood up and brushed the beach sand from his legs. "Thank you. But I am curious, what is Israel's interest in all this?"

Gabe did not answer at first.

"You knew her, didn't you?" Raphael said. "Leah's birth mother was in Israel when she died. It was in the Ramos article."

Gabe hesitated as if deciding what he could tell the young CSIS agent.

"Let's just say I help the daughter to honor the mother."

"I think I understand," Raphael replied.

*I am certain, my young Canadian friend, that you do not.*

Raphael turned and headed back across the sand to Avenida Atlântica.

It was mid-afternoon. He tried calling Leah, but she didn't answer. Once Raphael got back to his car, he sent Leah message.

**Raphael:** *Call me ASAP. Urgent*

His phone pinged with an immediate response.

**Leah:** *Is it my dad?*

**Raphael:** *Not yet. Critical you leave school now QUIETLY*

**Leah:** *Already gone. On bus to Boston. Agents at school with a warrant. They say I stole a data card with government documents*

Merde.

**Raphael:** *OK. Lay low. Use only US ID and cash. Understood?*

There was a pause before the next response. Finally, Raphael's phone pinged.

**Leah:** *Understood*
**Raphael:** *Will contact soon with address of a safe house*
Then Raphael's phone rang. It was a 613-area code. Ottawa. His time in Brasil was almost up.

## 38.

---

## DOES PRAYER EVEN WORK?

*BOSTON*

Nick left the bus and me at Logan Airport. It's where his hotel room was and where his dad would meet him later that evening. I was really going to miss Nick. Truth was, I missed all The Disappointments.

I stayed on the bus until Boston South Station, where I got off alone among the crowds of people coming and going. I had two immediate problems. I needed to buy some basics — a toothbrush, toothpaste, decent shampoo, a cheap change of clothes, and a phone charger — and I needed to find a place to stay. Something that wouldn't drain my cash reserves. I had a credit card, but I didn't want to use it. Turns out cheap and Boston don't go together. Still, a few hours after leaving the bus station, I'd done my shopping *and* found a place I could afford that would let me pay with cash. Once I was safely inside the room with the door locked, I headed straight for the bathroom and stripped off my clothes. I needed to wash off the day.

Hair washed, I stepped out of the shower and grabbed a towel. This was not the sort of hotel Dad and I were used to, with an abundance of thick towels, fluffy robes, and room service menus. It was a worn-thin, once-white towel sort of place, and there were only two of those. I used one to dry myself as best I could. With the only other towel, I wiped the steam from the bathroom mirror, then used the same towel to turban my freshly washed hair. My life had changed, but the face that stared back at me had not. My ear lobes were still too large, and I still had one brown eye and one blue eye. The difference was that now, thanks to Christina Ramos, I knew where some of those features might have come from. My birth mother. Rebecca Nowak.

Leaving the bathroom door ajar to let the steam out, I rummaged in my shopping bag for my new clothes. As I ripped the price tags off new socks, underwear, and T-shirt, I wondered, was this my life now? Living like Jack Reacher, buying a fresh change of clothes in every city? I shook off the thought and got dressed. At least I had clean clothes, and for those, and for this room, I had The Disappointments to thank. Still, even with their help, there was only enough cash to last two, maybe three days. *If* I was careful. After that? Well, I hoped Raphael had a plan.

After brushing my teeth and combing my hair, I checked my phone for the hundredth time. This time there was a message from Raphael.

*Rescue imminent. Will call soon. Imperative you stay hidden.*

I called him right back, but it went straight to voice mail. Unable to sit still, I began pacing the short space from the door to the wall and back again until, dizzy and more nervous than I'd ever been, I dropped into a chair and leaned forward. With elbows on my knees and my face buried in my hands, I tried to pray.

I'd never prayed before. Avery, Breine, and my Uncle Wally all prayed. Collectively, they were a Christian, a Jew, and a Muslim. They prayed in different ways and for different things, but it was to the same God, right? Abraham's God. And even though I'd never prayed before, never even thought about a capital 'G' God, I tilted my head toward heaven (and the stained motel ceiling) and hoped they were right. I hoped God was real and he (or she) would hear me. I prayed that no matter how confused and angry I was at Dad for keeping secrets from me (huge life-altering secrets!), God might really be up there, would hear me, and give my father back to me.

James Teague slid in and out of consciousness. He knew something was happening — he heard gunshots — but no matter how hard he tried to stay alert, he kept slipping back into blackness. The next time his eyes fluttered open, he was in the back of a van surrounded by four heavily armed men. One man spoke into a phone. At first, Teague couldn't place the language. Not Portuguese. Arabic? Closer, but no. Fighting pain and a body that was pulling him ever closer to darkness and the river Styx, Teague forced himself to focus, if only for a few seconds.

Hebrew. The men were speaking Hebrew.

A Lear jet sat fueled and waiting on the tarmac of Galeão International Airport. Its insides had been gutted and refit for medical transport. Also on the tarmac were Raphael and Jerome Hutchins, the Canadian Consul General. The two men watched as the van carrying James Teague pulled to a stop next to the jet, and four men jumped out. The men made swift work of loading Teague onto a stretcher and into the air ambulance where a doctor and flight nurse began assessing and stabilizing the patient. The pilot radioed the tower for a take-off position even before the doors to the jet were shut. Moments later, the plane had its emergency take-off clearance and began taxiing toward the runway. Three of the men climbed back into the van. The fourth, Gabe Atir, joined Raphael.

"Do you think he'll make it?" Raphael asked.

Gabe was noncommittal. "I would not choose to wager one way or the other. I am no doctor, but it is clear there was much damage."

"I probably should not be hearing this," Jerome Hutchins interrupted. He turned to address Gabe. "I don't know how you came to be here or why. And very soon, I will not be in a position to get answers — I've been ordered home. And so, because you will never hear this officially from my government, please allow me to say thank you." Consul General Hutchins shook Gabe's hand. "If you had arrived even one day later, this could have ended very differently."

With a head tilt toward his team, Gabe replied. "We were never here."

Jerome put a hand on the Mossad agent's shoulder, resting it there for just a moment before walking across the tarmac to his waiting car.

Gabe turned to Raphael. "We must go. We leave tonight."

"Thank you," Raphael said, extending his hand. Gabe shook it but didn't let go. Instead, he grasped Raphael's forearm with his other hand and held it.

"It will be difficult for you too, my young Canadian friend. You should also leave. Do not wait for Sunday. Whether or not Pereira wins, your association with Teague and his daughter has been noticed. Things here will become unpleasant for you very quickly."

"I'm leaving tomorrow."

"Good. And the girl?" Gabe asked. "You will send her to meet me at the safe house?"

"Yes. I'll call her now. I need to let her know her father is alive and heading home."

"She may be tempted to return to Canada to be with him. You must impress upon her that she must not. You realize that, yes?"

"Yes, but ..."

"Do not worry, my young Canadian friend. I will not let any harm come to the girl."

Raphael nodded. True or not, he wanted to believe it.

Sunday, October 2nd, 2022
Election Day in Brasil

# 39.

## WORRIED IN RALEIGH



*RALIEGH, NORTH CAROLINA*

It was noon Sunday, election day in Brasil, but right then the election was the furthest thing from my mind. Only forty-eight hours since Nick and I left Wentworth Academy, and I was in Raleigh, North Carolina, standing outside a bus terminal, waiting for my boarding call.

The bus was Raphael's idea. When I'd last talked to him late Friday night, he'd warned me that alerts had been posted at every airport along the eastern seaboard, along with my Canadian passport photo. Apparently, everyone expected me to fly north to Ottawa to be by my dad's sickbed. But Raphael warned me that if I tried to go through *any* airport, they'd grab me. What had me worried in Raleigh was that by now, the search could have expanded to bus and train stations. I was heading south, away from the border, but I still had to be extremely careful. I needed to heed every piece of *Spy 101* advice Raphael had given me over the phone. Starting with my appearance.

My hair was finger-combed into a messy ponytail and threaded through the D-hole in my new ball cap. Go Bruins. I wore large aviator sunglasses and stayed mostly out of camera range. When I *had* to pass a camera to access the washrooms or food, I kept my head down, pretending to read something on my phone. A week earlier, any of these precautions would have seemed tinfoil-hat paranoid. But a week ago, I wasn't hiding from the CIA.

In our last phone call before Raphael went dark, he'd talked me through a few *on-the-run* basics.

"You need to avoid using any ID. If you are stopped for some reason and required to identify yourself, use the American passport. It's in the manilla envelope I gave you back in New York. In fact, take it out now and keep it someplace handy. You do not want to be looking through that envelope in front of the police. Or anyone. In fact, Leah, take out every piece of ID from your wallet — anything that might suggest your name isn't Christine Louise Tyler — and stick it all into the manilla envelope with your other passports. Bury the envelope in your dirty laundry and shove that deep into the bottom of whatever bag you're carrying. And Leah ..."

"What is it, Raphael?"

"In case someone asks, Christine Louise Tyler needs a life. Where does she live? Where is she going? Understood?"

I understood.

I also understood that he said *other passports*. Plural.

The moment I'd hung up with Raphael, I tumbled the contents of that same envelope onto the hotel bed. Five passports. Five! From five different countries and a small pocket envelope with *'In case of emergency'* written on the front in Dad's familiar handwriting. For now, I left the small envelope untouched and focused my attention on the passports.

My Canadian passport was exactly as I remembered —
three years old, issued from the Canadian Embassy in Turkey with a cringe-worthy picture of fourteen-year-old me.
Its pages were decorated with stamps from all the countries
we'd visited. I plucked the American passport from the bed
and put that into an accessible zippered pocket in my go bag,
just as Raphael suggested. Then I checked the other three
passports one by one. The United Kingdom. Australia. New
Zealand. Each passport had a photo of me at different ages,
from very recent, to just starting middle school, with different names, birthdays, and even birth years.

I had a hard time wrapping my head around this. Last
week I would have been unable to imagine my dad capable
of arranging fake passports. But now? I clearly didn't know
him as well as I'd thought.

I reached for the smaller *In Case of Emergency* envelope.
Peeling open the flap, I dumped the contents out onto the
bed.

Credit cards, bank cards, tax IDs, and one tightly folded
note. Ignoring the note for now, I spread everything else
across the bed. Each card and tax number matched one of
the four passports. The *me* in each passport had a life in each
of these four countries. I *existed* in each place. I had a bank
account, credit cards. Apparently, I paid taxes? These were
farmed identities. Identities that my dad had grown for me.
And that's when it finally hit me. My dad was more than a
cultural attaché. With trembling hands, I picked up the note
and unfolded it.

*Leah,*

    *There's not much time. I promise that I'll explain
everything when I can. I hoped you'd never need these,*

*but if something happens, you <u>must</u> listen carefully to Raphael and do exactly what he tells you. If you need more money than the cards provide, call Birthday Max. I love you, Leah. I always have. You are my life.*

*Dad*
*PS I would have told you everything before college. I wanted you to have a normal childhood.*

I was jerked back to the present by the loudspeaker at the Raleigh bus station. It was time to board. Before the day was over, I'd be in St. Augustine, Florida, with Gabriel Atir, the Mossad agent who had rescued my dad. And just as important to me, a man who, according to Raphael, had known my birth mother. Rebecca Nowak.

# 40.

## IS SAYAN HEBREW FOR DOCTOR?

*SAINT AUGUSTINE, FLORIDA*

I got off the bus in Saint Augustine and hailed a cab to take me from the Old City across the Bridge of Lions to Anastasia Island — a barrier island on the other side of the Matanzas straight — where Raphael promised I would meet a man named Gabe who would help me. Gabe had known my mother, rescued my father, and offered to hide and protect me from the CIA; three precious pebbles of information that I'd tumbled round and round in my brain for the past two days until they'd become a polished, shiny gem of an idea. An idea that became even brighter and shinier once the condominium door opened.

Gabe Atir was old enough to be my father.

Gabe was dressed in pressed khakis and a golf shirt as though he'd just stepped off the links. He was powerfully built and tanned. Silver stubble sprouted across a shaved head. I didn't know it then, but Gabriel Atir was a chameleon, able to slide easily in and out of different personas.

"Leah, welcome. I've been expecting you. I am Gabe. Come in, please. You must be tired."

Stepping inside the small two-bedroom condominium, I was hit by a wall of cold air.

"Sit," he instructed. "I will get you some water. Are you hungry?"

"No. Thank you," I said, though I'd been ravenous twenty minutes ago. Now, I didn't think I could swallow pudding. Gabe motioned to the sofas and then headed into the small condo kitchen. He returned with a tall glass of ice water. I managed a small sip. When I looked up, Gabe was staring at me with piercing gray eyes.

"Raphael told me you rescued my dad. Thank you."

"Not me alone. I had a team."

A team from Israel's Mossad. What would Uncle Wally make of that?

"I'm told your father is in a medically induced coma, but the prognosis is good."

Before I could even ask, Gabe volunteered, "We have a Sayan working at the Queensway Carleton Hospital. A doctor."

"Is Sayan Hebrew for doctor?"

"No. A Sayan is any non-Israeli Jew who believes in and is loyal to the state of Israel. This condominium, for example, belongs to a Sayan who will loan it to us for as long as we need."

"Okay. And the doctor in Ottawa?"

"He will keep me informed of your father's condition. I thought you would want to know."

"I do. Thank you. Will your Sayan let you know when Dad wakes up? I need to talk to him. I have … a lot of questions."

"Because of the Ramos article, yes?"

I nodded.

"Understandable. Are you sure I can't get you something to eat, Leah? You must be hungry for food that hasn't been processed, fried, or from a vending machine."

He wasn't wrong about the crappy food, but I shook my head. I couldn't eat. Not yet.

"Then please, ask your questions. I will try to answer them all as best as possible."

"Raphael said you're from Israel. He said you're Mossad?"

"Yes."

"Okay. Then here's my first question. Why would Israel's Mossad want to rescue my dad? You must know who his boyfriend is."

"Ah, yes. Dr. Walid Masri does many *interesting* things for Palestine and the Palestinian cause."

"What do you mean by interesting?"

Instead of answering, Gabe asked his own question. "Have you never wondered why your father and Masri haven't married?"

I hate it when people answer my questions with a question of their own. Why make me go through a guessing game of clues when they know the answer? It ticks me off. I guess that's why, when Gabe did it, I shot a wiseass answer right back at him.

"Probably because Uncle Wally's already married?"

"What did you say?"

The muscles in Gabe's neck tightened, but only for a moment. If I'd blinked, sneezed, or reached for my glass of water, I'd have missed it. I hadn't intended to tell Gabe or anyone about the text Uncle Wally sent, but I hit a nerve somehow, and I wanted to know why.

"After what happened in Rio, I was supposed to go to London to stay with Uncle Wally. But when we landed in New York, Raphael got a text from Uncle Wally saying he was in Palestine for his wife's funeral." I did air quotes around 'wife.' "Maybe it was an autocorrect thing on his phone, except ..."

"Except what, Leah?"

"When I talked to Uncle Wally, I asked him about being married, and he didn't deny it."

"What did he say? Exactly?"

I began to feel more than a little uncomfortable with Gabe's curiosity. I decided to turn the tables on him and answer his question with a question of my own.

"Gabe, why did you ask me about Dad and Uncle Wally never marrying?"

His eyes narrowed for a moment, and then he relaxed and leaned back into the sofa.

"You have a lawyer who manages your mother's estate, yes? Max Klein. You must speak with him every year on your birthday?"

"How do you know that?"

"What questions does Max Klein ask you?"

There he goes again. Answering a question with a question. It was really starting to piss me off. If I wasn't so curious about Birthday Max and this whole Dad and Uncle Wally thing, I would have clammed up and refused to answer.

Instead, I said, "He asks me about ... about my life. But that's just a condition of my adoption. Isn't it?"

"And Masri — does Max Klein ask about him also?"

He did. Every year.

"Would you be surprised to learn it is a condition of your inheritance that Masri has no legal ties to you? Max Klein monitors this for the estate."

I let that sink in. This was yet another thread in my increasingly complicated story that would definitely need pulling. Later. Right now, I wanted answers.

"You told Raphael you knew my mother."

"Yes. Would you like me to tell you about her?"

I did. Desperately. But I'd had two days to consider what Raphael had told me about Gabe; as a result, I had an agenda.

"Why are you helping me, and how does my mother fit into all this?" I asked.

I searched his face for information — for clues — but he remained silent, giving nothing away.

"Never mind. I think I know."

"You do, do you?"

"Yes." I'd been polishing this answer since my phone call with Raphael when he'd told me Gabe Atir had known my mother.

"You're my father, aren't you?"

**41.**

---

# YOUR STORY BEGINS IN LONDON

Gabe's forehead wrinkled like he was considering whether he would offer the truth or a lie. I was sick of lies. I sat up straighter, my big Jay Leno chin stabbing him with my question.

"Well? Are you my father?"

"No," he said. "Your father is James Teague."

I blew out a frustrated puff of air.

"James Teague is my adoptive father. I'm asking you, yes or no, are you my *biological* father?"

"No."

There was no hesitation in his answer, no guile on his face. I was pretty good at reading expressions. Either Gabe was an Oscar-worthy actor, which, working for Mossad, he just might be. Or he was telling the truth.

"Why did you think I was your father?" he asked.

"You mean, aside from the fact you traveled halfway around the world to help my dad and me?"

"Yes, aside from that."

"Because you're Israeli, my mother died in Israel, and you knew her. Raphael told me as much."

Gabe's expression softened. He lifted one hand and held it under his nose, palm facing down.

"From here upwards," he said, motioning with his other hand from the bottom of his nose to the top of his head, "you look very much like her. But I can promise you, we are not related."

"Why should I take your word?"

"You should not, of course. But this is a problem easily solved. In the morning, we will get a DNA test. It will show you that I am not your father."

He seemed certain of what DNA results would reveal.

"If you're not my biological father, do you know who is?"

Gabe said nothing at first. Like he was weighing some logic problem.

"Child," he said finally. "James Teague is your biological father."

My body reacted to his news before my brain. My fists vice-gripped violently around my backpack strap. My arm and neck muscles tensed next, then my back, until I was rigid, stiff as Lot's wife, who'd been turned into a pillar of salt for looking back at where she'd come from.

Gabe reached for my backpack and peeled it gently from my hands, setting it on the floor beside me. Then he picked the water up off the table and handed it to me. I reached for it. My hand shook so badly that I had to wrap a second hand around the glass just to bring the rim to my mouth.

I managed a sip then Gabe reached for the glass. Stubbornly ignoring him, I returned it to the table myself. A small victory.

"You are suspicious of me," Gabe said, watching me closely. "Good. You may survive this, after all."

I *was* suspicious. And I was angry. I spat out, "Tell me, how is it possible that my adopted dad is also my biological dad?

"It is a long story. A story that begins in London, England. But I will tell you if that is what you want."

I nodded.

"Your father's NOC, his non-official cover, is cultural attaché, but your father works for CSIS. Your Canadian Security Intelligence Service. You are not surprised to hear this?"

I wasn't surprised. Not anymore.

"My dad doesn't... kill people, does he?"

Gabe laughed. He actually laughed. "No, Leah, your father does not kill people. He gathers information."

"Okay, but ..."

"You are curious how this is done, yes?"

I was. I'd spent fourteen years completely ignorant about Dad's real job. I blushed, remembering how I'd recently compared his job as a cultural attaché to being a booking agent. I nodded.

"There are very many ways intelligence agents gather information," Gabe explained. When a location — shall we say, destabilizes — CSIS sends in your father."

Destablizes. Like our postings to Belarus, Hong Kong, and Istanbul. That made *way* more sense than Dad's lame explanation about countries in turmoil being generative places for the arts.

Gabe continued. "In many instances, being Canadian is a great asset. It allows your father to operate unheeded and gives him more freedom to establish a SIGINT network. At least that is what Mossad believes."

"SIGINT?"

"Signals intelligence."

"Yeah, that doesn't help. What is signals intelligence?"

"Well, Leah, it's possible to ... shall we say ... extract information from various electronic signals."

"So basically, you eavesdrop on phone calls, is that it?"

"Intercepted communication is one of the ways. Electronic transmissions can also be gathered from ships, planes, satellites, land-based radios, and more. Radar and weapons systems emit electronic signals too. When we collect and analyze those signals, we can see what our enemies are capable of, what they are currently doing, and most importantly, we can predict their intentions."

"And that's what my dad does?"

"Yes, better than most. But he would also be developing human intelligence — HUMINT."

"You mean spies?"

"Sometimes. Usually, however, HUMINT is much more mundane."

"Is that what you do? HUMINT?"

"Yes. But when I acquire information, I pass it on to analysts. Your father operates differently. At least when it comes to Israel and Palestine."

"What do you mean? Different how?"

"Your father is sympathetic toward Palestinians, yes? Because of his relationship with Walid Masri."

"Yeah, but these days, lots of people are," I said, thinking of Breine.

"Sadly for Israel, that is true. But "lots of people" are not in the position to influence investigations."

"You're saying my dad does that?"

"Yes. And before you ask, we have proof. We had an asset inside CSIS for a time.

"Because of your father's reputation in the intelligence community, the information he provides is given special attention. It can be — and often is — shared with FVEY. And that has proven highly problematic for Israel."

"FVEY? What's that?"

"Five Eyes. It is an agreement between America, Australia, New Zealand, the United Kingdom, and Canada to share SIGINT. Signals Intelligence."

My eyes widened. I forced myself *not* to look down at my backpack, where passports from those same five countries sat inside, under my dirty socks and underwear. Gabe continued.

"The world's opinion of Israel has changed. After the horrors of the Second World War — the horrors, I might remind you, that in your family, only your great-grandfather Jakob managed to escape from — Israel had the support and understanding of the Western world. The world had witnessed first-hand the atrocities we had suffered and agreed we Jews needed a homeland to prevent that from happening again. Today, that support has eroded to the point where we believe our existence is once again under threat. But we will not give up the only homeland we've ever known. If we must, we will fight to protect ourselves. So, when your father's work began regularly undermining our operations, we took steps. We tried inserting someone inside your high commission in London, but that person was quickly rooted out. We needed someone on the inside. That someone was Rebecca."

"I don't understand."

"As you know, I am Mossad. As Mossad, I recruited your mother. She worked for me in London. I was her katsa, her case officer."

# 42.

## KILL TWO BIRDS

"My mother worked for Mossad?"

"You are imagining everyone in Mossad is James Bond, maybe? An assassin? A toppler of governments?"

I said nothing, but I admit that flashes of every spy movie and television show I'd seen popped into my head right then.

"An intelligence agency is not unlike any large corporation," Gabe said. "It needs a wide range of employees to function. Even custodians and clerical workers. Most especially, it needs computers and the people who understand them. That is where your mother came in. She was brilliant, and Mossad wanted that brilliance working for them."

"Because she had a master's degree in computer science and applied mathematics from Imperial College?"

Gabe raised his eyebrows.

I shrugged. "It was in the Ramos article."

"Yes, of course. But Rebecca's degree only tells part of the story. Even before London, when she was still an undergraduate student, she was recruited by all the big tech companies and Wall Street banks. But Rebecca chose us. She chose Israel and declared her intent to make Aliyah."

I'd heard that word before. Breine used it when she was talking about her family.

"We have a law in Israel: *The Law of Return*. It allows any Jew, including yourself," Gabe added pointedly, "to qualify for immigration. Rebecca was still an undergraduate at Canada's Waterloo University when she declared her intention to become a citizen of Israel. That is when I recruited her."

"Recruited her to do what? Hack computers?"

For the first time, Gabe looked uncomfortable.

He finally said, "To postpone her Aliyah and instead go to London and enroll at Imperial College for graduate school. The mission I gave Rebecca was to insert herself, body and soul, into James Teague's life. We needed to know what he was doing, who his assets were, and what he was looking at so that Israel could know what to expect and, if necessary, Mossad could intercept or mitigate."

All I heard was *body and soul*. My eyes bugged. Was this guy actually sitting there telling me he'd used my biological mother as a honey-trap like in some cheesy spy movie? This was insane! What kind of an f-ed up world did these people operate in?

"You're claiming that you aimed my mother — a woman barely out of her teens, by the way — at my dad, a man twice her age, and that I'm the result? Well, Mr. Mossad agent ... there's getting close to someone, and then there's close enough to make babies. You're forgetting one big thing. One huge thing. My dad's gay."

"Back then, your father's sexuality was not known. As a result, I believed that attention from a girl half his age would flatter him. And frankly, I did not consider it a great hardship for Rebecca either. Teague was handsome, fit, and considered an eligible bachelor. He was much older than

Rebecca, but the difference in their ages only added to my confidence that Rebecca would find her role ... acceptable."

"Acceptable? Why?"

"Orphaned at seventeen, Rebecca's profile suggested she would respond best to an older male. The absent father. But it was always difficult," Gabe said, shaking his head.

"Difficult? Try impossible!"

"If you're talking about sex, don't be naive, Leah. But if you're asking how your mother was able to seduce a gay man, that is something quite different."

"You are so seriously wrong it's laughable. You could take the most beautiful, charming, intelligent woman on the planet and aim her at my dad; he still wouldn't be interested. Do I need to remind you that my dad's gay? He wouldn't fall into any woman's arms."

"While I did *aim* Rebecca at James, as you so charmingly put it, James also aimed himself at her."

"Wait, *what?* Are you saying that my dad tried to honey-trap my mom?"

"That is exactly what I'm saying. It wasn't just Mossad and the big technology companies that wanted Rebecca's computer genius. Your father wanted Rebecca to work for him. For CSIS. And you, Leah, were the result."

I'd worried Gabe would lie to me. But lies flatter and coerce. Lies are velvet-covered things meant to be stroked and held because they feel so lovely and smooth. Gabe had just covered himself in sackcloth. My dad too. This all felt so ... so grubby.

"All I knew then," Gabe continued, "all I cared about at the time was that in Rebecca, I had what I believed to be the perfect asset. Her ideology was unwavering. And she was brilliant, a genuine computer prodigy. I assumed this brilliance would allow her to assess, process, and react to situations in the field better and faster than any other asset. Much like the computers she was so adept at using. What I did not understand, what I would not let myself see, was that Rebecca was completely unsuited to what I was asking her to do. She was not stable. When Rebecca first discovered she was pregnant, she spiraled."

"Back up. What do you mean, not stable?"

Gabe did not shrug off my question. The opposite. He took his time and answered carefully. "I am not a psychologist, so the answers I give you may seem ... trite."

"Go on," I said through gritted teeth.

"Your mother was... different. People, emotions, social situations — they all overwhelmed her. She preferred her computers. To her they were safe. Theirs was a language she understood and an environment she could control. But I pushed her to engage with the world outside, with Teague. It was too much for her. She could not cope."

Gabe looked outside through the sliding glass doors to the patio beyond. Perhaps he was collecting his thoughts, or maybe he was figuring out what pile of crap to feed me next.

"I assumed that Rebecca's superior intelligence would be an asset. It was not. Once again, I must assume responsibility. I turned a blind eye and insisted that she tell Teague about the baby. About you.

"Teague acted quickly. He moved Rebecca into his flat — separate rooms, of course — and she returned to graduate school. Teague created the cover story that he was an old friend of Rebecca's parents and was looking after her in their absence. Then you were born."

"It's you," I cried. "You were the source for the Ramos article!"

"I assure you I was not. This is *not* a story I want people to know."

God help me, I believed him.

"Rebecca was never a natural mother. Perhaps it was because of whatever disorders or social anxieties she suffered from. Perhaps it was postpartum depression, but Rebecca could not cope. She refused to even hold you."

That was a gut punch. I don't think I'm different from any other adopted kid imagining a kinder story; a teenage mother tearfully forced to hand over her baby daughter to strangers because she was too poor or too young to cope. I never once imagined having a mother who only kept her child because she'd been ordered to. By her handler!

"So you see," Gabe said, dragging me back to the present. "You are the child of two spies, each trying to outmaneuver the other for information. You were raised by a spy, and now it is spies who threaten you. So Leah ... do I call you Leah or Naomi?"

"Leah." Definitely Leah.

You asked me why I would help James Teague. I do not help him. I will help you. I bear some responsibility for your existence and carry guilt about how I used your mother. I cannot fix what I've done. But I can help you now."

I stood up.

"I need a shower."

Gabe nodded. "Of course. You must process what you've heard. It is late now. We will talk again tomorrow and make a plan."

"A plan? With you?"

"Yes, with me. There is no one else. You must see that."

I tried to think — was there someone else? Raphael was on his way back to Canada and a new assignment. My dad, who was apparently some sort of spy, could have helped me if he wasn't lying unconscious in a hospital bed. But even if he was well and standing right here in front of me, could I trust him?

Thing was, I didn't care that Dad wasn't really a cultural attaché; I get why he'd kept that secret from me. I even get why he didn't tell me about my birthright. He was worried that if the world found I was Naomi Nowak, I might be kidnapped again. It was why there'd been a Marcos and a Raphael. It was why Dad put his foot down about social media and why we had *security protocols*. It even explained *The Tank*.

Then there was his note.

*I would have told you everything before college. I wanted you to have a normal childhood.*

He planned to tell me at least part of the story, and I had to give him credit for that. But what I cared about, and what I'm not sure I could ever forgive him for, was how he'd used my mother. Rebecca. She'd been barely older than me when my then forty-something-year-old father had taken advantage of her — a young woman who, if Gabe's story was true, had been seriously neurodivergent. And now Gabe — this Mossad agent who, along with my dad, also took advantage of my birth mother — thinks I should make a plan with him?

I was disgusted. Disgusted by Gabe and, for the first time in my life, disgusted by my father. Until now, I'd believed that my dad was one of the most moral people ever. Okay, maybe not like Mother Theresa, but still ... a good man. But good men don't take physical advantage of young girls. And to think she was only a few years older than I am now? That's just ... that's sick. It would be a long time until I would be able to bring myself to trust either one of them.

I shook my head. "Make a plan with you?" I said. "You've got to be freaking kidding?"

"I am quite serious, Leah," Gabe said. "I will not sugarcoat your situation, nor will I coddle you. You have no other options. Your life is in danger. A connection exists between João Matheus Pereira, the CIA, and a man named Oren Glass. I don't know anything about Glass, not yet. Nor do I understand their connection, but all three — Pereira, Glass, and the CIA — are intent on locating your video and preventing you from bearing witness."

Bearing witness? That was a pretty religious-sounding way to describe being snatched by the CIA and tossed into some black site. Or worse. I tried to bury the image by changing the subject.

"Does it even matter anymore?" I asked. "It's Sunday. The election in Brasil is over."

Gabe shook his head. "The election is not over. Pereira did not secure the 51 percent of the vote he needed to be declared president. There will be a second round of voting in three weeks. And until then, the CIA will intensify its search for you. You've managed to elude them so far. That tells me you have some talent, either by nature or nurture. That is good, but it will not be enough. Allow me to help you. Let me help keep you safe, Leah. At least until your father is well enough to take over."

I hated that he was right.

"I wish I didn't know any of this," I muttered. "I wish I'd never gone on that mototaxi ride or shot that damn video."

"Do you have it?"

"No." I blurted out the answer before thinking.

"But you could arrange to have it released, yes?"

That's when it hit me. The video!

I knew exactly what I had to do.

I looked up at Gabe. "I *will* take your help," I said. "But we're going to do this my way."

"And what way is that?"

"Tell me, Gabe," I asked. "Do they have the phrase in Israel, *Kill two birds with one stone.*"

"From the Greek," Gabe answered. "Daedalus was trapped in the Labyrinth on Crete. He needed the feathers from two birds, but he had only one stone. With one throw of his stone, Daedalus managed to kill two birds, then took the feathers from both birds and made wings so that he could fly to freedom."

"That's it. That's the story," I said. "The video is my stone, my freedom. Release it, and Pereira will never be president. He'll go to jail. That's my first bird."

"And your second bird?"

"You said it yourself. There's a connection between Glass and Pereira and between Glass and the CIA. Right?"

"Correct."

"Okay. So I already knew that Pereira wanted the video. He sent the goons who killed Marcos. But you said that Oren Glass also wanted it."

"Yes."

"*And* you said that both Glass and Pereira wanted the video to bury it — prevent it from being released, yes?"

Gabe nodded.

"Well, the only thing that makes sense is blackmail. Oren Glass wanted to use my video to blackmail Pereira."

"I agree. But blackmail Pereira into doing what? And why?"

I shook my head. "I dunno. But follow me on this; if I release the video, Pereira goes to jail for murder. Right?"

Gabe nodded.

"Glass can't blackmail Pereira with the murder video if Pereira's already in jail. So whatever the blackmail was about … it won't work anymore. And that means Glass doesn't need my video."

"Keep going."

"Okay. So if you're right and Oren Glass is connected to the CIA-"

"He is."

"Okay. So then, if it was Glass who sicced the CIA on me and Glass no longer needs my video, then it's over, right? The CIA won't have any reason to come after me anymore, will they? And that means I'm safe. I can stop running. Second bird."

The corners of Gabe's mouth ticked up. "Very good. Very, very good, Leah. You have a talent for this. After you release the video, then what?"

"Then I intend to find out who the hell Oren Glass is and why he wanted my video so badly. Once I know that … I'm going to take the bastard down."

A look of admiration flickered across Gabe's face but disappeared quickly, replaced by a smile that didn't quite reach his eyes. I was pretty sure I knew what that bogus smile meant; he didn't believe I could do it.

That's fair. I wasn't sure I believed it myself, but I was damn sure going to try. As Naomi Nowak, I had virtually unlimited resources and two aces up my sleeve — a Mossad agent and a bloodhound of an investigative reporter. Christina Ramos. Gabe was already invested in helping me. To get

Ramos hooked, I'd only need to wave this story under her nose and let her get the scent. I had a plan for that.

"I will help you," Gabe said, surprising me. "But I am curious; how do you plan to do all this?"

It was my turn for a hollow smile.

"By turning a lie into a truth."

Gabe's forehead wrinkled into confusion. "What does that mean?"

It meant that, for the first time since our climbing trip to Bric Pianarella, I finally had an answer for my dad. I knew what I wanted to do with my life. I'd finally found something I was passionate about — expose the liars and make them pay.

But to Gabe, all I said was, "It's nothing. Never mind. What I need now is to make two phone calls."

"As the person charged with concealing you from the CIA, I must caution you against making any calls."

"Two calls," I insisted. "Max Klein and Christina Ramos."

Before Gabe could protest, I added, "And after I've talked to them, I'll need your help. I need to get to New Haven, Connecticut by Friday the thirteenth? That's two weeks from now. Can you do that, Gabe? Can you get me there safely without the CIA knowing?"

He looked at me through squinted eyes, the way art teachers tell you to do when they want you to better see the shape of things. Gabe was trying to take the shape of this new me.

"I can do that."

"Thank you," I said, and I meant it.

"Al lo da-var. You're welcome, Leah Teague."

# 43.

## IT WON'T BE LONG NOW

*YALE UNIVERSITY, SCHWARZMAN CENTER*

Gabe dropped me off at the New Haven Bus Station in a car borrowed from his seemingly unending supply of Sayanim, then left to do a surveillance sweep.

Heading north on Union, I spotted my reflection in a window. I barely recognized myself. My hair had been blackened with a bottle of rinse. I wore it slicked back and tucked into a black hoodie under a black down sweater. With dark violet lipstick and eyes thickly rimmed with eyeliner, I looked more like Evie than myself. I was a study in teenage gothic blackness. Importantly, at first glance, I would be unrecognizable. Pleased, I picked up my pace.

On foot, it was only half an hour from the station to my destination — plenty of time for Gabe to surveil the area. We didn't anticipate any trouble, but along with vigilance, Gabe had been teaching me tradecraft. He said I was a natural, which seemed to make him very happy.

Hoodie up, head down and map in hand, I took every opportunity to check for tails as I made my way to my destination — Yale University's Schwarzman Center.

I spotted her right away. She was standing on the steps of the Schwarzman Center studying a campus guidebook, just as we'd arranged.

"Excuse me. Do you know if there are public washrooms inside?" I asked.

"Ja. You can't miss them. Look for the signs."

"Thanks," I said.

"Graag gedaan."

She returned to studying the guidebook, and I climbed the short flight of steps and headed inside.

I found the washrooms and checked each stall. Empty. Then I waited at a sink, pretending concern about my makeup. A few moments later, she appeared and took her place at the mirror next to mine. Janneke.

"I didn't recognize you," Janneke said. "It was only your voice."

"That's the idea," I said smiling. "It's great to see you, Janneke."

"You too, Leah. Thank you for the plane ticket. But you should not have included the scholarship," she scolded me. "It was a little insulting. I would have helped you without it."

"I know you would. The money wasn't to convince *you*," I said. "It was to convince your parents to let you come."

She laughed. "Of course. How clever of you. It worked. They were verheugd."

"We should do this," I said with a head tilt toward the door. "Someone could come in."

Janneke nodded. She pulled the data card from her pocket and placed it on the counter between us. "Here," she said. "From Avery to Nick to me, and now to you. Just as you asked."

"Thanks, Janneke. Any trouble?"

"For me, no. Nick was not so lucky. While he was in Virginia with his father, they searched his room at school and his computer. They found nothing, of course. He was back in class by Monday."

"How is Nick?"

"A little shaken by all that's happened. But this weekend together is helping. Thank you for that."

"You're welcome, but you better go," I said. "Just in case."

"I wish we had more time, Leah. And I wish you could see the finished cut of our project. It's geweldig."

"I really want to see it, Janneke. But there's no time."

"I understand. When will you do it?" Janneke asked.

"Today. Soon. I'm meeting Christina Ramos in thirty minutes. She's set up to do a live interview-"

"Live? Looking like that?" Janneke's eyes bugged wide.

I laughed. It felt good to laugh. "Don't worry, Janneke. My face will be hidden during the interview — pixilated, in shadow ... something. I'll have to stay in hiding until we're certain it's safe, but it shouldn't be long. Once the video goes out on the web for the whole world to see, they'll have to arrest Pereira. He doesn't have *all* of Brasil on his payroll."

Her eyes widened as though she wasn't convinced. After everything that had happened, I can't say I blame her. But I knew I was right. I had the benefit of some inside information courtesy of Mossad.

"It's okay, Janneke. Really. Pereira will never become president. He'll be in jail long before the second round of voting. I can promise that."

Maybe I should have told Janneke that putting Pereira in jail wouldn't be the end, but I figured she'd find out soon enough, and I wanted her to have one carefree weekend with Nick.

And me? I had my sights firmly set on Oren Glass. The man who almost cost my dad his life by making sure no other countries — including my own — would help rescue him. The man who sicked the CIA on me, threatened my friends, and drove me into hiding.

And I wouldn't be alone. Gabe was sticking around. Once I finished my interview with Christina Ramos, Gabe and I were heading to Washington, DC. Gabe wanted information; I wanted revenge.

Oren Glass may be a kingmaker, connected to all sorts of important people, not to mention the CIA. But I have a few billion dollars now, a Mossad agent, and a secret weapon: The Disappointments.

"Prima," Janneke said. "We'll be watching."

She gave me a hug, then she was gone.

After a brief wait, I pocketed the memory card and left the washroom and the Schwarzman Center. The interview with Christina Ramos wouldn't repair the world, but it would go a long way to mending one small corner of it. After that … look out, Oren Glass. I'm coming for you.

# EPILOGUE

# THE KIRYA, TEL AVIV, ISRAEL

*MOSSAD HEADQUARTERS*

The director stared at the file on his desk. He was considering what to do about this new information when a small, angry woman with one brown eye, one blue eye, and floppy earlobes threw open the door to his office and stormed inside, waving a thin sheaf of computer printouts. The woman slapped the papers onto the director's desk and pecked the headline repeatedly with her finger.

The article was by Christina Ramos — an in-depth story about João Matheus Pereira, his crimes, and the schoolgirl who broke the story live on television. Leah Teague, née Naomi Nowak.

"Zona, Noam," she said. "What have you done?"

The director tried to calm her and motioned for the woman to sit. In a near frenzy, she waved him away.

"Promises were made!" Her chin lifted, and so did her voice.

"Made and kept, Rebekah. Made and kept. The girl does not know. Almost no one knows. The circle is tight."

"Ben elef zonot! Gabriel knows, and he is with her!"

"How do you know this?"

"Pah! How do you think I know?"

The director cursed silently. Parts of Mossad were slick, streamlined, and could operate with speed and stealth. Other parts lumbered under the often-crippling weight of bureaucracy with its endless reports all filed and stored on computers where it would be simple for someone like Rebekah Katz, formerly Rebecca Nowak, to discover.

"I trust him," the director said.

"Forgive me if I do not. Gabriel is the last man I would trust. The second last man."

Rebekah Katz faced off in front of the director. She was vibrating with anger. He knew he must calm her down. This woman was nothing short of a national treasure. Her current work made Pegasus Spyware seem like a middle school science project. Her work, and by extension, Rebekah herself, was a top priority for his government and Mossad. They needed her calm, focused, and on task.

"Gabriel will not say anything," the director promised.

The director reached for Rebekah's arm to guide her into the chair, but she recoiled. They had had so little day-to-day contact that he had forgotten — Rebekah Katz did not like to be touched.

She shook her head. "Zine beh sechel," she said accusingly, a tremor in her voice. "You're fucking my brain, Noam."

"It will be fine, Rebekah. Gabriel is only there to keep her safe until her father is well enough to take over."

"And what if James tells her?"

"Teague? There is zero chance that will happen. Teague adores the child. He would lose her forever if he admitted you were alive, and he knew about it. You have nothing to worry about, Rebekah. I promise you with my life."

"I will hold you to that," she said, then turned and left his office just as abruptly as she'd arrived.

The day had barely begun, but he already had a headache. Closing the door firmly behind Rebekah, the director returned to his desk and picked up his phone. He needed to talk to Gabriel Atir.

It was early in America, but that couldn't be helped. When the director first signed off on the mission in Rio, he'd been concerned that Gabriel was unrealistic — rescuing James Teague in no way guaranteed the girl would agree to be an asset. But after reading the report that had landed on his desk earlier that day, having eyes inside Teague's world was more important than ever.

Gabriel Atir answered his phone. "Noam?"

"Can you talk, Gabriel?"

"Yes. Leah is asleep in the other room. Is something wrong, Noam? It's the middle of the night here."

"Your report about Masri — the information was good, brother. Masri *was* married."

"How did we miss that?"

"He was married in London."

"When?"

"2016 to Nasreen Hamed. It was a paper marriage. The two never lived together. She returned to Palestine shortly after and resumed her life there."

"There must be more than that for you to be calling me at this hour."

"There is. Nasreen Hamed is the widow of a known PLFP member — the Popular Front for the Liberation of Palestine. She loudly and publicly blamed us for his death."

"Yes, and?"

"Do you remember Mohammad al-Halabi?"

"Of course. "The Gaza aid worker who was arrested for funneling millions in aid money to Hamas. But Noam, that was not a good moment for Israel, if you recall. Our American and British friends were quite upset with us about that."

"Yes. Because of how the trial was conducted."

"Mostly in secret, yes. They accused us of railroading al-Halabi. But that was years ago, Noam."

"It was 2016. The same year Dr. Walid el Masri married Nasreen Hamed."

"Pardon me, Noam, but I remind you it is the middle of the night here. Why is that important?"

"It is important if we believe al-Halabi's arrest was justified. If he was guilty of what he was convicted of, it would mean that when he was put in detention in 2016, an important source of funding to Hamas would have dried up. Enter Dr. Walid Masri. He marries Nasreen Hamed that same year. After their marriage, Hamed returns to Gaza City while el Masri stays in London, sending regular financial support. A husband sending funds to his wife is above suspicion, yes?"

"A tidy theory, but is it true?"

"We don't know. Not yet. We have only just begun to look. But if our suspicions are correct, now that Nasreen Hamad is dead, the good professor will be looking for other channels to bring money into the region, and that makes the girl a priority, yes?"

"Very much so."

"You have been with her a few weeks now, Gabriel. What is your assessment?"

"I have been teaching her tradecraft. The girl is a natural, Noam. Mossad could use a dozen like her. More importantly, she's asked for my help."

"With what?"

"Oren Glass. He is behind everything that happened to her, and she is determined to prove that and hold him accountable."

"What about her father? Teague is conscious now, I hear, and asks to see her."

"She refuses to see him."

"And why is that?"

Gabe hesitated. "She knows about London and my part in recruiting her mother. She knows Teague is her natural father and how that came to be."

"Ben elef zonot, Gabriel!"

"No, no, this is good, Noam. Trust me, brother. The girl and I are working well together. She is focused. Each day, we learn more about this kingmaker, Oren Glass."

The director shook his head. "It is difficult to accept that a country as powerful as America has allowed itself to be so easily manipulated by one man."

"Not one man," Gabe said. "A small group — a cabal if you will — that orchestrates laws and policy changes to advance their own wealth and power."

The director rubbed his temples. "America is our greatest and most powerful friend. But how do we deal with a country that allows itself to be run to line the pockets of a few select men?"

"We cannot. It makes them an unpredictable and dangerous ally."

"It does indeed," the director said. "Help the girl, Gabe. Win her trust; we need her inside Teague and Masri's lives, but not as much as we need our American friends. Do you understand what I'm telling you?"

"You are saying that there can be no trail that leads back to us."

"Yes. Be careful, brother. Help the girl unmask Oren Glass and his cabal — that alone will benefit Israel. But – and this is very important, Gabe — take great care that our fingerprints cannot be found anywhere. America must remain our ally. Understood?"

"Spell it out for me, Noam."

"Leah Teague is expendable."

The End

*The most painful state of being is remembering the future,
particularly the one you'll never have.*
– Søren Kierkegaard


Watch for the upcoming sequel,
THE BURNT CHILD.

# Bibliography

Though this is a work of fiction, a great deal of research and reading went into creating these characters and situations. Of particular use were the following books and website articles:

**BOOKS**

Crumpton, Henry. *The Art of Intelligence: Lessons from a Life in the CIA's Clandestine Service*. New York: The Penguin Press, 2012.

Dulles, Allen. *The Craft of Intelligence: America's Legendary Spy Master on the Fundamentals of Intelligence Gathering for a Free World*. Guildford, Connecticut: The Lyons Press, 2006.

**WEBSITES**

Jodi Kantor, "Rio, With Eyes Open," *The New York Times*, February 15, 2013, https://www.nytimes.com/2013/02/17/travel/rio-with-eyes-open.html

Brian Harris, "Brazil's criminals turn to flash kidnapping as they take advantage of new tech," *Financial Times*, September 3, 2021, https://www.ft.com/content/225fd97c-ef82-4dfa-b09b-97b1671e1e00

David Bernstein, "Blacklisting of pro-Israel watchdog organization NGO Monitor by the Associated Press," *The Washington Post,* December 2, 2014, https://www.washingtonpost.com/news/volokh-conspiracy/wp/2014/12/02/blacklisting-of-pro-israel-watchdog-organization-ngo-monitor-by-the-associated-press/

Marisa Kabas, "Young American Jews Have Reached a Tipping Point With Israel," *Rolling Stone,* May 21, 2021, https://www.rollingstone.com/culture/culture-commentary/israel-palestine-jewish-american-support-1172309/

Ben Lynfield, "Israeli court sentences director of Gaza charity to 12 years in prison," August 30, 2022, https://www.theguardian.com/world/2022/aug/30/Israeli-court-sentences-mohammad-el-halabi-director-of-gaza-charity-to-12-years-in-prison

"Timeline of the murder of journalist Jamal Khashoggi," *Al Jazeera,* February 26, 2021, https://www.aljazeera.com/news/2021/2/26/timeline-of-the-murder-of-journalist-jamal-khashoggi

Zeinab Cheaib, "40 days of mourning: Breaking down Islamic funeral rituals," *WTOL11,* July 8, 2020, https://www.wtol.com/article/news/local/islamic-scholar-breaks-down-the-mourning-process-according-to-muslim-faith/512-a1098b59-eeb2-4c24-b4b8-f5cad21464a5

"Brazil profile – Timeline," *BBC,* 3 January, 2019, https://www.bbc.com/news/world-latin-america-19359111

Teo Spengler, "Gardening Know How: Cannonball Tree Characteristics and care," *Gardening Know How,* https://www.gardeningknowhow.com/ornamental/trees/tgen/cannonball-tree.htm

Amy Catherine Kirchheimer, "A Comparative Study Of Humint In Counterterrorism: Israel And France," 1970 – 1990," *Thesis submitted to the Faculty of the Graduate School of Arts and Sciences of Georgetown University*, April 16, 2010, https://repository.library.georgetown.edu/bitstream/handle/10822/553531/kirchheimerAmy.pdf?seque

"What is a SCIF Room? A Deep Dive into the Fortress of Classified Information." https://www.panelbuilt.com/blog/scif-room-security-unparalleled

"Canadian Security Intelligence Service," *Government of Canada*, https://www.canada.ca/en/security-intelligence-service.html'

"Flora and Fauna of Rio's Epic Jardim Botânico," *Almas*, https://almasdelsol.com/flora-and-fauna-of-rios-epic-jardim-botanico/

"Five Eyes Intelligence Oversight And Review Council (Fiorc)," *Office of the Director of National Intelligence*, https://www.dni.gov/index.php/ncsc-how-we-work/217-about/organization/icig-pages/2660-icig-fiorc

"Bric Pianarella, Crag Info," *Vertical Life Climbing App*, https://www.vertical-life.info/en/outdoor/liguria/finale/bric-pianarella

"Intelligence Studies: Types of Intelligence Collection," *United States Naval War College Library Guides*, https://usnwc.libguides.com/c.php?g=494120&p=3381426

"The Establishment of the Institute for Intelligence and Special Operations (Mossad),"

*Mossad, Israeli Secret Intelligence Service,* https://www.mossad.gov.il/history

"Red Command," *InSight Crime,* July 17, 2022, *https://insightcrime.org/brazil-organized-crime-news/red-command-profile/#:~:text=The%20Red%20Command%20(CV)%20is,thousands%20of%20members%20from%20prisons*

Tim Lau, "Citizens United Explained," *Brennan Center for Justice,* December 12, 2019, https://www.brennancenter.org/our-work/research-reports/citizens-united-explained?ref=indi.ca

Davied Oziel, "The Most Dangerous Favela," *Bē,* https://www.behance.net/gallery/879211/The-Most-Dangerous-Favela-of-Rio-de-Janeiro

"Israel and Palestine Events of 2022," *Human Rights Watch. World Report 2023,* https://www.hrw.org/world-report/2023/country-chapters/israel-and-palestine

"Israel/Palestine: Designation of Palestinian Rights Groups as Terrorists," *Human Rights Watch,* October 22, 2021, https://www.hrw.org/news/2021/10/22/israel/palestine-designation-palestinian-rights-groups-terrorists

"CUI Awareness and Marking," *Department of Defense,* Novemeber 2020, Cleared for Open Publication April 1, 2021, https://www.dodcui.mil/Portals/109/Documents/Training%20Docs/21-S-0588%20cleared%20CUI%20Awareness%20Training%20Nov%202020.pdf?ver=eOMZuMPrdLXcnhS6egUe2w%3D%3D

"Search for adoption records," *Province of Ontario,* https://www.ontario.ca/page/search-adoption-records

Neelabja Adkuloo, "10 Best Destinations For Rock Climbing In Europe In 2023," *Travel Triangle*, https://traveltriangle.com/blog/rock-climbing-in-europe/

"Israel Intelligence Agencies," *Jewish Virtua Library, A Project of Aice*, https://www.jewishvirtuallibrary.org/israel-intelligence-agencies

Brendan Brown, "13 signs someone is a genuinely good person (and not just faking it)," *The Expert Editor*, August 23, 2023, https://expert-editor.com.au/blog/signs-someone-is-a-genuinely-good-person/

Justin Bariso, "An FBI Agent Shares 9 Secrets to Reading People," *Inc.*, https://www.inc.com/justin-bariso/an-fbi-agents-9-ways-to-read-people.html

Cory Doctorow, "How To Create Perfect Fake Identities," *Boingboing*, September 3, 2008, https://boingboing.net/2008/09/03/howto-create-perfect.html

Michael Ellmer, "The Sayanim: Mossad's International Volunteers," *Grey Dynamics,* April 16, 2021, https://greydynamics.com/the-sayanim-mossads-international-volunteers/

# Acknowledgements

Many eyes saw this manuscript, and many more supported its creation and its creator. Some were sensitivity readers, some had expertise in a sport, subject, language, or location. Some were there for the writerly bits and some poured wine and made meals. My thanks go out to all of you (in no particular order), and I sincerely hope I haven't forgotten anyone.

Kate Clarke, Heather Tekavac, Ilene Cooper, Katherine Warren, Mic Laguë, John Warren, Barbara Jean Scott, Rina Nichols, Rebecca Welton, Keely Meyer, Esther Hershenhorn, Cindy Roorda, Gary Fabbri, Elisabeth Norton, Nell Pierce, Angela Cerrito, Alexia Roy, Mina Witteman, and Jacqueline Baric.

But most of all, thank you, Geoff. Thank you from the bottom of my cold and wicked heart. I could not have done this without you.

T Bjørn

# About the Author

Thomas Bjørn has spent half his life living in, or traveling to, every continent except Australasia and Antarctica. After three post-secondary degrees and numerous aborted career attempts, he has turned his attention to writing fiction and chronicling his adventures.